To Face the Universe

Sea Changes

Starship
Book II

BRIAN MICHAEL HALL

DEDICATION

To my children, and their children. May they continue to be a constant source of joy and wonderment.

CONTENTS

ACKNOWLEDGMENTS

This book was made possible by the many Authors I grew up reading (you know who you are) and it is my solemn hope that one day you too might pick up this book.

Many times, I find myself listening to music while I write and these audio interludes tend to fill me with inspiration. The range of artists and genres of music that I listen to are so diverse as to preclude any listing that would do justice. Just remember this very important adage - music is life.

BLOOD IMPLICATIONS

1

The crew of the Starship *Iwakina*, having evaded both Ros'Loper's and the New Rangelley Alliance's ships, moved on towards their next set of adventures, first having to drop their guests off at the Andalii homeworld...

Kimberly Rosel, the *Iwakina's* resident doctor, was excited that she would be able to work once again with her old friend, the Andalii Dorigethra. The Andalii were naturally telepathic, and now she, whom Dorigethra had constantly chided for not having any ability in this arena, would be able to show her old friend that she was able to reach his level due to experiments she had been conducting. She would show him what Humans were capable of. Maybe she would even bring Marishima on board; *perhaps not*, she thought. Marishima was dangerous and could derail months of research. Better to let her stew in her suspicions. *Exciting times*, Rosel thought as she observed the latest tests from her lab subject.

* * *

Captain Saitow entered the bridge and relayed coordinates to Sanae, who was disguised as Kintaro Sagura. She had just about gotten the jump sequence set when her board lit up again; this time with a distress signal. "Captain, contact detected: a faint distress signal bearing 200/20 at sixty-thousand klicks; Too far to determine the source."

"Wonderful. Take us over there Sagura; nothing like a little more adventure when adventure is afoot." Saitow responded dryly.

* * *

As the *Iwakina* approached the source of the distress beacon, Saitow called his officers to the bridge. Sagura confirmed it was a ship of unknown design, a little bit bigger than the *Iwakina* at five-hundred meters length and one-hundred-thirty meters at its widest points. Saitow took reports from his bridge crew. There was no voice message; only a constant signal. Visuals showed severe scarring as if the vessel had been in a battle. Scans showed two distinct heat signatures that suggested two life forms in an isolated part of the ship. The rest of the place was dead.

"What do you think?" Saitow asked in general.

"This is a big unknown, Sir. I've never seen this technology before. It could be dangerous, but it's worth a look." Takagawa spoke up. He had the look of a kid in a candy store.

"Of course, there are the life forms to consider..." Doctor Rosel seemed a bit perturbed at Takagawa's

2

lack of concern for them.

"Yes, there's that." Takagawa retorted.

"Simpson, I want you to put two small teams together. One will escort Takagawa and a couple of his engineers on an examination of the ship, while another escorts Marishima to check out the inhabitants. Everyone remains on high alert while we are tethered to that thing. Use the maintenance access airlock and tether across. Takagawa, any ideas on accessing the ship?"

Takagawa poured over the visuals. "Sagura, can you get us within one-hundred meters of this point? I believe this is a breach we can get in through. Once inside we can see about a way out."

"Very well then, let's check it out." Saitow wasn't sure what would come of this expedition, but he had an odd feeling about it. He didn't like the odds given his past record with odd feelings...

*   *   *

Goh Takagawa was the first to go EVA. The extravehicular suits the *Iwakina* had were less bulky than the ones he had trained in. He used a gravitic maneuver module to shoot across to the mystery ship and attached the tether. The breach was large and led to a great open space like a cargo bay. He signaled for the rest of the expedition to come over. While they came, Goh searched the space for an access hatch. The place seemed somewhat familiar, but he couldn't quite place it. When he found the hatch he was looking for, it hit him. This was a variation on Old Earth technology. This stuff was easy; mostly two-polarity electrical signals through metal wiring. He pulled out his tablet and started a scan for the proper power requirements. He popped the panel open that controlled the hatch, scanned the wiring, and jacked in with a portable power pack after calibrating it to the proper settings. The door opened. There was no sound as the space on the other side was not pressurized. It looked to be a containment corridor. This would be a space to keep contaminants from filtering through to the rest of the ship. *Clever*, Goh thought. He checked the other hatch and found that the space on the other side of that was fully pressurized. Scanning the corridor, he found the main power panel and jacked the power pack into that. That way he could power the whole corridor, controlling the hatches and pressurization from their respective control panels. He checked on the rest of the boarding party. They had all made it across. He radioed Simpson to bring everyone into the corridor. Once everyone was inside, he sealed the outer hatch and pressurized the corridor. A purple light came on above the other hatch; Goh took this as a sign that the pressurization had equalized. A quick scan confirmed his assumption. He tested the air and found normal volumes of breathable oxygen. He took off his helmet and bade the rest to do so.

"We can leave these EVA suits here." Goh suggested.

"No can do, Boss. Ours are combat rigged." Simpson told him.

"Suit yourself." Goh half giggled as his own lame pun.

Everyone got their gear in order. Goh got a good

look at the Marines' gear. It *was* different; they had all sorts of attachments to them, mainly weapons. He jacked into the main control panel with his tablet. The whole ship was offline, but enough power in the right place would get him what he needed. It was easy to get access to the ship's secondary systems. However, he would need to get access to the ships core systems to get anything useful beyond the map he was downloading. He transmitted it to Simpson's tablet. "It seems pretty simplistic in layout. This is where the life forms were detected. My team will be heading here." Goh indicated the two points he referred to on the tablet.

"Right. Let's head out. Ross, you're with the geeks." Simpson commanded.

*   *   *

Marishima was weary about doing an EVA. She had training for it, sure, but it was unnerving none the less. She felt more comfortable once they were in the other ship and out of the suits. The whole group stuck together for a few minutes, and then it was time to split. The 'geeks' as Lieutenant Simpson called them, went down a couple decks at one point while her team went up. She was apprehensive about this whole adventure, so she made small talk with Simpson to get her mind off of it.

"Lieutenant, what exactly is a 'geek'?" she asked.

"It's a technology driven smart guy I guess; ancient lingo we learned at the academy." Simpson replied.

Then he stopped short of a large hatch. "We're here."

*   *   *

Takagawa and his team reached the computer core center as indicated on the map. He had his team break out their gear and set up a data relay node so he could access the ship's mainframe. They had just gotten the start on a complete system download; the interface was so easy to handle. It was only the language that was odd and would take time to decipher. Just then he got the call over his comm unit that Simpson needed access to the chamber where the life-forms were. Goh accessed the secondary systems again and was able to route some power to the hatch there and get it opened. "Good luck..." he bade them and then got back to the task at hand.

*   *   *

Marishima watched anxiously as the hatch opened with a whoosh. The Marines went inside with more caution than usual. Simpson motioned for her to enter after the room was secure. The two life forms they had detected were Humans; a man and a woman who were lying on separate tables near a large container. Both appeared to be asleep or unconscious. Marishima pulled out her portable scanner and checked the man out first. He was alive, but his vitals were very weak. Her diagnosis suggested that he was in some sort of state of hibernation. Her knowledge base indicated that a booster would bring him out of it, so, after obtaining Simpson's agreement, she gave the man the booster. The man awoke somewhat startled, but then muttered something in a language other than standard codex.

"Do you speak English?" Marishima asked him.

"Yes. Who are you?" the man replied in a heavy accent.

"I am Marishima, a medical assistant from the starship *Iwakina*, here to rescue you."

"Ah... a rescue." The man looked around the compartment. Marishima noted that his gaze lingered first on the large container and then on the woman. He sat up rather abruptly, which caused him to wobble a bit before he caught himself with a straight arm. Marishima found the man rather handsome, but in an odd way, as if there was some weird reason she could not place for his attractiveness. He had long brown hair which was a mess and deep eye sockets which framed these piercing grey eyes; eyes which had a slight red tint around the edges of his cornea. The man pressed the edge of his table which she could now see had a padded top, and a drawer slid open. He pulled an opaque bottle of some kind out, opened it, and downed the contents in one gulp. Marishima noticed a small bit of dark red liquid at the corner of the man's mouth before he quickly licked it away. The man now looked a bit more alert and was scanning the room once more; this time it seemed to Marishima that he was sizing up her Marine escort. It struck her as odd that they were not reacting more cautiously at this man's movements. He straightened up in his seat but did not get to his feet.

7

"Ah... thank you. I feel much better. Please accept my apologies; I have yet to introduce myself. I am the Postulant Collin of the house Bartholomew. That woman there is Esme; she is my charge. Here..." Collin indicated the large container, "... lays my patron the Lord Bartholomew in stasis. Please accept us into your care."

* * *

Takagawa and his crew finished up and were heading toward the deck access area. He marveled at how such ancient technology built solely by Humans could last so long. It wasn't quite as old as the Pruatha tech, but it was several thousands of years old. It didn't even have an Anomaly Core, yet something he couldn't figure out must have given it power when it was fully functional.

* * *

Marishima wanted to know more about the situation these people were in before bringing them aboard the *Iwakina*, but she didn't want them sidestepping the questions she would ask, and she didn't want the Marines knowing that she was more than just a medical assistant. She attempted to probe Collin's mind. Oddly, he seemed to be blocking her without even knowing it; he gave no indication that he detected her actions.

"Dear people. Might I trouble you to go to this level here and retrieved some space suits there for us two? I see we will need to go through the breach in the cargo bay." Collin snapped his head sharply to the right and his face seemed to blank out for a moment. "There are others here with you; an engineering team. I must speak with the head engineer. Please fetch him here at once." Collin looked at the nearest Marine who, despite the demanding tone of Collin's request, headed off as he was bade. Collin began putting small items, including more of the opaque bottles, inside a bag of some kind. He then went to where the woman lay and kissed her full on the lips. Marishima was shocked, then surprised, as the woman began to stir. She opened her eyes, but it seemed as if no one was occupying them.

Marishima took this opportunity to probe the woman's mind. She immediately withdrew, sensing something dark and horrible there that would turn her own mind to madness. Marishima sensed that these people were far more dangerous than even Sparrow 64. This Bartholomew, whose mind she could not even sense, must be a powerful being to be the lord of such as these.

*   *   *

Goh and his team had reached the level of the life form chamber when a Marine from Simpson's team came hastily toward them. "Mr. Takagawa, you must come with me at once; it's very urgent!"

"Why, what has happened?" Goh asked as he went

along with the Marine.

"You just have to come quickly. You are being summoned."

"Summoned? By whom? Your Lieutenant?" Goh was starting to get anxious.

The Marine said nothing more, only continuing ahead as the hatch to the place came in view.

They entered the room. Goh surveyed the area noting the large container and the two Humans, besides those from the *Iwakina*. The Marine that had come and gotten him went straight to the man and pointed to Goh saying something Goh didn't catch.

"Mr. Takagawa, I presume? You have taken some data from this ship. It must remain here. Give me the device that it is on." The man held out his hand. Goh felt a strange desire to do as the man said. He had learned to gauge Qi energy, in himself and others and this man had a great quantity of it. It was almost overwhelming him, but he had learned to channel his own Qi as well and felt that what he needed to do was channel his Qi to block whatever strange influence this man's Qi was performing. The data he collected must be of great value besides the benefit it would have for Goh's research. Goh gave the man his interface device in the hopes that the man would not realize that he had downloaded a copy to his personal tablet.

"Thank you, Mr. Takagawa. I am glad that you have allowed us to avoid some unpleasant events."

The man introduced himself and his companion, and mentioned his 'patron' who was supposedly inside the large container. He indicated that the container would need to be transported to the *Iwakina*. He showed Goh the mechanisms for moving it; four gravitic platform points controlled by a panel. He insisted that Goh be the one to operate it. Goh was more than happy to; he would get to operate ancient Old Earth technology first hand. The Marines sent to collect the couple's space suits returned and Goh was surprised when the two stripped naked in front of them to suit up. He noted that Marishima seemed to be blushing as she looked away. *Odd behavior for a medical assistant,* he thought. Collin placed their clothing in one of the bags they carried. Goh noticed that he left his interface device on a table along the far wall.

"Shall we be going?" Collin asked indicating the hatch.

"Let's do this." It was Lieutenant Simpson who led the way out of ship.

2

Doctor Rosel was readying the Sick Bay for her new guests. Marishima had radioed ahead and notified her of the visitors. Doctor Rosel had insisted that they be screened in Sick Bay before being allowed access to the ship. The rescued were brought straight to her while remaining in their space suits, along with the container with their patron inside. With the room sealed she had the two expose an arm and then she took blood samples, assuring them that they would be tested for all sorts of things that might quarantine them from the rest of the ship.

Collin, as the male introduced himself, grudgingly agreed for the both of them. Rosel analyzed the blood samples and was astonished. This was no ordinary blood. Collin volunteered the information that she wanted to know without her even asking.

"Good Doctor, we do not have the ordinary blood of Humans within us. The blood of our patron Bartholomew courses through our veins; more so in me than dear Esme. You see, our Patron Bartholomew and I, to a lesser extent, are Kyuketsuki. Kyuketsuki is the name given us by your Old Earth ancestors; in your language it means vampire."

"That's astonishing!" was all Rosel could manage. She had heard stories of vampires; mostly assumed to be mother's tales to frighten children to obedience, but to have a living specimen right in front of her was remarkable. The look on Collin's face brought her back to reality.

"Are we clear Doctor? I would like to have Esme wake the Master."

"Right. Go right ahead." Rosel replied. If this guy was a lesser vampire, she really wanted to meet this Master. His blood was teaming with antibodies and other stuff she could only guess at. However, none of it hit the filters as dangerous to the crew. She watched as the two undressed from their suits, but only Collin put on some clothing taken from a bag he carried. The woman called Esme walked naked to the end of the container and pressed a few places; a door opened at that end just big enough for her to crawl into. It closed behind her. After a few moments the entire top portion of the container split in two with the two sides raising and then sunk down into each side. Rosel could see the naked Esme laying atop another person who was clothed; this was a large man with flowing white hair and pale skin. What appeared to be blood flecked the corners of his mouth. Esme rose from atop him and stepped out of the container. The man's eyes shot open as if he had just lost the warmth of his mother's breast and he struggled to rise out of the container himself.

This man or vampire Bartholomew spoke in a strange language that Rosel had never heard; even though she had visited hundreds of worlds. Collin did his best to answer what Rosel assumed were numerous questions. Then the vampire offered his arm to the Doctor. "My patron assumes that you wish to examine his blood as well Doctor?"

"Ah! Yes." Doctor Rosel quickly took a sample of Bartholomew's blood and added it to the analysis. It was truly more vigorous that Collin's blood. *Fascinating* she thought.

"My patron wishes to propose a bargain with you.

He wishes to purchase passage to our homeworld for a vial of his blood. Do you realize the worth of such an offer?"

Rosel thought what great luck she was having. *First, she would get to have the Andalii scientist Dorigethra assist her in her work and now to have a whole vial of vampire blood to experiment with!* Her plans would soon bear fruit.

"Tell your patron that we have a deal. I will speak with the Captain of the ship."

"Very good. Now, I would like to leave my patron and Esme here in your care for a while. I need to go to your bridge and speak with the operator of the ship. Please have one of your military men escort me."

Rosel did not want this opportunity to slip by. She unsealed the room and spoke to the escort that had been standing guard outside. Collin spoke once more with his patron who got a very sad look on his face. Collin then spoke in the same language to the woman who had still not dressed. She had a streak of fresh blood that must have originated at her neck and went down to her small breasts to linger there. Rosel motioned to check it out, but the woman stopped her with a universal sign of the hand palm outward. She then wiped the blood away with a cloth to reveal that there was no wound to be seen. She then took clothing from the bag and put it on. Esme helped Bartholomew out of the container and into a nearby service bed. Collin must have been satisfied with the outcome because he immediately left with the escort. Rosel offered Esme a chair to sit next to Bartholomew. As she watched the two of them, she thought that fortune was smiling on her indeed.

*　　*　　*

Sanae as Kintaro Sagura was manning her station awaiting orders from the Captain. She knew that they were supposed to jump to Andali and had the jumps already calculated and inputted into the navigation system. She was curious as to what the survey party had found on the contact; however, nothing had been relayed to the bridge except that there were three survivors taken aboard. She glanced at the Captain at the Conn. He sat there looking stoic yet impatient; his head resting on one hand at the chin while the other tapped steadily on the arm of the command chair. A sudden feeling of anxiety gripped her as she struggled with the thought of how the Captain was feeling. Such empathy was uncharacteristic of her and it confused her all the more. She shook her head and looked away; such feelings were not in her training and that scared her just a little.

She got a much-needed distraction when the Bridge lift doors opened and a Marine came in escorting a handsome young man that was not part of the crew. The man paused and seemed to be sizing up the entire Bridge. He focused on the Captain and, moving toward the front of the command chair he stopped and bowed deeply. "May I presume you are the Captain of this vessel?"

Captain Saitow was brought from his melancholy to look up at the young man. "Yes. Yes I am."

"Please allow me to introduce myself. I am the Postulant Collin of the House Bartholomew. I and my companions came from the ship tethered to this one. I must ungently speak with whoever steers this vessel."

"Ah yes…" Captain Saitow keyed up a visual on the visitor's ship. "Sagura there has the navigation." The Captain indicated Sanae with a hand. He seemed distracted as if he was getting a message by neural-net. The visitor came to her and bowed. Before he spoke, he got an odd look on his face, but then smiled politely.

"*Sir*, it is urgent that you untether this ship and move us away to more than two kilometers from *my* ship. It will shortly self-destruct." Sanae quickly did as she was asked. She keyed in the disengage command for the tether and moved the ship to the required distance. Out of the corner of her eye she noticed the visitor fumbling inside a pocket of his robes. Everyone on the Bridge watched the display of the visitor's ship as they moved away from it. Suddenly the screen went bright white as the other ship exploded.

The Captain addressed the visitor then. "Well, now that that problem has been solved, my Doctor has given all of you a clean bill of health. She also has offered to generously pay any transportation cost to wherever you may desire to go. I would like the honor of having you as a guest for dinner this evening. What say you?"

The visitor smiled and Sanae for some reason did not like the particular way that he smiled at her Captain. "We would be delighted, Captain…?"

"Glenn Saitow, of the Saitow Conglomerate family. Pleased to meet you."

"I assure you Captain; the pleasure is mine as well."

"Nanami, please escort our guests to the client

suites; Doctor Rosel has the others in the Sick Bay. Collin was it? We shall call on you for dinner soon. Please get yourselves settled and refreshed. We have much conversation to exchange. Oh, and please give your dining preferences to Nanami before she leaves you."

"Thank you, Captain, you are most gracious."

Sanae watched as Nanami Oliver escorted the visitor along with the Marine he had entered with into the lift. After they had gone, she felt as if something was not quite right, but she could not figure out what it was.

* * *

Stephen Jing was adjusting to the modifications that the Chief Engineer Goh Takagawa had made to the ship's chapel. The lift no longer opened to the center of the room; now there was a dividing wall that split the chapel in two to the point where the lift had been. It was still there of course, but now it no longer opened to the chapel. It was just as well. The lift being a distraction to services for the few who did come on appointed times to hear of God's grace. Suddenly, Jing felt the presence of a great deal of Qi and it felt as if this Qi was not of the pure and spiritual kind, but corrupted and tainted by the forces of time. Its foundation was ancient, and so powerful that he decided to investigate its source. He went into the sanctum passing Gunter who was reading at the small table they had there. He fished out a weather-beaten leather satchel from one of the many cabinets here. He had been a Priest of the Order for so long that he had accumulated quite a collection of useful artifacts; one of which he pulled out of the fur-lined satchel. It was a semi-rectangular piece of dark opaque glass and he handled it very carefully. He noticed Gunter eying him very curiously. "My friend, have you ever seen one of these before?"

"No Brother, I have never seen it. What is it?"

"This is a Glass of Saint Albert. I suspect a great evil has come to the ship. This will show us what it is." Stephen rubbed the glass with his left hand back and forth while chanting a prayer; his eyes closed and concentrating on the Qi that he felt. The use of the glass was part of the Arcanum; he would have to teach Gunter how to use it soon as well. He felt a sharp pain in his hand and stopped moving it, spreading out his palm as flat as he could on the surface of the glass. He opened his eyes and saw a slight bluish glow form under his hand and run the length of the glass. *There are at least two Class E creatures on the ship* he thought. The glass would indicate the class of a presence by the color it pulsed. His Qi detection abilities told him how many there were; the energy was focused in two different parts of the ship. He told as much to Gunter.

"So, what kind of beings are these 'Class E' creatures?" Gunter asked.

"From where we are in space-time, they can be only one thing: Vampires. We must inform the Church at once. Dig out the Dimensional Communicator; we will just have to risk its detection. Information of this sort has to be given to the Holy See immediately. The Vampires are not known for leaving their construct unless something grave is afoot."

Stephen watched Gunter pull out the apparatus that would allow instantaneous communication across vast distances without the requirement of a GCN connection. Stephen prayed that the ship would not run afoul of these creatures, whatever they may be.

* * *

Marishima was taking care of some paperwork in regards to her only *real* patient Lowey Jax. He was sleeping peacefully in the nearest of the many sick bay berths. There were numerous bruises, a couple of wounds, and he had a nasty bump on the back of his head, but he was recovering nicely. It would probably be about another week before he could be released. She looked up to see the Kyuketsuki Collin standing in the doorway. "Esme darling, what are you doing?" He said looking toward her patient. Marishima looked in that direction to find the woman Esme standing beside the bed of Lowey; that blank expression still on her face. *How was she there?* She certainly did not pass her by coming through the door. Marishima could have sworn that she was the only one in the room. She stood and watched as Collin escorted the girl out into the corridor. She walked over to Lowey suspecting some sort of foul play, but the man seemed to be sleeping restfully. She checked his wounds and was astonished to find that the bruises were gone and his wounds were all healed to the point of not even being visible.

She stepped out into the corridor to find Nanami Oliver escorting the three visitors out of sick bay. She made to speak, but seeing the ever-blank look on the woman Esme's face, she held her tongue. She stepped back into the room upon hearing Lowey Jax stirring from his slumber.

*   *   *

Stephen Jing received word back from the Holy See; do nothing, they said. It was not in the best interests of the Church to interfere with the machinations of such creatures unless it directly affected the laity. 'Watch over the ship and report any occurrences that were beyond prudence for such beings' were his orders. Stephen thought on this for a moment. He should inquire at least as to who these creatures were. He started toward the new chapel doors; that was when he sensed them. They must have come up in the lift towards the client quarters on this deck. Their Qi signature at this range was very clear; they were indeed vampires. The only other time he had encountered vampires was on Oculus III. Stephen shuddered at the thought and forced it from his mind. He would follow the orders of the Church and steer clear of these creatures.

*   *   *

Collin inspected the cabin that was provided to them. He gave explicit instruction to Ms. Oliver for his Patron's cabinet to be brought here immediately. She would do it right away. All of the weak-minded Humans were easily bent to his will. There was no need to involve the Master in such petty affairs. He looked to the man. *How long had he served the house of Bartholomew as a Postulant?* He had lost count through the centuries. It was long enough to know all of his Patron's innermost desires and the very things that frightened him. *What ambition!* He thought; to go against even the Ancients in his pursuit of technologies to improve the lot of his people. His choice in a Betrothed, however, was questionable. Esme was a telepath; another slight against the Ancients. He intended to find out what she was doing inside that young man's room in the Sick Bay. The Master was lying upon an elaborate bed under a gaudy looking tapestry of some forgotten forest scene. Esme was sitting on a divan staring blankly in his Patron's direction. Collin sat next to her and faced her to him. He thought, *Esme what are you up to?*

I am sharing in Master's dream…

Enough of that. What were you doing to that man in the Sick Bay room?

Healing magic. The Master would have wanted it to foster good will among the crew here.

It is not your place to make such decisions! Am I clear? Collin loathed conversing in this way. However, Esme was under the Master's trance otherwise which rendered her mute. Even the little amount of blood of the Master that coursed through her veins tended to turn a Betrothed into an automaton. It amazed him that she kept her full senses on the inside. What bothered him was that she was both adept at magic and full telepathy. He thought her to be too much of a liability; she could get into even the Master's head with a thought and he would not even know she was there.

Yes, My Lord. She replied in his head.

*   *   *

Doctor Rosel paused outside the Officer's Mess. She checked her neural-net to verify that they were on a course to the Kyuketsuki Warusei; *what an odd name* she thought. It meant Vampire Planet. She had heard about it in her younger days. It wasn't a planet at all; actually, it was a Mechanismoan Mega-Construct. These massive structures were created from an entire solar system and built directly around the system's star during the Great War between the Pruatha and the Mechs. She would have to go there to get her payment from the Kyuketsuki Bartholomew. They would be taking a roundabout route to avoid Ros'Loper controlled space; at least until they left there and went to Andali. She so hoped that Dorigethra was available. She would need his expertise to finish her little project. The ship was on the move even though one would hardly notice.

She keyed the hatch and entered the mess. Mess men were scurrying about to get the final preparations in order. The table was already set and she noticed Kuremoto at one end of the table and the First Officer at the other end. A Mess man motioned for her and seated her next to Kuremoto.

"My word Doctor, you are looking quite fetching!" Kuremoto beamed at her. She wore a formal gown as was protocol. She didn't *feel* 'fetching' at all. She smiled politely at him.

"For the life of me I do not know why I am seated at the head of the table…" Kuremoto began. She wasn't interested in the man's conversation style; in fact, she didn't care for the old man at all.

"Well, with there being three main guests... I'll assume they will be seated there... that puts you at the fringe now doesn't it?" She beamed back at him. He had a shocked yet disappointed look on his face that made her turn away for a moment. She saw that the First Officer just rolled his eyes.

The Captain came through the hatch escorting Princess Shirae. The Captain sat next to Rosel in the center and placed the Princess between him and the First Officer. They exchanged pleasantries. Then the guests entered the Mess. Everyone at the table rose while the three were seated. Esme was seated across from her, Bartholomew in the center, and Collin on the other side. Collin made introductions all around for them. The Captain introduced those of his crew who were present, as well as the Princess. A soup was served as was custom in a formal dinner setting. It was some sort of thin base that tasted like meat. Bartholomew made a sound as if he were clearing his throat. Collin addressed the entire table.

"My Patron would like to say a few words about our circumstances. As he is forbidden in using the language of Humans, I will interpret for him." Collin motioned for Bartholomew to begin. The Kyuketsuki spoke in that strange language he had used in the Sick Bay. His voice was deep and seemed to have an echoing effect in her mind. Collin interpreted. "As you know our ship was disabled and drifting dead in space. For rescuing us we thank you deeply. Now I will tell you the circumstances of our arrival in this situation. We were on a mission to test some new technology that was developed in secrecy by our House. Unfortunately, one of our subordinates decided that, since the technology was forbidden, he would use the opportunity to usurp our seat and informed the authorities in the hope that we would perish at their hands. Three warships from our world came at us, but we fought bravely, having destroyed all three in battle. However, we were badly damaged and disabled, with almost the entire crew contingent killed.

"It is our understanding that this ship is not entirely of Human manufacture. The technology we were working on was also alien to us; it was Mechanismoan in nature. Perhaps once we have our house back in order, we can strike a deal for a technology exchange."

The Captain sat back as if contemplating the offer. "Your offer sounds intriguing but it is not in my office to make such deals. Perhaps I can get you in contact with my family who ultimately finances this enterprise."

Rosel heard a small sound come from the direction of the Princess while Collin was translating what the Captain had said. After receiving a reply from his Patron, Collin said, "Yes, please do so. Once we arrive at our homeworld, I will give you a communications device with which your family can contact our house." Rosel noticed that neither Collin nor his Master was eating their soup; rather they nonchalantly slid them toward the girl Esme who was eating heartily. That was the most lively she had seen the woman since making contact.

"I am fascinated to hear about your homeworld. Please tell us what you can about it. We will have to lie over for a few hours there to recalibrate the ship. Would we be able to make port?" The Captain asked.

"I am afraid making port there will be impossible;

it is the Kyuketsuki Warusei after all." Collin answered. Rosel was startled when Kuremoto all of a sudden dropped his soup spoon with a clatter in his plate.

"Kyuketsuki Warusei? So that means you are all Kyuketsuki? I had heard stories but to actually meet real Kyuketsuki…" Kuremoto stammered a bit as he said this.

"Are you *OK* Doctor?" The Captain was concerned for the old man as well as the possible offense this could be giving his guests.

"Yes Captain, forgive me. Forgive me honored guests. It is just that I had only heard of Kyuketsuki in wives' tales to scare children. I had no idea that they actually existed with their own homeworld even."

"Here we are; in the flesh." Collin was all smiles. He interpreted what was said for his Master. The pale man grinned as well, showing pearly white teeth past his thin lips. This was the first time Rosel took full notice of his appearance; his hair was as white as the snow she had seen as a child and his cornea were a deep crimson color.

It was the Princess's turn to protest. "Your world has made raids on Human settled worlds along our borders…"

"Dear lady, we do only what is permitted by our Andalii allies; perhaps you should bring this up with them? My Patron is of a minor house that specializes in engineering. We do not deal in chattel." The look on Collin's face seemed to flare for a moment, but returned to its normal sanguine state. Rosel heard not another word from the Princess as the next course was served: Steak with steamed vegetables. Bonifacio was outdoing himself this day. Esme was devouring the contents of her entire plate, while both Collin and his Patron were only taking small bites of the meat.

The Captain did his best to steer the conversation in a positive direction. "So, what is life like on your homeworld?"

"For us Kyuketsuki it is very pleasurable. We have all the comforts that one needs to live a long healthy life. This applies to most Humans there as well. Entire generations live, work, and play on the inner surface without even knowing the true nature of their rulers." Collin replied. Rosel was starting to wonder if he was testing them. He was giving them enough bait.

"Does anyone ever plan to leave your world? I've heard rumors of rogue Kyuketsuki who have left there." The Captain was throwing bait of his own.

"We have had an occasional exile. However, we tend to take care of things in-house. Those that wish to leave without authority are dealt with severely. We have ships that patrol the surrounding space when the need arises." Collin was translating the back and forth for his Master; perhaps wanting him to add to the conversation. It appeared that he was not game for it.

Rosel watched Esme as she passed her empty plate to Bartholomew who passed it to Collin. Collin placed all of his and his Masters vegetables on the plate and passed it back. Esme began to devour these as well. The two Kyuketsuki finished their meat.

The First Officer started in on some tale of being on Patrol near the Adalii border near their homeworld. Suddenly Rosel felt an odd feeling in her head. *You should change your mind you know.* It was a woman's voice speaking to her *inside* her head. She looked up to see Esme staring straight at her with the same blank expression as always. *The Master's blood is very powerful. In such quantities as he is offering you, it could be very bad for you.* It had to be Esme. *Do not speak aloud; only think.*

Esme, is this you?

Yes. You are a telepath. That is why you can hear me. Perhaps you do not know?

What...what do you mean?

In time you will know. Mark me; do not take the Master's blood. It will go badly for you.

Rosel then felt as if the voice was no longer there. Looking up she saw Esme again consuming the vegetables on her plate; a mess man standing by patiently to take the plate from her. Rosel almost sensed that her eyes lit up for just an instance when a portion of strawberry tart was placed in front of her.

3

Denton Bret finished showering and took the offered robe from the *Arbiter* Avatar. It was great to have her around. She provided all sorts of information on the Pruatha. She was even creating one of their teleportation cabinets so that he could exploit some of the worlds that the Pruatha had been observing and the other species had not found yet. Of course, she would have to go down first to load the other end with organic stock; as she had explained it to him, he wasn't sure that he wanted to be disassembled and made whole again with different molecules. She assured him that her old master had found it exhilarating. They reached Saragothra rather quickly. Reconnoitering the surrounding space, they found the perfect place to lure the *Iwakina* to battle; an asteroid field at the edge of the Saragothra system. He brought the Arbiter Avatar planet-side disguised in a hooded cloak to see if there would be issues; there were none. They received the occasional odd look, but most people just ignored them. Some major political issue was keeping everyone's attention which was fine by him.

He had put in a request to hire the *Iwakina* by the normal channels and was waiting patiently. They would take the bait soon enough. He wouldn't even need to rely on Chiampa's beacon. The enemy would come straight to him. It *would* help to know when they arrived.

*   *   *

The *Iwakina* was well underway to the Kyuketsuki Warusei. Goh Takagawa was having difficulty with the language of the visitors. It was like no other language in his datasets; although he had quite a collection gathered. The one that came the closest to it was the ancient form of Latin; an archaic form at that. There were maybe two or three loan words that may have matches but he couldn't be sure. The symbols used for letters were the easiest part to figure out once he found patterns of usage, but he was not even 100% sure of that. There were even a small set of diagrams and text in another language altogether. They seemed to indicate tiny spheres which attracted entire starships from one place to the next. *Spaceballs!* Goh thought in amusement. The best part of the whole download for him was the numerous schematics of ancient Earth technology. *He just needed to get at the language to make sense of it all...*

* * *

Ken Edwards was getting very apprehensive. He just had a very bad feeling about leaving Benoba in the sick bay. It did not have anything to do with the location; it was something about the good Doctor that made him edgy. Besides, Benoba was not getting a great deal better with her skin condition, but to Edwards, it made her even more exotic to be honest. He got permission from the Captain to move her to an unoccupied cabin right next to his; purely for protective reasons and so that he could be more available to her in her studies. Doctor Rosel was nonplussed on the issue; she stated that it appeared to her that some of the coloration in Ms. Benoba seemed to be permanent like the woman's hair color. The pink pastiness, like the skin of a very fair person, shown like tiger stripes across normal healthy-looking skin on what parts of Benoba's body Edwards could see. He spent a great deal of time with her and insisted on escorting her about the ship; for her own protection of course. Most of the crew would gawk for just a moment when they first encountered her, but otherwise did their best to not make her feel awkward. For his part, Edwards did his best to be gentlemanly, but it started to become apparent that his feelings for her were becoming more than platonic in nature.

*   *   *

The jump sequence ended forty minutes out from their destination as was instructed by their guests. Sanae hailed the Captain and Collin as instructed. Both reached the bridge on the same lift.

"Collin, if you would do the honors…" The Captain was rather cordial to the visitor. *Perhaps they had discussed a plan on the way up here* she thought.

"Navigator, please take us in this direction at full impulse. We must be assured of a smooth approach toward my Patron's holdings." Collin instructed her in her disguise as Kintaro Sagura by pointing at a holo-map. Sanae punched in the course and the ship headed in the direction indicated.

After thirty minutes of full impulse, Collin had her enter hyperspace, changing course to head for the construct. A visual representation was displayed on the main board; the real view would blind any normal person. Still the construct when it came into full view was burning white.

"Take us to within five-thousand kilometers and stop. We will exit hyperspace once we determine that there are no other ships in that space." The sensors indicated no other ships, so Sanae pulled the ship out of hyperspace. The visual of the construct on screen changed to its true form; a vast blackness filled the screen in front of them with a myriad of faint lights of various hues on its surface. To Sanae it was oddly beautiful.

"Captain, we are in your debt for the hospitality you have provided us. However, we must impose on you for a short time longer. We require a shuttle to take us in and we will be accompanied by your Doctor Rosel, who insists on seeing the Master's house. I will give her escort the communications device you will need to contact us further." Collin almost seemed to be instructing the Captain rather than requesting.

"Just send her back in one piece." The Captain replied.

* * *

Doctor Rosel was scared and excited at the same time. The warning given her by Esme just added to the excitement. She watched as the shuttle approached the blackness and Collin was having an apparently heated exchange with someone on his communicator. He finally fell silent and, turning to his patron, said something abrupt. He then instructed the shuttle pilot to head toward a particularly bright spot which turned out to be an access bay. She watched the monitors as the shuttle entered the construct and flew several kilometers inside.

They touched down on a landing pad and waited for the whole area to pressurize. After a few expectant moments, Collin seemed agitated. He told the Marines who would be escorting her to be on guard and stay in a tight group. Apparently, it was a bad sign that a welcoming party did not come to meet them. They left the shuttle and headed down a short corridor into a large bay area. Rosel was so enthralled by the structure and texture of the walls here that she had wandered from the group. Collin called to her, warning her to stay close, but it was too late; she fell, feeling many sharp pains all over her body as if she were hit by many needles. She felt her body was wet with blood. Holding out her hand she saw it all over; her own blood that she was losing. Just then she saw a blinding blue light emanate from the group, and saw many blue flames engulfing figures in the distance. She looked up from where she lay and saw Esme bending over her.

I should let you die here and avoid the suffering that fate will bestow upon you. But the Master would be saddened by such a waste of his efforts. Live and suffer well. Esme was once again in her head. She felt Esme touch her and a great feeling of relief took hold of her as if the needle pain never existed. She sat upright. *Did you heal me?* She thought at the woman.

Yes. Do not curse me later on. Esme helped her to her feet. They passed a number of burnt bodies before they reached a tram-like vehicle.

"Pitiful fools. Did they not know that having the

Master's blood flowing in them was enough to seal their fate?" Collin had a look of both pleasure and sadness that was disconcerting to Rosel as he said this.

The Tram took them to the House of Bartholomew. As they exited, many people prostrated themselves before their Master in the hopes of gaining mercy for what had transpired. Collin told her that an upstart Postulant of his rank named Stephan had taken over in the Master's absence. The bodies they passed before were underlings who had set up an ambush. Stephan was not among them.

They went down several corridors, many filled with prostrated servants until they came to what Collin called the Inner Sanctum. As they entered more servants prostrated themselves save one. This was the usurper Stephan. Words were exchanged in the language of the Kyuketsuki. Then suddenly Stephan produced a handheld device which he activated after stepping into a circular area. A harsh light filled the area of the circle and Rosel watched as the deviant's flesh burned off of him; his body collapsing in a heap of ash.

"Hmpf. The weakling took his own life rather than face the wrath of our dear Master." Collin was all grin as he said this. "Dear Doctor, it is a shame that you had to witness these events. However, it would do you well to remember what happens to those who cross our Patron. Unfortunately, some of those servants you see here before you will not live to see tomorrow; the Master will likely call for a Decimation."

Rosel was familiar with this term from ancient history. Every tenth man from an enemy camp was killed on the spot to ensure obedience from the rest.

Bartholomew said a few words from where he was seated in a grand chair; probably a throne of sorts. Collin had Rosel and her escort approach. "It is now time for you to collect your reward, Good Doctor." A vial was brought forth to Bartholomew who unceremoniously bit his own wrist drawing blood. He poured a great deal into the vial.

"Dear Doctor the ways of the Kyuketsuki are very strict. The only way you will be permitted to leave here with the Master's blood is by drinking it." Before Rosel could object, Collin had the vial in his hand and was by her side in a flash, tilting back her head, making her drink. She coughed as the warm liquid ran down her throat.

"Do not worry, Good Doctor; these Marines will forget everything they have seen here. This is what you wanted all along is it not? You will have immortality, in addition to your enhanced Human abilities. You will be an agent for the Master. Can you feel him? He is there with you now, down your throat, into your stomach, coursing through your veins."

Rosel felt an intense heat overtake her for a moment, but as suddenly as it was there, it was gone. She felt somewhat renewed.

Collin was handing her a thick book. "This is the book of the Kyuketsuki Initiate. You will not be able to read it now, but in time you will understand its meaning. It will guide you on the path. Now go and be well until the Master calls you to service."

Doctor Rosel and her escort were given Collin's communications device, returned to the shuttle, and sent off. She shuddered at the implications the ordeal meant for her. As the shuttle headed up the great passage to the surface, the outside monitors showed that they became surrounded by bodies floating in the zero-gravity of the corridor; the Decimation had begun.

4

Saitow waited for the shuttle's return with an uneasiness that was uncharacteristic of him. Now that the visitors had left his ship, he almost felt as if he had been manipulated in some ways. Although he couldn't quite put a finger on it, he just felt it was so. He checked with the calibrations crew; they were almost done. Apparently, they didn't want to be in this place a second longer than necessary either. The only person who had anything positive to say about the place was Takagawa, who was using the ships visuals to record as much footage as possible of the construct's surface. Saitow ordered Sagura to plot a rapid course to Andali. As soon as that shuttle docked, and the contingent was accounted for, they would get underway.

* * *

The jump sequence to Andali would take just under an hour. Marishima helped Doctor Rosel set up billeting and extra lab space for their guest hopeful, the Andalii Scientist Dorigethra. She had asked Doctor Rosel about him and found out that they had been friends at the medical university that they both had attended. She was told the Andalii was a genius, able to figure out almost any biological conundrum with ease. He tended to have an ego to go along with that. Although he could be quite irritating, he was always quite friendly with Rosel. Marishima hoped that the friendliness would spread to those close to the Doctor. She did not need an egotistical ass for a boss right now. She had enough to deal with in Sanac, Doctor Rosel's possible telepathic talent, and her anxiety over not knowing the status of the other rogue Sparrow members, including her beloved Wilhelm.

*   *   *

Nanami Oliver was escorting Doctor Rosel down to the surface of Andalii. She had been on several trade missions here as Sakura Nechenko, but had no worries about being spotted; the Andalii rarely remembered such petty details as who traded with whom or what was being traded after the deal was secured. She remembered the most striking features of the inhabitants: thick rear neck muscles to support great bulbous outcropping brain cavities at the back of their hairless heads. That, and the fact of their rather flat faces, was the only trait that distinguished them from Humans. They did tend to have thick brow ridges and broad noses. It was ironic that their heightened intellect had led them down a path of economic decay that was diverted only by their contact with Humans of the Old Earth Empire. Humans lived with them for a time, but soon tired of their penchant for always needing to be right; a trait which subsequent generations endeavored drastically to overcome. Now there are few humans on the planet, but other worlds in Andalii space had comingled populations.

They landed in a clearing on the outskirts of a large village marked by many extravagant mansions. Rosel had insisted that she contact Dorigethra herself through the comm-link. She somehow smoothed over the presence of the *Iwakina* being in orbit with the Planetary Government Authorities. It was agreed that Dorigethra would come with them *and* arrange for a transport of the Kadihri and Pendari Ambassadors. Nanami mused at how the drunken fools had holed up in one or the other's cabins drinking heavily and missing the whole Kyuketsuki evolution. She had to threaten them again to get them to sober up long enough to be transported off the ship to a Human controlled transport.

Dorigethra arrived in a gravitic service vehicle. He had several pieces of luggage; each of which was exceptionally heavy Nanami noted. As the shuttle headed back up to the ship, Nanami rolled her eyes as the two hugged each other and exchanged pleasantries like two sisters who had not seen each other in years.

* * *

Dorigethra Fan was a little annoyed at being among so many Humans. They always tended to be direct in their thoughts which were very difficult to tune out. It was worth the burden being able to work with his dear old friend Kimberly Rosel after all these years. She had assured him that he would not have to mingle very often with the rest of the ship; she had set up a lab in the Sick Bay for the two of them to use. The only other Human he would most likely have constant contact with was her medical assistant Marishima who was escorting him now. He was musing on this as well as detecting inorganic biorhythms within the walls of the corridors down which he was being led. This magnificent ship was made of trillions of nano-units. This fascinated him and kept his mind off of the thoughts of the various Humans he passed.

He was shown his quarters and the passage from there to the lab they would work in. It just then occurred to him that the thoughts of this Marishima were not getting to him; he would think more on that later. Doctor Rosel showed him a comatose patient that she needed help with, although he sensed that there was more to this patient than Kim let on. It occurred to him that Kimberly's thoughts were not getting to him either, so he probed. To his astonishment he found that he was being blocked! He probed harder and harder, but the block grew in intensity to thwart his every attempt. His concentration was broken when Kimberly addressed him.

"Fan, what's wrong? You seem agitated."

"Oh, Kimberly dear it's nothing. You don't know what just occurred?"

"Umm… You were staring intensely at me and started biting your lip. I thought I had done something to offend you."

"No, no! Nothing of the sort. Seriously though; you don't know what just happened?"

"Do I have something on my face?" Rosel was very confused at this point. Dorigethra pulled his tablet out of his robe pocket and started typing furiously. *His old friend had developed telepathic abilities and was completely unawares!* This merited a great deal of research. He didn't regret accepting Kimberly's invitation in the slightest.

"Kimberly, let's just say that you just did something

extraordinary that merits further study. I believe I will be of great service to you in the coming months." Dorigethra looked about for Marishima, but the young woman was gone from the room.

*   *   *

Marishima took the first opportunity to take her leave of the two doctors. She knew that she could get onto *Unity* from here and needed news of Wilhelm before she lost her mind. Besides, the Andalii seemed to be scanning everything without even realizing it. She had never encountered a creature with natural telepathic abilities until now. She would ask Wilhelm about it.

She keyed her cabin's hatch to lock and donned her VR gear. She arrived in her mansion and found her cats wanting attention. She dismissed them, although it pained her to do so, and checked her messages. There were the usual calls to check the *Unity* news; elections to decide on a referendum to align with the New Rangelley Alliance were coming up. She loathed politics, so she dismissed them quickly to find a coded message from Wilhelm with new contact information. He had almost been found, but was still a step or two ahead of the others. She called for him. His feed indicated that he was unavailable and offline, so she sent him her own coded message asking for him to contact her as soon as possible. She logged off of *Unity*; she was too worried to contact other friends of hers there before she heard back from Wilhelm. A coded email was awaiting her on her personal terminal. It advised attempting an encrypted video link. She did as it indicated. Wilhelm answered the line and greeted her with a smile much to her relief.

"Now, now, dearest, why are you crying?" Wilhelm said with much concern.

"I am just so happy to see you…" Marishima choked back a sob.

"I am sorry, little one. I cannot risk going into VR just yet because we are on the run right now. How are things there?" Marishima saw that Wilhelm was trying to be more positive than he otherwise felt. He and the others had been on the run for a long time, but the efforts of the enemy were getting more and more resilient.

Marishima wiped away her tears and told him about what had transpired on the ship from the point that they had parted until now.

"So, your current dilemma is that an Andalii is on board the ship?"

"He is in the cabin next to mine and in the lab in Sick Bay where I work."

"That could be dangerous. The Andalii are natural telepaths. That is what led to their decline before Humans came to their rescue. Since Human thoughts are easily read by them, they had great reasoning to ally with us. You must be careful around him. If he seems to be probing you, let loose some normal surface thoughts like what you ate today, or what video you want to watch, or even some boring analytics you are working on; that will cause him to tune you out."

Marishima was thinking about mentioning her love of him; it was hard to keep it suppressed. Then

41

suddenly she heard a voice beckoning Wilhelm. It was a woman's voice telling him they were about to bug out. *Was that Angelie?* She thought. Wilhelm wished her well and said his goodbyes before the screen went blank. Marishima wondered who Wilhelm had there with him. She so wanted to be there too.

* * *

Dorigethra was excited to begin his tests. The ship had stopped short of their next destination for interface calibrations of some sort; nothing that concerned him of course. He would help Kimberly with her experiments in blood transformation and this thing she called psyche transference. As if someone could actually transfer their psyche to another person. He reviewed the notes she had provided, but could not make much sense of the mathematics; it wasn't biology after all. Plus, it was riddled with ancient Pruathan technological data. He would help her with all that in due time. First, he would perform his experiments. It was apparent that she had latent telepathic abilities; he would find out just how many and how much she could perform. His people had a catalog for the various telepathic abilities measurable by his portable training device. He only possessed five of the fourteen cataloged abilities, so he brought along the training device to use in his spare time. It was quite expensive but worth the investment; he had already raised his telekinesis rating a level in the half-cycle that he had used it. He still marveled at how such things could be quantified. It had something to do with brainwave patterns or the like. There were rumors that it contained a living psyche that reacted to telepathic ability in a certain way, but he did not believe such nonsense. He would go through each of the indicator exercises with Kimberly and monitor the device for a level indication. He finished his breakfast of rolled protein and unpacked the device from his belongings. It looked like a Human head created out of silver. There were ten dark circles across the brow and a hand-held remote sat in a recess in the top back portion. This is so exciting he thought as he hefted the device and keyed the hatch.

*   *   *

Kimberly Rosel was nervous. She had not seen Dorigethra Fan in many years. They had been colleagues at the same medical academy for several years and had become very close friends. She remembered him telling her that she was his one and only Human friend in the entire Universe. Sure, he had Human acquaintances that shared work with him, but she was the only Human he had ever confided in; she knew some of his deepest secrets. When he came in to the lab, he was all smiles.

"Kimberly, it is so good to be able to work with you again; not just as classmates but as scientists! I cannot wait to get started. Ah, but first I would like to do some minor exercises to get our minds finely tuned so to speak. Won't you join me?" Dorigethra had the most endearing smile he could muster on that flat face of his. *How could she refuse?* She thought.

"What did you have in mind?" she resisted an urge to giggle at her own silly pun. She watched as

Dorigethra produced a silver-plated head and placed it on a table. He then placed a lab stool on either side of it. He offered her the seat facing the back of the silver head and took the other seat for himself.

"We are going to play a little game. I want you to ignore our little friend here between us and concentrate on trying to think of what I am thinking. Try to read my mind. Ready? What am I thinking?"

"Ah, I can clearly feel that you are thinking of how awful Human food is probably going to taste when you run out of protein roles. Honestly, have you ever even eaten Human food?" She looked expectantly at Dorigethra as his face lit up.

"Wonderful! Let's try a new one. I want you to think of an image. It can be anything; perhaps your favorite flower. Now I want you to think of it as if you are showing it to me by directly putting it in my thoughts...Concentrate harder now... Have you got it? No, no, I suppose that one will not work out. Let us move on.

"For the next exercise, I want you to think of a random innocuous event that has happened to you; something I have no idea about. Have you thought it? Very good. Let's see..." Rosel thought of the last time she went hiking on Euphrosyne. She looked up to see Dorigethra's gaze fixed steadily upon her. His expression turned from one of concentration to confusion, and then excitement, but he rapidly calmed down.

"Kimberly, well done! Now..." Dorigethra turned the head in her direction and came around the table, removing the hand-held remote from the back of it, "I want you to concentrate on this silver head. I want you to think about what kind of person this may have been if he were alive, how smart would he be, how cunning, how clever, however detailed." Rosel concentrated and saw that two of the ten dark spots on the head's brow flashed green. Dorigethra continued.

"Now think of how this person would feel about being concentrated on so deeply, would he be nervous, angry, hurt, amused?" Rosel had a slight inkling that the silver head was actually nervous and angry at being stared at in such a way. She said as much as the two green lights flashed again.

"Very good. Now I want you to think about where this silver head may have come from and how it came into my possession." She did so, but nothing came to mind for her and the lights remained dark.

"Good." Dorigethra returned the head to its original position and sat back on his stool. "Next, I would like you to try and read my mind once more…"

Rosel tried to think about what he was thinking like before. However, this time she could not sense anything; it was as if his mind was blank.

"Well done. Now if you would…"

"Hold on." Rosel interrupted. "There are more things going on here than mere mind exercises aren't there? When this is done, you are going to explain it all to me, correct?"

"Most assuredly. However, initially it helps if the examinee is unawares as to what she is being tested on. Shall we continue?"

"Fire away."

"Now I want you to concentrate on something that you would desperately like me to do. Tell me to do it, but only using your mind to do so. Be sure to concentrate fully on the attempt to persuade me." Rosel thought of something completely silly that no Human has probably ever seen an Andalii ever do. However, Dorigethra just stood there looking bored.

"Enough of that. The next one is going to be a real rough one to conceptualize, but I am sure you can manage. I am thinking of a very dark and dangerous looking place. I want you to think about causing my thoughts to change. I want you to make me see this dark and dangerous place as a place of light and safety. Can you do it? Concentrate…"

Rosel tried desperately to think this through to him. He simply frowned as if she were a disappointment to him.

"I failed, didn't I?" she mumbled. She saw that he was taken aback by this reaction and began apologizing.

"No, no, there is no pass or fail in this. I assure you. There are only a few more exercises to go, ok? Now I want you to concentrate very hard on making me think that you are not there in front of me."

Rosel could not suppress a giggle at this point, but sobered as she saw Dorigethra was very serious. She did as she was bid.

"Great, you can stop. Good. Now I want you to concentrate on the silver head. Think of it as if you were lifting it off of the table gently… Hmmm, no luck there. Alright. Now I have to give you a word of caution before you attempt the next exercise. If it works, you will be rather amazed at the result but you may become disoriented. It is a very normal reaction for first timers, so be ready. What I want you to do is think as if you are looking at the front of the silver head from my point of view. Concentrate on seeing what I am seeing…"

Rosel did as she was bid. It did actually appear as if she was looking through Dorigethra's eyes; four green lights on the front of the head were lit. She blinked and her vision returned to normal. "Was I really…?"

"Yes! I will explain it all after one more test. This final test is a bit dangerous, but I am healthy enough to withstand it so do not worry; just do as I instruct you. I want you to concentrate on the center of my brain. There at the center I want you to think of me as having a headache. I want you to gradually increase that pain up and up until I tell you to stop. I am ready; please begin."

Rosel concentrated on causing pain to her friend; it was an exercise after all. She saw him flinch just a bit but then his eyes opened wide with wonder as she increased her thoughts of causing him pain.

"Stop! That was magnificent! Although it is one of the dangerous abilities…" Dorigethra seemed absently contemplating this latest development with much thought. "Kimberly, what do you know of telepaths?"

Rosel was taken aback by this question. She knew that most Andalii were latent telepaths, but among most Human populations, telepathic abilities were outlawed. She said as much to Dorigethra.

"Well, whether you knew that you were one up until now or not; you, my dear, are a telepath."

Kimberly Rosel shuddered as she remembered her

encounters with the Kyuketsuki; particularly the girl Esme.

*   *   *

Dorigethra had used the training device as an indicator; it showed the level that Kimberly had acquired for each of the fourteen abilities. He wondered how she had developed them. "Do you have any idea as to how you came to get these abilities?" He asked her, but before she could comment he continued, "If you had been born with them you would have naturally came into the knowledge of them, but it appears to me that you did not even realize..." Dorigethra trailed off into deep contemplation.

"My experiments." she replied.

"Your experiments? How so?"

"I have been experimenting with psyche transference using some Pruathan technology and a few drugs that I have developed. I gave you the notes remember?" Kimberly looked slightly upset that he seemed cavalier about her work.

"Dear Kimberly, I just only arrived on the ship, surely you did not expect me to get fully into things the first night? Now, now, don't fret; it's unbecoming." Dorigethra saw that she was frowning, so he tried to pick her spirits up. "Darling, do you know what this means? You have extraordinary abilities! Let me break them down for you." He again offered the lab stool, but moved the silver head training device out of the way. "There are fourteen telepathic abilities among my people. We determined that among the few sentient species who can obtain these abilities, these fourteen abilities are universal. A being that possesses them has varying degrees of power over them and we rate this as levels from one to ten. Most beings have from four to six abilities at most; you my dear have an incredible *eight*! The device indicated no development of *Broadcasting*, *Clairvoyance*, *Sensing*, *Suggestion*, *Alteration*, or *Telekinesis*, so I won't go into those. However, you have the normal ability of *Telepathy*, which all telepaths have; it is sort of a basic requirement. You have a good level five in this. This ability allows you to speak mentally with another telepath, but does not allow you to speak mentally with a non-telepath; you would need to be a high-level *Broadcaster* for that. You have low level abilities in *Psychometrics* which allows you to gauge a person's mental abilities, and *Empathy* which allows you to determine someone's emotional state.

"Remember when I asked you to concentrate on making me think you were not there? You did just that, but barely. At a level three, your *Blanking* ability made you fade a bit, but it might work on a non-telepath. You can make them believe you are not there. *Probing* is basically mind reading; at level four you can go moderately deep into someone's thoughts. As you saw you are also a level four in *Sight*. This ability allows you to see through the eyes of another telepath who is willing to allow you inside their head.

"The most interesting abilities that you have are level nine in *Blocking* and level eight in *Psychic Attack*. At Level nine you have probably been subconsciously blocking any attempt to probe you, as I have to admit, I have attempted once or twice since arriving. Finally, as you probably have figured out, *Psychic Attack* is just that; a means to cause pain in the mind of both

Telepaths and non-telepaths, without causing permanent damage." Dorigethra finished his descriptions and looked expectantly at Kimberly, who, to his surprise looked quite astonished.

"Just think of the implications if I have developed external means to induce such abilities…" was all she could muster.

5

The *Iwakina* crew were on the one quick jump needed to reach Uprising. Kuremoto had been extremely anxious when he learned that they were going to stop short and calibrate the ship in hyperspace; the Captain did not want to be near Uprising too long. They would come out far enough from the planet for Kuremoto and an escort to sortie to the coordinates that had been smuggled out with the virus samples. These coordinates were supposed to be a point where the planetary defenses would not detect a couple of starfighters approaching once the planet-wide defense shield was dropped. Kuremoto hoped the two men who risked it all to get him this information would evade their government long enough for it to fall. He got a call on the comm-link. "You ready Professor?" It was Corporal Bastian, his escort.

"Ready as I'll ever be." Kuremoto tried to sound confident but he was sure it didn't turn out that way.

"Don't sweat it. I've seen you burn one of these; you're a natural."

"Thanks." Kuremoto felt a bit better at the confidence this young man had in him. A green light lit up on his indicator board. The Captain was on the comm this time. "Doctor, you are GO for launch."

Kuremoto waited for the whoosh his escort's Ethla made going out the adjacent tube and punched his own launch sequence. The Gees he was pulling always gave him a little thrill and he admonished himself as being too old for such elation. He followed his partner in a long arc around to the other side of the planet and then eased up, waiting for the signal that the defense grid was down. Several minutes passed, but then he saw the indicator bands on the satellite in front of them change from blue to red; this was the sign the grid was down. His wing man wagged his Ethla and headed in. Kuremoto followed.

*   *   *

Shirae was on the bridge at the invitation of the Captain. He wanted her there for two reasons; to impress the Administrator of Uprising, and because he had assured her that she would be involved with the ships business from now on. She did not like being used, but was happy to be by his side. When the Administrator came on the vid-screen in her violently purple uniform, the woman's eyes widened with astonishment, and then she bowed deeply.

"Your Highness, what a pleasant surprise. We did not expect a State Visit…"

"Administrator, we are not here on a visit; we are merely here to observe the business of this ship. Please think of me as if I am not here at all." Shirae giggled a little inside; she hoped the woman did not notice.

Captain Saitow took his cue from that, "Administrator, I am Captain Saitow of the Starship *Iwakina*. I believe you have a passenger for us to pick up? Please drop your defense grid for our shuttle to come down. My First Officer will be aboard and can discuss terms."

"You are not coming down? We can provide refreshments from your long voyage perhaps?"

"I am afraid I have duties aboard ship that require my immediate attention. Please be assured that your daughter will be well cared for on her journey to Saragothra." *The Captain is in full statesman mode* Shirae thought to herself.

"Thank you, Captain, she is in your care." The vidscreen went blank and the Captain sat back in his chair. He offered the First Officer's chair to Shirae.

"Shirae, what do you think of the Administrator?" Saitow asked.

"I don't know what you are asking; I have only seen the woman for those few moments." Shirae replied.

"Our visit here today is historic. It will be the end of her rule here on Uprising."

Shirae was taken aback by this statement. *What could he possibly mean by that?* She was about to ask him to explain, but having glanced around the bridge she noticed that the Navigator was looking at them in an odd way. Perhaps he could hear their conversation. Not only that but it was probably unexpected for them to be speaking so informally in front of the crew. She said as much to Saitow who just smiled at her. After a few moments of contemplation, he said, "You are right dear Shirae. Perhaps we should take our conversation to my quarters…"

*　　*　　*

The two Ethlas were landed at the designated coordinates. Corporal Bastian would stay with the Ethlas and remain in his cockpit to avoid contracting the Uprising inhabitants' disease.

Kuremoto wore protective head gear as the contagion was airborne and contracted through the lungs; besides that, he had inoculated himself with vaccine for the ailment. A land crawler type wheeled vehicle approached and his friend Marcus departed the interior.

"My good friend! It has been so long! Come aboard. We can talk on the way to my underground lab."

Kuremoto made sure they loaded the several cases he had brought with him, and then climbed aboard. The vehicle sped then off in the direction from which it came. His friend looked fit, if not much older and with the addition of a large sequence of numbers tattooed on his right cheekbone area. Kuremoto must have been staring because his friend reached up and stroked the number.

"This is our legacy old friend. If your cure works for us, the whole galaxy will know us from these tattoos. Enough un-pleasantries though; how have you been faring?"

Kuremoto told him of some of his accomplishments since they last parted. Both men were ancient; the Uprising government provided Marcus with Rejuve because he was the foremost medical officer among the infected. Surprisingly, Rejuve staved off the wasting of the disease. He was also considered by them to be a well-known pacifist leader. That would all change soon enough.

*   *   *

Saitow was weary about telling Shirae about the plot to cure the diseased people of Uprising. He needed to though, in order to gain her trust. He waited until she was done looking around the room and offered her a seat in an overstuffed lounger; she had never been in his quarters before. He then sat in the seat next to hers. First, he told her of the structure of the government. It was run by a handful of uninfected officials under the Administrator. The infected would work in their factories manufacturing weapons in exchange for food and medicine. A secure system of transference was implemented which decontaminated any inorganic items; mainly the products made by the workers. It was fatal to anything organic. The workers were overseen by an elite corps of biohazard suit wearing storm troopers. Any form of dissent was dealt with swiftly. He ended this part by mentioning the population's facial tattoos.

Next, he told her of Kuremoto's plot to fix this inappropriate system by providing a cure to the infected. He showed her Kuremoto's notes on the disease and how it appeared to be manufactured for the purpose of creating slave labor. Then he sprung the final details on her.

"Kuremoto is at this moment down there on the other side of the planet providing the cure to these people, while we are maintaining the ruse of playing transportation for the Administrator's daughter."

Shirae looked contemplative for a moment then lit

up as if she had a brilliant analysis on her mind. She said as much. "Knowing as much about you as I do at this point, I would have to deduce that you are going along with this in order to deny further weapons shipments to our empire, thus depriving Aisou of more power. Otherwise, I do not believe you would endanger the ship in this manner. Am I correct?"

Saitow smiled amusedly at the audacity of the Princess's statement. However, she was mostly correct in her evaluation of the situation. His admiration of her was increasing tenfold.

"Princess, *you* will make an extraordinary Empress someday."

* * *

Goh Takagawa was sitting in his office admiring his latest accomplishment; an organized working schedule for his entire engineering compliment. Things were finally going smoothly despite the loss of Misaki. He uploaded the schedule to *Iwa* and had it disseminated to all involved parties. He sat his tablet down and rubbed his eyes. Setting his hands down he touched something unfamiliar and pulled back his hand. It was the small piece of circuitry he had found in Sagura's cabin. He had forgotten all about it with all that had transpired with the ship, and the myriad tasks he had to do and supervise. He keyed up the diagnostic on his terminal. It was indeed a piece of sophisticated communications hardware. This brought thoughts of the spy he was supposed to be tracking. He keyed up the sniffer program he had running. There were several more hits on it. He swore under his breath for forgetting to monitor it.

Now he was thinking wearily about the possibility that his best friend of several years could be a spy for the Imperials. Goh had even recruited the man for the mutiny. He sat there contemplating the odd occurrences that had taken place since the mutiny. Something was just not right about his friend. He was getting more and more hard pressed to realize that Kintaro Sagura could in fact be the spy he was looking for. He was soon in conflict with himself between loyalty to the ship and loyalty to his friend; he even began rethinking his loyalty to the Empire.

He decided that he would keep his theories to himself for now and just keep a sharp eye of Sagura. He decided to start carrying a sidearm; if the time came for action, he would be ready. Now if he could just remember if he had given the information to Nanami Oliver that he had been told to…

*   *   *

Kuremoto glanced out the narrow windows of the vehicle on occasion to see them pass through a small community where most of the people looked destitute and lifeless. He was grateful that he would be able to change things for these people. They pulled up alongside a nondescript building and Kuremoto was escorted down several flights of stairs. There was a corridor that led to a large steel door. His escort stopped short of that and pressed a recess that looked like just another crack in the wall. A hidden door recessed into the wall and Kuremoto was led through. They went down another corridor with a couple of turns in it for defense. Finally, they came to another large steel door. This one they keyed open and Kuremoto found an elaborate laboratory set up.

"Edward, please set up over here. I have several test subjects ready for you." Marcus indicated a table near some patients in beds. There were five of them; Marcus's daughter Margo was among them.

"Marcus, I am not one hundred percent sure the cure will work; there may be complications and..." Kuremoto glanced nervously at Margo who smiled at him.

"Edward, this is our moment of truth. I have selected patients within various stages of the disease. Margo is here because she must be cured before the coming troubles, and you must take her with you."

Kuremoto was shocked. He did not suspect for a moment that Marcus would be willing to part from his only daughter whose own mother had been taken by the disease. The girl was maybe seventeen years old. Kuremoto suspected that the plans these people had for the future would begin with a terrible darkness if Marcus wished for his daughter to be absent from their experience. Kuremoto owed this man his life; Marcus had saved him from a dreadful bought of addiction that had nearly killed him and left him in ruin.

"If the cure takes, I will; I promise you she will be well cared for." Kuremoto replied.

"Good, I have an encounter suit ready for her so that you can get her properly decontaminated on your ship. We don't want to cause trouble for your benefactors;

but I am getting ahead of myself. Shall we begin?"

*   *   *

Marcus listened intently as his friend Kuremoto explained the nature of the disease and the cycle for administering the cure. Kuremoto had enough doses for possibly two-hundred infected, and the time it should take for full regression was minimal depending on what stage the patient had already developed. Marcus knew the stages, but listened intently to be sure that Kuremoto had them down himself. He also knew that the diseases had been manufactured; his own experiments had determined as much. That was the reason that they had prepared for the time this day would come.

The disease was a virus that at onset, formed in the lungs and reproduced there, making the carrier spread the disease by airborne means to anyone nearby. It was also almost always passed from mother to child in the womb. When the patient reached an age where they were less able to maintain working fitness, the diseases mutated and grew substantially, slowly filling the lungs with fluid, and eventually drowning its victim. This took a course of several agonizing months for the infected; the Administration kindly offered these people 'Serenity', a program aimed at humanely putting an end to their suffering. No one knew what happened to the volunteers for the program or where they were taken.

Marcus helped administer the cure to the five patients including Margo. It would be a half an hour before they could test their blood for the disease's reaction to the cure. If it worked, he would have the remaining doses given to the able-bodied men who had secretly volunteered to take up arms. Each would give blood first in order to reproduce the cure through natural means, instructions for which Kuremoto had given in minute detail.

The first blood sample was taken and showed that the disease was in fact being destroyed by the cure; Marcus hugged his friend and then his daughter whose blood sample they had checked. They were about to test the other patients when an aid came hurriedly to Marcus and told him he was getting a call from the Administrator. Marcus bade his friend to continue, and then hurried to a side room which had been created as a replica to his office in his poorly equipped official lab several miles away. The call came on a video feed that was secretly rerouted here. He sat at his pseudo desk and answered the call. The Administrator in her horrid purple uniform came on the vid-screen. "Marcus, darling, how are you?" Marcus noted that her smile looked a bit more sinister than usual.

"I am doing well Administrator, and you?" He replied calmly.

"Oh, I am doing well... it's just that I am a little confused. It seems that I am talking to you there in your office, but my courier is being refused entry to that same office. You see he is there to deliver your supply of Rejuve, yet you refuse to see him. Why is that?"

Marcus began to sweat. His monthly resupply of Rejuve was not scheduled to appear until several days from now; *why was it early and why did it have to appear at such a critical time?* Several options went through his head about how to deal with this situation;

60

none of them provided a viable way of getting out of the jam he found himself in. Marcus got up from his seat and walked hurriedly around his desk toward the vid-screen while saying, "That's very odd! I'll go at once to see…" at that point he feigned tripping and landed full into the vid-screen ripping it form its mount and in turn ripping the connecting cords. The screen went blank as it crashed to the floor. Marcus picked himself up and brushed some dust off of his lab coat. He hurried out the hatch and gave the aid instructions to capture the courier at all costs, ensuring his comm-unit is disabled. He hurried over to Kuremoto who was just finishing checking the last of the blood samples.

"All done; it's a success!" Kuremoto beamed. Marcus's look must have been grim as Kuremoto's expression became serious when he looked up at his friend.

"Margo dear get into the suit and wait for us at the door please. That's a good girl." Marcus stroked his daughter's head for what may be the very last time. He led Kuremoto away from the patients.

"Edward, it seems that our plans will have to be sped up a bit. I just had a run in with the Administrator on the vids. She will likely send her goons after me. I cannot express my sincere appreciation enough for all you have done for us. You are enabling an entire planet the chance to have a new life without tyranny and injustice. For this we are all grateful. Hopefully we will be able to talk again soon. However, you must take Margo and go. Now." Marcus embraced his old friend once more and sent him off with an aide. He quickly swiped at a budding tear as he waved to Margo when they left the laboratory.

*   *   *

The shuttle pilot had been given instructions to wait for clearance from the Captain before lifting off from the surface. This would allow Saitow to coordinate the shuttle's exit from the defense grid with Kuremoto's return. The shuttle pilot was to give some excuses about a coolant leak he had to fix or some other impromptu maintenance. Vic Soto was there to keep the passenger engaged. It had been almost two hours; Kuremoto had assured him he would be in and out rather quickly. Kuremoto and Corporal Bastian were to await a toned signal before leaving the planet. The client was already waiting aboard the shuttle and the pilot had reported she was impatiently waiting at that. Suddenly he got a message from Bastian on an encoded channel, "All packages accounted for, but we may have been compromised by flyover. We may have to shoot our way topside."

Saitow swore to himself and ordered the shuttle pilot to hightail it up to the ship. He may need some collateral. He had Simpson scramble the remaining Ethlas and begin defensive patrolling.

*   *   *

Kuremoto had experienced a much bumpier ride on the way back to his starfighter than when he arrived. They were making no pretenses in getting him and Margo back to where the Ethlas were parked. Once they were dropped off, Kuremoto got Margo loaded into the second seat of his Ethla as the vehicle sped off in a direction different from which they came. He got on his comm-unit and told Corporal Bastian about their need to expedite leaving. When asked about his passenger, Kuremoto assured him that she was no threat. They fired up the Ethlas and did preflight checks on the fly. Suddenly, they heard a roar as an atmospheric vehicle flew low over their heads. Bastian sent his message to the Captain; if need be, they would have to destroy one of the defense grid's satellites. Kuremoto thought that it was ironic that these satellites had been manufactured and installed by the Saitow Conglomerate.

* * *

Vic Soto got the message from the Captain and curtailed the fake maintenance the pilot was acting on. He gave his goodbyes to the flight controller and the shuttle was airborne in no time. The Administrator's daughter, Beatrice was her name, was mumbling something about it being about time. As they made it past the defense grid, the pilot reported that it had been reactivated as soon as they were clear. Soto felt a tug on his sleeve. "Mr. Soto, have the pilot turn on the monitors. I want to see the planet and surrounding space." Beatrice urged him. She was a mere child of sixteen; she did not need to know about the troubles that were soon to befall her planet.

"I'm afraid the monitors are malfunctioning at the moment dear Miss." Soto did his best to be serious.

"Well, I certainly hope that the ship we are headed to does not have so many problems as this darned shuttle." Soto spared a glance at the girl's official escort. The woman just rolled her eyes.

*   *   *

Corporal Bastian was sure that they had eluded the atmospheric vehicle, but there was still the possibility that the government had scrambled fighters. He did not want to be around when they arrived. The two Ethlas shot full bore up out of the atmosphere only to encounter proximity warnings that the defense grid was active. Bastian knew there was only one option if Doctor Kuremoto and his passenger were to get back to the ship. He throttled is Ethla in the direction of the nearest satellite.

"Bastian! What are you doing? That's suicide! Those satellites have-"

"Don't worry about me Doc. Just get yourself and that little lady back to the ship!" Bastian cut him off.

Bastian got within firing range of the satellite and got off several plasma bolts before feeling his cockpit and himself being ripped up by projectile loads. He managed to flip on the autopilot and see the satellite explode before he lost consciousness.

*   *   *

Kuremoto saw the satellite explode, but he noticed

that Corporal Bastian's Ethla was flying in an uncommon pattern to that of a live pilot. He angled close only to see the cockpit riddled with holes and a few splatters of blood on the inside glass. He got on the horn to the ship; to damnation with radio silence at this point.

* * *

Saitow was contemplating the latest events. He had the shuttle aboard and in docking procedures. Nanami Oliver had been sent to see to his newest guest. His Ehtlas were doing deep arcs looking for ships from the surface. So far none were apparent. He just wished he knew what was going on with Kuremoto and Bastian. Just then a frantic radio message came over the open channel; it was Kuremoto.

"*Iwakina*, this is Kuremoto! Bastian is on autopilot; send immediate escort! I repeat, Bastian is unconscious and on autopilot; send immediate escort!"

"Comms, patch me in!" the Captain ordered. "Kuremoto, this is the Captain. What is your status?"

"I and passenger are fine. Both Ethlas are out of the defense grid. However, Corporal Bastian's Ethla is on autopilot; I'm afraid he's unconscious… or worse." Kuremoto replied.

"Passenger?" there was silence from the other end. "I'm sending Ethlas to intercept. Bastian's Ethla should be heading in the direction of the ship. Can you confirm?"

"Roger, we are inbound. Should I transmit IFF?"

"Go ahead. At this point if they are going to come, they will come at the ship."

"Captain! A priority signal from the planet. Audio and video." It was Communications.

"Kuremoto! Keep an eye on Bastian and continue heading our way. Saitow out." The Captain finished with Kuremoto and composed himself for the coming storm. "Patch the Administrator through."

"Aye, Captain."

The vid-screen lit up with the torso of a purple clad and very angry Administrator.

"What can I do for you Administrator? Your daughter should be comfortably settled in by now." Saitow did his best to sound nonchalant.

"Captain Saitow! My Defense people tell me that there are two small unidentified craft heading your way that destroyed part of my defense grid escaping the planet. They also tell me that you have several other small craft prowling around the perimeter of your ship. Would you mind explaining what is going on?" The Administrator seemed a bit flustered.

Saitow weighed his options carefully before deciding bluntness was called for. His family would not take kindly in his messing with the affairs of a major weapons supplier. He would talk to Kuremoto in order to get some leverage with the new regime, whoever that turned out to be.

"Dear Administrator, it has come to our attention that your little arrangement comes at the expense of the suffering of several hundreds of thousands of people. It has also come to light that the suffering of these people is caused by no natural disease; this disease is of a manufactured origin. I and my colleagues could not in good conscious let this pass. I'm afraid your reign of terror on Uprising is about to come to a bitter end." Saitow ended it there to let it sink in for a bit.

"Captain, I demand you return my daughter at once!" The Administrator was almost turning red. Apparently Saitow had struck a chord of truth.

"Oh, I'm afraid that it would not be in anyone's best interests for the child to return to such a world with all the trouble that will be taking place there soon. Don't you think that the child would be safer on Saragothra with her father? We think so. Worry not. She will be well taken care of I assure you."

The Administrator was silent for a moment. Perhaps she saw the wisdom in having her daughter gone for a while.

"Come on, tell me Saitow; what have you done? Don't you want to gloat about it, now that you have me in a bind? You abscond on a merry-men's folly with a ship of the Empire, kidnapping a royal person – oh yes, I did some research on you – and now you have come to right some great wrong in the galaxy - here on Uprising?" The Administrator was more cunning than he gave her credit for.

"Now, now, dear Administrator; I do not want to spoil all of your fun. Besides, gloating is for tyrants and poor sportsmen." Saitow saw a flash behind the vid-screen and looked to find Sagura holding up a tablet with big letters scrolling across it: ALL ETHLAS ON

BOARD AND IN DECON. SHALL I PLOT A COURSE TO KALK SIR? Saitow flashed him a thumbs up; the universal sign for get-us-the-hell-out-of-here. They would avoid a lot of Imperial space by heading into Yolandan Conglomerate space and taking their Jumpgate to Saragothra. He cut off the Administrator who was going into a tirade of angry embellishments.

"Administrator, I would love to continue this conversation, but I have a delivery to make. Best of luck." With that he keyed off the vid-screen. "Somebody, get me a report from the hangar deck!"

* * *

Kuremoto had preprogrammed the Uprising disease into the decontamination chamber's detection apparatus. After the Ethla was decontaminated, he escorted Margo to the chamber for inbound pilots. Once she was in, he had her remove the bio-suit and do some breathing exercises. The chamber pronounced her clean, but he would do some more tests in his lab once he got her there. First though, he needed to get the status of Corporal Bastian. They had got him out and onto a gurney for transport straight to sick bay. Kuremoto thanked the gods he was still alive. He was sure that Doctor Rosel could fix him up as long as she got to him while he *was* still alive. There was no love lost between Kuremoto and Rosel, but he had to admit – the woman could do medical miracles.

He took Margo up the lift straight across from the chamber which went all the way up to his laboratory.

Besides him, only the Command Staff had the code to open the lift doors to access it. He took a good look at the girl. She was short and a little skinny, but she was pretty in a plain way. A few hearty meals should get her in better shape. He was sure that malnutrition was as common as the infection on Uprising. She looked shyly at him as he offered her a seat.

"Don't worry dear girl. I'm far too old to be chasing after teenagers. Are you hungry? I think I have some travel rations around here somewhere. You don't want to just jump into the food on this ship in your condition. Oh, but you will get to enjoy it soon enough; Bonifacio is an excellent cook..." Kuremoto lost his train of thought as he saw the girl was sobbing into her palms.

"Now, now; don't fret. Your father is a brilliant and resilient man; I am sure he will get things straightened out on Uprising in no time."

"It's not that... I... I'm just so happy to be here with you. My father has told me so much about you every evening while we waited for the day you would come to save us." She was practically beaming at him as she wiped the tears from her face.

It was just then that it hit him; he had possibly saved hundreds of thousands of lives. He turned and hurriedly set up the makeshift bed that he used when he was too exhausted to go down to his quarters; busy work to hide his own overwhelming emotions.

The door to the lift opened startling him. It was the Captain. He took one look at the girl and glared at him, then came hurriedly to Kuremoto's side. The two men went to the far side of the lab.

"Professor, I think you have some explaining to do." The Captain sat in a chair; Kuremoto thought it ironic that it was the very chair where the Captain had proposed he join the mutiny from. Kuremoto took the other seat.

"Well Captain, where would you like me to start?" Kuremoto did not feel like being bullied at the moment.

"You can start by telling me who that young woman is, that is on my ship without permission. I see she has an Infected's tattoo. What is going on?" Saitow was tapping the arm of the chair.

"Have I ever told you the story of when I first came to the *Iwakina* Project? No? Well, you see, I was extremely distraught at the lack of progress I was making with understanding the Pruathan technology at the time. I took to stims, and then to booze, and then to... well let's just say I was on a downward spiral. I ended up in the hospital there on Euphrosyne. Marcus, the friend you helped me to help, was an intern at that hospital. He somehow decided that I was his personal crusade and got me off of the addictions. I owe the man my life. While we were on Uprising, he had me cure his only living offspring, that girl there, and made me promise to take her with me. You see, I am repaying a long-owed life debt. She is completely free of infection; I was right about the nature of my cure. It was almost instantaneous. I hereby respectfully request permission for my charge to remain aboard the ship until further notice. By the way her name is Margo." Kuremoto finished his request and looked earnestly at the Captain who seemed to be in deep contemplation.

"Doctor, you know you never cease to amaze me! What will it be next; imported Vasuvian muskrats flying about the ship on their little wings? Fine. What is another young female added to the growing female population of this ship going to hurt? Now tell me what in the hell went wrong down there? Did you get the mission accomplished?"

Kuremoto told him all of the details as he observed them. At the end of his report he added, "I do not know if the plan succeeded to this point, but the place we were taken to was pretty secure. Marcus is a brilliant man; if anyone can get this done it is him. Now let me introduce you to our newest guest."

*   *   *

Nanami Oliver had been given yet another unpleasant task by the Captain; most likely to make up for all the trouble she had caused him. It did occur to her that she was usually the best suited for the jobs he gave her. She owed him a lot anyways. This time she was to inform the current client's keeper in no uncertain terms that their status had changed dramatically in the past few hours. Saitow family spies had reported that fighting had already broken out on Uprising and that the Conglomerate was ferrying media to the planet for confirmation of the alleged malpractice of the Administration. Apparently, Thane Mercenaries had also been hired by the Infected. This came over the Captain's 'special' secret communications terminal. Nanami decided it was above her paygrade to wonder on the nature of that terminal; the ship being far from the GCN lanes. It had come with the Augments from the Conglomerate.

She arrived at the client's cabin with one of her security personnel and hailed. The hatch opened with the keeper standing just inside.

Nanami spoke before the keeper could get a word in edgewise. "I am Nanami Oliver the ship's Security Officer. I need to speak with you about an urgent matter. Alone."

The woman who was in charge of taking care of the Uprising brat glanced inside. "She's asleep. How about speaking out here?"

"That will do." Nanami waved her escort back and stepped aside for the woman to exit the cabin. She was of medium build and strong looking; much like Nanami herself. Nanami was sure she could take her though. Once the hatch sealed, Nanami gave her the news.

"I am assuming that you know that you left the planet under uncertain circumstances. There has been a revolt on Uprising caused by the news that the disease that quarantines the planet was of artificial manufacture. At this time the government city complex is being stormed by those infected who have been cured of the disease. It has been determined by the Captain that your status on this ship is no longer diplomatic. However, the Captain guarantees your safety to the point of delivery of the girl to her father as originally contracted. I need you to hand over your sidearm and remain in your quarters for the duration of the voyage." Nanami put out her hand to receive the weapon.

"And if I refuse?" This woman was too much like Nanami for her liking.

"Then I will be force to kill you on this very spot." Nanami did her best to show the woman that she truly meant that which she did.

"Very well. Please give the Captain our thanks." The woman handed Nanami the two automatic pistols she carried.

"I'm told that it will be less than two hours before we hit the Jumpgate, but I will send some sandwiches for you two." Nanami offered as a gesture of condolence.

"Thank you." The woman said as she activated the hatch.

*   *   *

Sanae had stopped sending messages to Contact Sigma. She thought that it was pointless to risk her cover by sending messages that remained unanswered. Besides, it would be smarter for her to remain under radio silence when the host receiver may have been compromised. She had other things on her mind at the moment. It seemed to her that the relationship between the Captain and the Princess was going beyond captor and captive and progressing to an amicable affair. This bothered her very much. The fact that it bothered her bothered her even more. She had never felt love before, but she knew what it was; she had been trained to use it effectively. It seemed as if it was being used against her at the moment.

She put her mind to studying the Pruathan Galactic Database. The coloration for the place they were going, Kalk, had the same dark bluish hue that the Kyuketsuki construct had. However, it had the symbol for an organic planet not a construct. Several of the surrounding worlds were also bluish, but some were the familiar orange of the normal sort. She found this odd. She supposed it didn't matter since they were only going to be there for the time it took to get Jumpgate clearance and go through. It was connected straight to Saragotha's gate.

*   *   *

Beatrice had awoken rather hungry. She insisted that Mona, her escort for several years now, take her to the ship's dining facility at once to get something to eat. She became sullen and angry when Mona told her that the voyage would only last another hour or so and sandwiches were being brought to them. There was a hail at the hatch and before Mona could intercept her Beatrice keyed it open to find a porter with a covered rolling tray out in the corridor. She went to go out and throw off the cover, but before she got both feet outside, she saw someone behind the porter trying to get past. That someone was a girl with an infected tattoo. *How could she be here on the ship?* Beatrice had to do something before she infected the whole vessel. *She had to kill her; that's what Mother would do.* She nearly screamed, but instead pulled out the dagger her mother had given her on her thirteenth birthday; the dagger she never let out of her sight. Beatrice was about to lunge at the girl but found her hand with the dagger in it locked in the grip of Mona. The woman was powerful, while Beatrice was helpless. She screamed obscenities as she helplessly watched

74

the infected girl scurry away past a security man. The porter just stood their aghast. Mona twisted Beatrice's arm to the point where she had to let go of the dagger or be injured; it clattered to the deck with a tinging sound. Mona then tossed Beatrice unceremoniously toward the divan where she landed, then grabbed the tray from the bewildered porter and closed the hatch. Beatrice began to protest, but went silent as she saw *that look* on Mona's face.

"Beatrice, dear. Let us not make trouble for our hosts, okay? Be a good girl and have a sandwich. I'll explain everything to you when we are safely on Saragothra." *She was using 'that' tone of voice again* the girl thought. Beatrice knew when to behave; it was when Mona used *that* tone of voice.

* * *

The *Iwakina* arrived at Kalk and hailed the Jumpgate Command and Control facility. Saitow had all his vid-screens up and was marveling at all the Kalkish ships in the vicinity. They were all a strange yellowish-green color and had several connected round parts to them. Round was a sacred thing to the Kalk. They most likely saw the sleek lines and blackness of his ship as disgusting. A response came by video. A rotund round headed reptilian filled the screen.

It was apparently male from the voluminous tufts of hair coming from its three facial discs. It peered at a round tablet in its hand.

"Captain Saitow, it has come to our attention that some trouble has occurred between you and our business partner the Uprising Administrator. Is this true?" It hissed at the Captain.

"We had a little extra business to conduct there, yes, but we only wish to fulfill our contract. We need clearance to Saragothra please." Saitow bowed low in his seat as was the custom between Kalkish business partners. He knew the only way out of this would be to keep it at a business level, The Kalk were all about business.

"Well Captain, it appears that a hefty sum has been added to our contract with the Administrator in pursuit of your vessel. This is quite a devilish detail I'm afraid. Will you surrender your ship or…"

Saitow saw that as his cue to grease the palms of these creatures. It was the only way to save face and save his ship. He keyed his token ring to the ships Token Data Drive and sent a sizeable amount of MU to the jumpgate *fees* account.

"Ah, I see we have come to a mutual understanding. Please allow five minutes for gate activation. Trade be with you." The creature hissed his species' mantra and disappeared off the screen.

*   *   *

The shuttle ride planet-side at Saragothra was a bumpy one. It was a rather stormy day when they arrived, but they were assured the landing site at Beatrice's father's compound was safe. Nanami escorted the two off the shuttle and bid them well. It was raining lightly which just added to the misery this young girl would soon face. Nanami turned and re-boarded the shuttle. She would tell her frustrations to Lo; he always knew the right things to say to get her out of her depressions.

NEMESIS

1

The shuttle had just returned and Saitow was considering his next client. The messages he had sent from Kalk and when they arrived here at Saragothra remained unanswered. Perhaps he would skip this client and take the gates straight to Roseglade; the crew could use some relaxation time and he would be better off smoothing things over with his family in person. Just then Communications stated that there was an incoming message from sources unknown. He had Comms put it on screen. He was surprised to see his former Assistant Watch Officer Denton Bret filling the screen.

"Ah! Dear Captain, it has been too long. How fares the happy mutineers?" Bret was leering at him in an almost psychotic way.

"We are well; and you?" The Captain was weary, but played along. *What could his former officer be doing here? Was there an Imperial cruiser nearby?* He tapped a message to Comms on his tablet to find out where the signal was coming from.

"Don't bother trying to find me; I've got this feed going half way across the galaxy. Now Captain, I dare say that it pains me so to see you fat and happy in that command chair; especially since you only got a B minus in the battle simulations at the academy. What was it? Your record? I believe it was zero to twenty-six..." Bret was toying with him now. If there was one thing that could get Saitow fuming it was the mention of his academy records in battle simulations. "Now, now Captain, don't blow your top just yet. I have a proposition for you. Come to these coordinates and we will have a *real* battle." Bret turned a bit to look at something off screen, made a *tisk* sound, and screwed his face up. "See you soon!" he said hurriedly and was gone from the screen.

Takagawa came on the radio and reported he had detected a programming breach in *Iwa's* systems and stopped it. Sagura then reported a ship matching the contact that had fired on them the first time they were attacked was coming close then veered off and heading out of the system. He also reported that he had received a set of coordinates on his navigation console.

Saitow ordered a pursuit of the ship. Just then the engines died and the whole system rebooted. Sagura could not get them restarted. Takagawa reported a system wide failure. It would take about an hour to get the ship working again. Saitow cursed under his breath.

*   *   *

Shirae noticed that the ship seemed to power down and then power had cycled back up. She grabbed Haruka and headed out of her cabin. It seemed that the Chief Steward's staff was in an uproar. She could hear them passing rumors of an attack or an impending battle back and forth. She wanted desperately to speak with the Captain. Just then an all-call came over the Ship's Communications system; it was the Captain.

"*Iwakina* personnel, this is the Captain. We are about to go into battle. This is not a drill. I repeat; this is not a drill. All essential personnel man your stations. All non-essential personnel return to your quarters until further notice. Get moving people; this is not a drill."

"Oujo-sama?" Haruka asked, jerking her head toward their cabin.

"Come, Haruka. We must speak with the Captain." Shirae commanded and headed off in the direction of the lift, Haruka in tow. As they rounded the corner to the corridor where the lift was located, they practically ran into Captain Saitow.

"Ah, Dear Shirae, I was just coming to locate you. I want you to gather your girls and go below to the Deck Four Recreation Lounge; it is the safest place on the ship at the moment. Come; I'll escort you." The Captain grabbed her hand before she could get a word in and was bringing her back to her cabin. Once they were inside and the other girls were being roused, Saitow filled her in on the situation.

"You see, if we don't accept this challenge, we will be under constant threat from Bret who has a formidable ship. I do not know how he got it or what his strategy will be, but I have to do this for the *Iwakina*, the crew, and you my dear Princess. While you are in the lounge, I am sure one of the crew will put the screens on external view, so you will be able to watch the battle unfold. We will be leaving shortly for the battle site. Is everyone ready? Good, let us go."

Again, Shirae was following this man as he escorted her down to Deck Four. When they arrived, Shirae was not surprised to find Lowey Jax inside the Recreation Room.

"Safest place on the ship." Was his only greeting. Shirae knew that Nanami Oliver would be on the bridge.

Captain Saitow made sure the four women were comfortable and took Shirae's hand and kissed it.

"Wish me luck." he said.

Grabbing hold of his hand she pulled on it to bring his face down to hers and kissed him on the cheek. "For good luck!" she replied before letting go of his hand. She almost thought the man was blushing as he left the room. Turning she saw Haruka blushing too, yet with a furious look in her eyes. Ran-chan and Amane were all smiles. Lowey Jax just stared wide-eyed, then muttered, "Well, would you look at that…"

* * *

Ken Edwards had brought Benoba to his office in the Cargo Bay. He thought that his office would probably be the safest place on the ship where they could be alone. It was not as if he wanted to take advantage of the situation, but he desperately longed for her company; the woman was almost his equal in intelligence. She seemed happy enough to be with him; even alone in the spacious office. He had one of those new vid-screens installed in there so he could watch recorded news while he worked. He brought up the

Iwakina's external feeds on it so that they could watch when the battle unfolded. Benoba was almost starting to look normal, or as normal as she was going to get with that stunning white hair of hers. Her skin was almost an even shade of pale.

"Do you think the Captain is capable of defeating this Denton Bret?" Benoba asked him once they were settled in.

"Well, the Captain is a pretty capable commander, but that has only been tested on pirates and smugglers; never an Imperial Navy Officer." Edwards hesitated, but decided to come out with the thing that was probably on every officer's mind about now; the thing that was a taboo topic on the ship.

"The truth is the Captain flunked every battle simulation at the Naval Academy. He was given a passing grade of B Minus because of his reputation and status. No one mentions it because of his success against the aforementioned pirates. That is a ship's secret, so keep that to yourself." Edwards saw that his statement had made Benoba a little anxious, so he added, "I am sure he will persevere; this is *his* ship on the line now."

* * *

Goh Takagawa was heading to his cabin to collect some tools before heading to the bridge. The repairs were almost complete and he was sure that the Captain would want him there for damage control. He was rounding the corner where the hatch to his quarters was and ran into his friend Kintaro Sagura. Goh subconsciously patted the sidearm he carried and stepped back a bit.

"Goh, do you have a moment?" Sagura asked.

"Sure. You are on your way to the bridge, right? I just need to grab something." Goh keyed the hatch and went inside with Sagura in tow.

"So, what is on your mind?" Goh asked as he placed items in his tool case.

"I am wondering what you think of the Captain rashly going after Denton Bret? Do you think he will be able to defeat him? That ship looked pretty formidable..." Sagura asked, *seeming a bit too timid* Goh thought.

"The Captain knows what he is doing. You should know that as much as any other man on this ship. It is our part to man our stations and back him up; you will be surprised once you see what this baby can do in a battle." As he finished speaking, he felt a piercing cold surge through his body. Glancing over his shoulder he saw that Amara had come up very close to him; she had a wide-eyed look on her face.

"That is no man... it is a woman in disguise." Amara said placing her cold hand over Goh's mouth lest he give away the fact that he could see ghosts. He shook his head, and then his limbs as if he were shaking off lethargy.

"Right, let's get up to the bridge." Goh said and headed out the hatch.

* * *

Sanae was worried more for the Captain than for the crew of the *Iwakina*. It was not the thought that he might fail that bit at her; it was the fact that he was putting himself into danger. It wasn't that she doubted him; it was only that she needed to say something to someone. That is why she sought out her best friend Goh. She regretted that they had been distant lately. The man seemed to have lost most of his boyishness in gaining so much responsibility for the workings of the ship. When the battle was over, she would try to be more cordial toward him. It struck her as odd the behavior he displayed just before they left his cabin. Also, she had thought she had seen some hazy movement in front of his face; something that made her feel a little uneasy. She dismissed the thought and followed Goh to the bridge. He was right; the thing to do now was to fully support the Captain as Navigator of the Starship *Iwakina*.

* * *

Saitow felt alive like never before. This was going to be his vindication; *Bret be damned*. He sat at the Conn checking to ensure everything was ready. He had security personnel stationed on each deck to keep all non-essentials inside their quarters. He did not need any senseless casualties. His top officers were all manning their stations on the bridge; all he need do was give the order. "Sagura, is the navigation programmed for our destination?"

"Aye, Lor-…Aye, Captain." Sagura replied.

"Very well, jump." Saitow ordered. It would only take half a minute to get to Bret; he was so close.

Suddenly a claxon brayed warning that they had exited the jump but leaving them in hyperspace.

"Sagura, report!"

"Captain, the failsafe protocol has engaged due to… Sir, the coordinates we received led to a massive asteroid field." Sagura pulled up the representative display of hyperspace; there were indeed gravitational signatures of massive asteroids all around them. The failsafe would keep them from getting too close; these rocks would be much closer in normal space.

"Sagura, drop us a few klicks out of the field and bring us into normal space."

"Aye, Captain." Saitow watched the holo-display as Sagura deftly maneuvered the ship downward out of the field.

Saitow got on the Comms, "Simpson, are your Ethlas ready for launch again?"

Simpson came on the channel. "Sir, we have one Ethla down – Bastian's, but the rest are fueled with pilots on standby; myself included."

Saitow was furiously tapping on his tablet. "I'm sending you a plan right now. When we come out of Hyperspace, execute it."

"Aye, Captain."

*   *   *

"Master, we have multiple contacts fanning out within the asteroid field. Shall I pursue?" *Arbiter was itching to cut her teeth it seemed* Bret thought. He had a plan, although her idea of picking them off one by one throughout the field was a good one. He had only one prize in mind though; the *Iwakina*. He could feel her determination through the sensory device she had made for him. She called it a Neural Quantifier – something she had gleaned from contact with the *Iwakina's* AI – it allowed him greater control over the ship if he needed it.

"No, no. Let them come to us. We have plenty of time to pick them off." He replied.

* * *

Simpson gave the go order once the ship exited hyperspace. He and seven others would fan out and search the Asteroid field while the two remaining Ethlas escorted the *Iwakina*. *It's too bad Bastian is laid up in Sickbay; he is my best pilot* Simpson thought. The ship would pursue once his Ethlas made contact. It did not take them very long to find the enemy; he was hiding just inside the asteroid field. Corporal Osano got first contact and radioed the coordinates to all ships. Then his signal was lost. Simpson and his pilots went full bore to the coordinates provided.

* * *

Saitow got the signal that Bret's ship had been spotted. He ordered full speed to those coordinates. His Communication's Officer indicated a Message coming in from the enemy.

"On screen." Saitow ordered.

"Well, Captain, it did not take you long to find me. Welcome to my playground! Now that you are here, I would like to introduce you to my ship. This…" he stepped aside to show a humanoid form that could only be a metallic android. "…is the *Arbiter*, my ship. Surrender now and we might let you live; albeit drifting in space in a shuttlecraft."

Saitow found it beautiful and grotesque at the same time. He had only one answer for Bret.

"Be gone, I do not parley with dead men." Saitow gestured with his hand across his throat to indicate both a neck slicing blow to Bret and to kill the video feed to his Comms Officer. Instead, the screen went to a view of space. Saitow raised his hand to stop the Comms Officer. A small form grew on the screen. It was one of his Ethlas.

He heard Bret say, "A parting gift then." And the Ethla got off a few shots before it was destroyed in a silent explosion. Then the screen went dark like the mind of the *Iwakina's* Captain.

*   *   *

"Whoa! Now that's more like it!" Lowey Jax had jumped up out of his seat and was gazing at the monitor. Dark shapes were buzzing by at a dizzying rate of speed. Shirae looked at the screen and back to the man.

"Mr. Jax, what is it?" she asked.

"Dear Princess, our Captain has entered the asteroid field. He's taking it to the enemy." Jax sat down again, but was leaning toward the screen. He flinched a couple of times as the ship had to course correct to avoid one or two of the bigger rocks, as a huge grin showed on his face. Flashes were seen as some much smaller ones hit the shields.

Shirae was once again confused by the marshal world of men.

*   *   *

Doctor Kuremoto did his best to calm his charge Margo down. She was huddled on his cot in the lab hugging him tightly; she would not let him go. Luckily, he had given the remote controller to the vid-screen to her so she could follow the news in case something of Uprising was reported. He reached for it and pulled up the *Iwakina's* external feeds; the ship was cruising through an asteroid field. *What in the hell was the Captain up to? Seriously? A battle?* Kuremoto thought. He realized it would be in poor timing to inquire to their status at this point; he had just to console the girl and pray that the ship survived.

*   *   *

Simpson's Ethla was in the lead and following the most likely course of the *Arbiter*. The enemy had fled deeper into the asteroid field and his flight of Ethlas was in hot pursuit. He could see the *Iwakina* was also coming deeper into the asteroid field on his tactical display. This place was great for Ethlas because they could take advantage of their secondary gravitic propulsion system. It was too bad his sensors were practically useless with all the metal in these rocks; there was just too much interference for them to be effective. He would find the enemy and the Captain would bear down on him like a typhoon; of this he was sure.

*   *   *

The *Arbiter* had stationed itself at point number two; the ambush point from which Bret would get his revenge. The ship's finely tuned sensors had all of the tiny bothersome Ethlas positioned and the hated *Iwakina* was coming, in accord with his plans. It was too bad that the crew was able to thwart *Arbiter's* programming hijacking, but it appeared that the scrambling she had done as a decoy had affected the *Iwakina's* sensors. The *Iwakina* did not give any indication that she was able to detect the *Arbiter*. As a matter of fact, the *Iwakina* was slowing down as if she were about to stop. Perhaps Saitow was baiting him. It did not matter; he had nothing but time.

*   *   *

Simpson was just about reaching the point where his frustration was turning to anger when his sensors lit on something other than a large asteroid. He wasn't about to go charging at the enemy like Corporal Osano did. He got close enough to verify that it was in fact a ship and sighted the coordinates. He made sure to put a large rock between him and it, and then radioed the coordinates to the *Iwakina*.

*   *   *

Saitow had this nagging plan forming in his mind. It was dangerous, but would be just the thing to get the jump on Denton Bret, who had the advantage of the field in this battle. It was bold, but it just might work…that or it would spell doom for the whole ship. It was his lack of risk taking that had got him into this situation. He had been the most cautious Naval Officer, swearing off his days of youthful bravado; doing everything by the book. Even in the simulations, he did things by the book… and lost every time. With the pirates it was different; yet the pirates were third rate strategists at best. He was now up against one of his peers, and one that was adept at bending the rules. After analyzing the sensor data from Saragothra, he knew he was up against a powerful ship as well. It also appeared to have a fully functioning AI; fully functioning AIs had been outlawed ever since Daphne.

He had the ship slow to a near stop. The space here was relatively free of large asteroids. Maybe Bret would come to him. If not, then he would have to do *that*. He steeled his resolve and started the sequence to do what he had never done in his entire career; he was going to throw out the book.

"Takagawa, can you override the jump fail-safes manually?" He inquired.

"Why yes, Captain, but whatever would you want to do that for?" Takagawa was properly concerned.

"You need not worry about that. If we succeed, we are freed from a very powerful enemy. If we don't then we'll all be dead anyway. Just do it." Saitow ordered. Takagawa did as he was commanded.

"Sagura, I am proposing to do something extremely dangerous. I am about to give you an order. I take full responsibility for the execution of the order; no fault will be laid upon you for following it. Do you understand?"

Sagura let out a breath like he had been holding it the whole time Saitow was speaking. He replied after a few more seconds, "Aye Captain."

"Good. When next we get report of coordinates on the enemy ship, I want you to jump the *Iwakina* within a klick of those coordinates. If luck is on our side, we will be facing the enemy ship and will open up on it with all that we've got. You will have to maneuver at the blink of an eye; are you up to it?"

"Yes, Sir." Sagura replied, if not a bit apprehensively.

"Weapons, I want full volleys on whatever contact Sagura reports immediately from whichever batteries are facing it, do you understand?"

"Aye, Sir." Takagawa answered. Saitow watched his display and saw all batteries being primed. That would drain a hell of a lot of energy from the ship's stores, but they only had one or two shots at this at best.

Just then the radio call came in; it was Simpson with the news he was waiting for.

* * *

"Master, my sensors detected another Ehtla; this one has turned tail and ran. Shall I pursue?" the *Arbiter* Avatar sat beside him keeping him updated on the developing battle.

"No. We want them to come to us. We have range over there weapons; they cannot touch us. Did it radio our position?" Bret was contemplating the destruction of the *Iwakina* and was getting impatient. However, he knew the best course of action was to let the enemy come to him. His was the stronger ship after all.

"I cannot say; the Ethla has gone around the great rock. There is too much interference."

"I am more than sure that it did. What is the *Iwakina* doing?"

"It is still loitering- wait, the *Iwakina* is gone."

"What? How could that be?"

"It was there and then not- Master! The *Iwakina* is bearing right on top of us at less than a klick! They're firing!"

"Return fire! Now!" Bret screamed.

* * *

Takagawa was not much of a religious man, but at this moment he was praying to God they made it through this in one piece. The Captain gave the order to jump and they did just that; jumped less than seventy-five thousand kilometers in about five seconds. There was a delay in hyperspace as the failsafes were called for, but the override allowed the ship to come out into normal space just like the Captain had ordered; less than a kilometer from the *Arbiter*. However, they were facing the wrong way. Goh fired everything he had from the aft batteries.

"All aft batteries depleted Captain." He reported.

"Sagura bring us around so we can have at her once more!" The Captain ordered.

The monitors indicated the maneuver; however, the ship was rocked by several explosions. "Sir, the enemy has returned fire and the aft shields are depleted; they got a lucky hit on our propulsion system." Goh reported.

"Captain, we are still turning, but the ship is listing and there is no maneuver control." Sagura chimed in.

"Damage to the enemy?" the Captain wanted some good news.

"Sensors indicate their shields are down in some places and we took out some of their gun ports.

However, the remaining three are charging." Goh did his best to sound positive.

They had no idea how long the enemy needed to charge their guns. At this rate it would take another thirty seconds to bring all of the *Iwakina's* forward guns to bear.

*　　*　　*

The *Arbiter* thought she found the reason that her former master had wished for her to no longer have emotions. Her new master lay slumped in his chair unconscious; an overhead fixture had been jarred loose and had landed on his head. He was bleeding, but still breathing. Her remaining batteries facing the enemy were still charging. She felt horrified at their current situation, and started to know an emotion that was new and overwhelming; she began to feel fear. She knew how to save herself; the ship would explode and she would ride a charred but sturdy hard-drive within her avatar out into space just like before. What of her master? She could not just leave him to die, but the escape pods were facing the asteroid they were hugging. Suddenly she had an idea. The odds of success were several thousand to one, but it was really her only recourse. She lifted the body of her master and headed deep inside the ship.

*　　*　　*

When the *Iwakina* had turned enough under momentum for the forward batteries to be fired, Goh let loose his barrage. He thanked God that the enemy had not had a chance to fire. The monitor indicated that the *Arbiter* exploded in multiple areas before the tell-tale 'Big One' explosion of the anomaly core. It sent a shockwave through the *Iwakina* and multiple pieces of the asteroid the *Arbiter* had been hugging flying in all directions. Unfortunately, it hadn't been enough to remove the entire thing from their path.

"Sagura, can you jump us out of here with the remaining charge?" the Captain asked in desperation.

"I could if the navigation console was taking my commands; it's locked up." Sagura looked longingly at Goh. Goh attempted to override the controls from his console. He looked at Sagura, shook his head, and then looked to the Captain.

Captain Saitow got on the All-Comms. "Attention, all personnel! Brace for impact!"

2

Captain Saitow watched aghast as the *Iwakina* impacted the remains of the asteroid. The ship was jarred and some very harsh noises came from deep inside the ship. A reverberating tremor took hold of the bridge. Holding tightly to the conn, he saw Sagura thrown to the deck, his head hitting rather hard. One of his cherished decorative wooden ceiling beams came loose and threatened to crush Sagura where he had landed. Saitow leapt into action, catching the beam with his body while straddling Sagura, his left elbow on the deck and his forearm touching Sagura's body. The blow dazed him a bit. Saitow's hand felt like it was squeezing a pillow; in his semi-consciousness he thought that Sagura was a big man, but not *this* fat. When he opened his eyes, it's was as if he were atop a rough looking version of the Princess! He exclaimed loudly and tried hard to move, but the beam was just too heavy. *How could this be Shirae when it was Kintaro Sagura who he had dove to save from his prideful antique beams?* He felt the beam lifting and scrambled out from under it as members of the crew moved the heavy wood.

*   *   *

Sanae saw the beam falling but had no time to move out of its path. Her fall had been pretty hard and she felt a bit groggy. Her training kicked in and she brought her arms up to shield her face, closed her eyes, and braced for the impact. Perhaps this would be her final breath; thoughts of the Captain filled her head. The beam didn't strike her, but a heavy body landed on her mid-section. Hearing a startled cry, she opened her eyes to see the Captain's head above hers; a horrified expression appeared on his face just before he scrambled from atop her. The feeling of his hand was still fresh upon her left breast. Confused, she deftly moved out from under the beam as she could see other crewmembers holding it aloft. Each had an astonished look on their face. Confusion turned to dread as she reached for the Transmutor Device at her back and realized it had been damaged. She no longer held the appearance of Navigator Kintaro Sagura it seemed. She turned quickly toward the lift doors and found the barrel of a pistol pointing straight at her face. Behind the pistol was the bewildered face of her best friend Goh.

* * *

Goh Takagawa had braced for the impact of the collision and was doing mental calculations of the damage that it would cause when he saw his friend Kintaro being saved by the Captain from one of those annoying antique beams the Captain loved so much. Suddenly his friend was no longer there under the Captain, having been replaced by a smallish woman with short hair. He blinked twice and rubbed his eyes to be sure. *This woman looked remarkably similar to the Princess!* Other crew members lifted the beam and Goh moved between the main bridge and the lift entrance to get a better look. The woman looked confused at first, but quickly got to her feet, her movements like that of a soldier. *Amara had told him that Kintaro was not a man, but this?* Goh thought quickly about the things that didn't quite add up about his friend, and the indications that all pointed to Kintaro as the spy on board. He drew his sidearm even quicker as the woman turned in his direction. He needed to capture this girl because he needed answers.

* * *

Saitow watched with awe as Goh prevented the intruder's escape. Nanami motioned for two crewmembers to grab the girl. Saitow stepped up then.

"Goh and Nanami, take this… *woman* down to the Brig. Check for damage as you go." He ordered, and to the imposter, "I don't know who you are, but your story had better be a good one. I'll deal with you once the ship is back in working order." Saitow stepped aside and let the escort by. He watched as they entered the lift and the hatch closed. At least that was working.

* * *

They had placed the imposter woman in the Ship's Brig; a high security containment room that was seldom used. It had a camera for watching any occupants which covered the entire room except for the toilet; even criminals rated a little privacy.

Goh had meant to speak to this woman several times, but hesitated. *What would he have to say?* Betrayal hung over him like a dark cloud about to burst forth a deluge. She seemed to be rather sullen and tight lipped anyway. Nanami had asked her several questions getting no response whatsoever. Nanami was even a little rough in depositing their charge which elicited a rather fierce angry look. However, whenever Goh caught her eye, she would look away quickly. *Was it guilt?* Goh was determined to find out, but the ship demanded his full attention; he would come back later and have his say. It wasn't like the prisoner, or anyone for that matter, was going *anywhere* anytime soon. He had observed that what he could see of Deck Six on their way to the Brig was sound; no damage as far as he could tell. They passed some people headed for Sick Bay; none of them seemed badly hurt, but a few were quite bloodied. He marveled at how the nanite's in the ship would clean the deck wherever their blood had been spilt.

He excused himself from Nanami Oliver and her detail to go inspect the rest of Deck Six; there were a few key systems on this deck. First, he got direct communications through his neural-net to the rest of his team and got reports of their positions and status. He directed them to check the vital systems first, and then check for structural damage on the decks they were on, flushing out any injured crewmembers they found and sending them for aid. Life support was their first priority. After that he wanted to get the shields fully up because they were still in the middle of a damned asteroid field. He hoped they could get all that done in about an hour because that is when he was sure the Captain would call for a key personnel meeting.

*   *   *

Shirae had heard the explosion and felt the ship reverberate. They watched as the vid-screen had cut out momentarily when the ship jumped and then the battle that lasted less than two minutes. Lowey Jax and the few other crewmembers present cheered, and Shirae even sensed a bit of enthusiasm from Haruka. Ran-chan cheered with the rest of them and Amane raised her fist in a victory salute. Just as quickly as the cheers went up, they died and an eerie silence gripped the room. Everyone's eyes were focused on the vid-screen. Shirae looked too and saw a rather large asteroid growing on the screen. The Captain's warning to brace for impact came just as the realization hit them; they were going to collide with that thing. Everyone grabbed at something to brace themselves, but there was little to do except hug the floor. As the ship collided with the asteroid the room shook and several people lost their footing. As the tremor cleared, Shirae took toll of the room; everyone seemed alright except for some minor scrapes. Her girls were better off than most. She bade Ran-chan take Amane and assess their quarters. She and Haruka would go to the bridge to check on the Captain.

As they came to the lift, it was heading down, so they had to wait; Shirae became more and more impatient with every minute. Finally, it returned and they got to the bridge. The place was in disarray; a large beam of wood was lying next to the Navigator's station. She hoped that Kintaro Sagura was okay; she did not see him among the people trying to straighten up the bridge. That is when it hit her; everyone she looked at was staring at her strangely. She caught sight of the Captain and quickly went to his side. She waited for him to finish speaking to the First Officer.

"Ah, Shirae, you should not be here on the bridge... but I am glad to see you are safe. We seem to have run into a bit of tough luck." He said when he noticed her there.

Shirae was suddenly overcome with emotion and rushed into the Captain to hug him. She did not even consider where she was or who was there; her thoughts were only of the Captain's safety.

"Oh Glenn, I was so worried." She buried her head in his chest. After an awkward few second, she felt Haruka-chan gently trying to pull her away. She took a deep whiff of the Captain's clothing before letting go.

He smiled down at her. "Worry not dear Princess; it will take more than a big ugly rock to do me in. Now, it is best that you go to your quarters while we get the ship back in shape. I will call you and Haruka to the next Officer's Call so you can get the latest information on what's going on."

Haruka pulled her toward the lift and she obeyed, looking back as the Captain's smiling eyes followed them into the lift. When the lift doors closed, she heard Haruka take a big sigh.

"Oujo-sama, that was rather unexpected." She finally said; then, "I suppose that I will have to resign myself to the fact that you are madly in love. There is no helping it."

Shirae did not know what to say; she felt that she had needed this acknowledgement from Haruka for a long time now. She grabbed the woman and hugged her, tears starting to flow.

"Thank you so much Haruka-chan!"

*   *   *

Goh looked at the damage caused by the explosion and thought that it did not seem as bad as the impression it made. Only the port side gravitic repulsion unit had been taken out; the explosion causing feedback to the system that took out all of the Navigational controls, including the propulsion and jump drive controls. The ship had spares for most of that. They would have to use the costly ion drive for impulse power; it required fuel replenishment after use, unlike the gravitic systems that tapped power from the CHAR.

Life support had been at one-hundred percent; the hull not so good at ninety-seven percent integrity, but there were no breaches. *Iwakina's* autonomous systems were repairing that and the damaged shield nodes. His teams reported minimal damage to all decks; mostly non-structural. *Iwakina* would repair that after the hull and shields. Goh got the teams coordinated on the various navigation controls just in time before the all-call from the Captain sounded.

*   *   *

Sanae sat in her cell contemplating her fate. She had protocols for this type of thing; be silent, plot escape, if necessary: death. However, things were not completely clear cut in her head anymore. She had been feeling emotions she had never been meant to feel: love, admiration, envy, scorn, and now guilt. These had been creeping over her slowly since the mutiny and the added silence from Contact Sigma. *What was she to do now; end it all and waste a life that she had just started living? What would be done with her?* She would not be turned over to the Imperium; that was certain. *Could she bargain for a place amongst them once again?* No, she had nothing to bargain with. *What of her friendship with Goh?* To her it was genuine, but to him surely it was just a ruse. *How could she face him now?*

She curled up on the cot and pulled the blanket over her head to hide the tears she had never shed before, from the ever-present surveillance camera.

*   *   *

Saitow called a meeting of key personnel once he thought that the crisis had settled down a bit. He needed to know what was going on. He did not like being dead in the water like this; God only knew what enemies were out there searching for him still. Maybe if he got the word out that he had defeated an Imperial warship, he might get a little more breathing room.

Everyone was assembled except for Kuremoto. He bowed out in order to manage his new ward. She had gone into a panic when the battle rocked the ship; apparently, she had been through some traumatic experience in her youth. Even the Princess was present, as well as Haruka; Shirae sat there trying to look regal while staring at him with what seemed like stark admiration.

Saitow got reports from around the table. Goh had his team going full-tilt on repairing what the *Iwakina* could not repair herself. He estimated completion in forty-eight hours or so given crew-rest requirements. Saitow knew it would be done in half that time. Nanami had all of her security personnel helping with cleanup; Oz's people were on top of that. Simpson's Marines were trying to get the Ethlas sorted out and refitted in their berths. Edwards reported ship's stores were one-hundred percent; his people were just tidying up in the cargo bay. Soto said that Song Ha's shift would have the bridge squared away within the hour. Rosel reported very few casualties; however, there were a couple of heavy bleeders that she would have to keep an eye on for a while. She gave the names to their respective leaders. She also reported that Corporal Bastian would pull through as well. She said her alien friend was helping out.

Saitow was satisfied with the reports. He simply ordered his people to get the ship in working order so the mission could resume. He felt he needed to give them some explanation of the events that had just transpired. He told them who had attacked them, and why he had pursued the course which led them to this point. It was a cat and mouse game that had to end. Better that he took the initiative than let it fester across the entire galaxy. Everyone seemed to accept his explanation; Rosel even gave him a wink and a thumbs-up.

Saitow dismissed the meeting and approached Shirae intending to invite her to dinner in his quarters. *Should he be so straightforward with her?* In the past few hours, he had seen something in her that had piqued his curiosity. He intended to determine if the feelings he had for her were reciprocal. Shirae eagerly accepted his invitation, and surprisingly, Haruka seemed nonchalant about it. Saitow held Shirae's hand for a moment and bid her farewell until dinner. He had business to attend to while his cook did his magic. First though, he called Bonifacio personally to ensure that the main course for tonight would be that meat called chicken.

*   *   *

Doctor Rosel was making her rounds of the patients that were still in sick bay. She had one of the Chief Steward's men hold up here because he had a rather nasty head wound and apparently his parents had not had him Protein-biased out for hemophilia. *Well, they couldn't catch them all* she thought. Suddenly, she became fixated on the man's blood. He was asleep and his dressings were becoming soaked. She pulled her attention away in order to get some fresh dressing. *This would take a synthetic skin treatment* she thought. She got the kit for that out of a cabinet. She was sensing this strong odor coming from the man. She knew what it was; it just had never seemed so strong of a smell to her before. It was the smell of fresh blood. She removed the soaked dressing and tossed it into the bio-waste container. She watched as a slowly moving trail of thick red blood moved down his scalp and toward his neck. It fixated her attention so much that she reached out and touched it with her finger. She brought the droplet of blood she had collected on her sterile glove to her line of sight and looked longingly at it; it was as if it was calling to her. She contemplated the reasoning for this sensation; it could only be the Kyuketsuki blood she had ingested. Licking her lips, and going against all of her medical training and better judgment, Rosel licked the blood off of her gloved finger. The sensation overwhelmed her to the point that she staggered a step backward. It was as if the taste of this man's blood sent an invigorating tingle through her very being. She looked again at the blood slowly making its way down the man's neck.

She forced herself to look away and quickly removed the gloves she had donned, throwing them in the bio-waste container. She called to Marishima, who was in the main chamber. Marishima came quickly and was ordered to take care of the man's dressing; Rosel having told her that she was feeling ill and needed to rest in her quarters. Once she was sure the young woman was busy with the patient, she headed to the medical stores and stuffed a cylinder of stored blood into a satchel. She went straight to her quarters, brushing past Dorigethra in her haste.

3

Marishima had just finished applying the fresh dressing to the patient Doctor Rosel had left her. She heard the tell tail swoosh of the hatch opening and looked up to find the Andalii entering. She hardly knew him; it seemed as if he had been avoiding her ever since his arrival. They had been in the same room several times, but hardly shared even a glance. It was just as well; she had no desire to come in contact with a full-fledged telepath. Now he was approaching her. She removed her gloves and tossed them into the bio-waste container.

"Can I help you Doctor?" she asked as politely as she could.

"Yes... Marishima is it? I passed Doctor Rosel in the corridor; she seemed quite distressed..."

Marishima knew this to be her cue to offer information, but she decided to remain silent. She wanted this awkward alien to stew in the awkward moment.

Dorigethra blinked his beady eyes at her and continued, "Do you know what could be the cause?"

"Well... she left me this patient and stated that she was feeling ill and needed to go rest in her quarters."

Marishima put on a look of mild curiosity that she hoped would end this Andalii's questioning. Just then she sensed that she was being lightly probed. She managed to suppress her instinct to block him and let her thoughts be read. However, when she looked into his eyes, she read there that he somehow knew she was a telepath. He probed deeper. She had no choice but to block him then. The cat was out of the bag.

Ah, how wonderful; there are more than one... Dorigethra spoke to her in her mind, *Don't worry. Your secret is safe with me.* With that, the alien turned and left the room.

Marishima's first thought was to kill him in his quarters. However, she knew the relationship he had with her boss; she owed her as much to let him live. What had he meant by 'more than one'? She felt she had better consult with Wilhelm about this as well. First, she needed to put that all aside and tend to the remaining patients.

* * *

"Yamano, take us here." Saitow pointed at an anomalous symbol on the holographic nav-display for the replacement navigator to plot. Renge Yamano was her name; one of his family's augments. She was supposedly an accomplished Astro-gator; that's what they were calling them these days. The point was the Carina Nebula; the perfect place for maybe the greatest plan he had come up with in his whole life.

He would show this to Shirae and then-

"Captain, now that we are ship-shape, shall we go look in on the prisoner?" Soto, his exec, interrupted his reverie. It occurred to him that he had neglected to prioritize this new development. He flushed a little at the remembrance of his hand on the woman's chest.

Composing himself he inquired on the Security Officer's progress with the woman.

"She is down there now…" Soto replied.

*   *   *

Sanae sat crossed-legged on the bunk in the cramped room. She had been contemplating her fate and the possibility of escape. Surely, they would move her off the ship; she could then make her move. It was bittersweet her betrayal of those she had come to know and love, especially the Captain. She felt abandoned by Contact Sigma and the Empire. *There was also her resemblance to the Princess; what would they make of that?* She tried to calm herself with meditation. That was interrupted by the opening of the hatch. She slowly turned her head to see Nanami Oliver swagger in. She turned her head back to face forward just as slowly.

"Now look here little miss, I want to know who you really are and what your mission here is!" The woman bellowed.

Sanae said nothing but continued to meditate; with a heightened sense about her this time.

"Silent treatment, eh?" Oliver stepped in front of her and bent her head down to Sanae's face. "I'll ask once more; who are you and what is your mission aboard this ship?"

Sanae remained silent. She was not about to turn

sides to this woman of all people.

"Say... I know all of your secrets. I have all of your messages decoded on my desk. Who is this Contact Sigma?" Oliver was undoubtedly looking for some sort of reaction. Sanae gave her none of that.

"So, you won't talk. Maybe I should just beat it out of you, eh?" With that Oliver took a swipe at Sanae's face.

Sanae grasped the taller woman's wrist, had her spun around, and took her down to her knees in a matter of seconds; Sanae's right hand grasped firmly around the front of Oliver's throat.

"I have no desire to kill you, nor will I give you any information." Sanae whispered into Oliver's ear. She then sent the woman face first toward the hatch. It swooshed open and two Security people entered.

Oliver picked herself up and looked wild-eyed at Sanae who had resumed her position of meditation. The two Security men stepped toward Sanae, but Oliver waved them off. All of them left the room. Sanae wondered who would come next. There was no one aboard the ship who could best her. Perhaps it would be thrilling to provoke them into trying. No, she had no desire for combat; or anything else for that matter.

*   *   *

Saitow rounded the corner that connected this corridor to the one leading to the Brig and practically ran into Nanami Oliver and her detail. The woman looked a bit disheveled and angry.

"Oh, Captain..." She said in surprise while straightening her clothing.

"Have you news of our prisoner?" Saitow asked noting the quiver in Nanami's voice.

Nanami cleared her throat and proceeded to give her assessment of the prisoner.

"That woman is a mute, my Lord. She is dangerous too. She may seem delicate, but she is hardened by military training beyond any normal Imperial, I can tell you that. I suggest caution."

Saitow detected a hint of respect for the prisoner in Nanami's voice despite her apparent anger at the moment. He would have to review the video of the two women's encounter.

"Thank you Nanami that will be all." Saitow turned to his Exec as his Security Officer left. "Get me two Marines and a folding chair."

Soto used his Neural-net to call for the Marines and chair. It took a couple of minutes for them to arrive.

They then preceded through the security apparatus that led to the Brig's containment area. There were eight cell rooms, each fully enclosed, and one preparation room. The prisoner was in the cell directly across from the preparation room separated by a small corridor. The cell doors could not be opened until the preparation room's door was secure.

The door to the prisoner's room was opened and the Marines went in; each taking up position on either side of the prisoner who was sitting crossed-legged on the bunk at the back of the cell. Saitow entered closing the door behind him. He unfolded the chair and set it opposite the woman directly in the center of the room. He sat. The two sat staring at one another for a few minutes. Saitow could not get over the fact that this woman had a striking, if not rather muddled, resemblance to his dear Princess. The similarities were uncanny. The face was almost the same; however, there was a look of hardness to it and her short hair was mousy and unkempt. Saitow decided to ask the obvious questions that he was sure Nanami had tried without success.

"Who are you and who sent you?" This was greeted with silence. "Are you a spy for the Empire?" Still nothing; jus that blank stare. It was a little un-nerving. Saitow dismissed the thought. He thought he caught a hint of curiosity in her stare.

"I know of all your dispatches to a Contact Sigma. Who is that, your controller? Your keeper?" Still nothing but that stare...

"You want me to get her to make a noise Captain?" it was one of the Marines; a big tan fellow named Finau. The woman did not even acknowledge the man's presence. She just stared that stare...

"No. If she is not going to say anything, beating her won't make her talk. I just wonder why she looks so much like my beloved Princess." Saitow started at the sight of the woman whose stare seemed to turn into surprise and then sorrow for just the fraction of a second; just long enough for him to catch it before that blank stare returned.

Saitow decided to play on that, "I suppose I should tell her about our encounter when I propose marriage to her this evening..." Saitow looked hard for a reaction, but the woman was still staring back at him defiantly. "We are through here. Let's be off." As he left the room he turned to the woman once more, "The sooner you cooperate, the sooner you will get out of this Brig."

* * *

Sanae waited for the hatch to close behind the Captain and then curled up on the bunk. She had the blanket completely covering her body in order to hide the sorrow on her face and the tears that threatened there. She was distraught at the fact that she completely knew now that what she felt was love for the Captain. Yet this man that she loved was going to propose marriage to the only other woman on the ship that looked like her...

* * *

The Captain had invited her to the Library deck for dinner. He had also showed her how to access the recorded video feed from the prisoner's cell. Shirae sat watching with fascination; this woman that had her face. *She was unkempt and hard looking, but there was no mistake; this woman could even be her twin!* Such a thing was impossible of course; she was an only child. Surely her father would have told her of such a person and raised them as sisters together.

Shirae suddenly remembered the message from the spirit Miriam, *Princess Shirae, do not blame the father; blame the one who controls the father. Tell this also to the one who is almost you when you can see her true self.* "

The one that is almost you..." could this be the one spoken of? A thought formed in her head. She called for Haruka.

"Haruka, I want you to do something for me this evening. Take this token case to a Security Officer named Metz while I am dining with the Captain. Tell him you need to deliver a message from me to the prisoner in person."

Haruka looked weary but Shirae knew she would do whatever she requested. She had no more loyal servant in all the Empire.

"Yes, Oujo-sama. The message?" Haruka asked.

Shirae proceeded to have Haruka memorize her message to the woman in the Brig.

* * *

Kimberly Rosel had slept for a considerable amount of time after getting her fill of blood. She thought back on the moment. She had rushed back to her quarters and used a spare scalpel she had lying around to open the container of blood. The smell filled her with desire. She greedily raised the container to her lips and sucked down the entire contents. Having satisfied her desire, she looked at the container in her hand with disgust, flinging the thing across the room. She removed her clothing and got into bed curling up under her blankets. She had fallen fast asleep and only woke up after many hours of restful sleep.

Her first thought was of the book given to her by the Kyuketsuki. She rose and put on a robe. She retrieved the book from the shelf among the many data cases she had on medical subjects. Bringing it to her table, she flopped down in the chair there and opened it. She was not surprised that she could understand the language the book was written in. She began to read and the horror she was now a part of began to sink in.

* * *

Nanami had covered every inch of the former Kintaro Sagura's quarters. It took her a while, but she eventually found the two terminals hidden there. She sent them to Takagawa for analysis. She went back to her Security Suite and found Lo waiting for her.

"Now, now, you know I am on duty."

"Oh my, am I being a nuisance? Shall I go lock myself in the Brig as well?" Lowey Jax said with a smirk.

"Oh no; I don't want you anywhere near that woman. Look at this…" Nanami keyed up the video from her encounter with the prisoner.

"Ouch! That is one rough lady. I see you made it out of there in one piece. A little ego bruised probably…" Lo chided.

Nanami punched him hard on the arm. "I can still take you out if I need to… At any rate that woman is dangerous. She has training beyond any Imperial military; even the commandos."

"I wonder what her purpose is on the ship. Surely they had no idea the mutiny was about to occur."

"It was pretty air tight. Maybe she was here to keep an eye on someone or just the ship itself."

"Well, I'm sure you military types will get to the bottom of it sooner or later. There is no sense in wasting time brooding over a sleeping prisoner. Why don't you come out of here for a bit? I'll buy you a drink." Lo was insistent.

"Ok. This thing is on a perpetual record anyway. It's not like the Captain has us doing shifts or anything." Nanami smiled her biggest smile at her man as they headed out the hatch.

* * *

Saitow gazed admiringly at Shirae as she finished her Vrel which, if he recalled correctly, was the second most prevalent beef-like meat in the galaxy. They had talked about the coming days and how he would soon show her his ancestral home on Roseglade. The subject of the prisoner had come up briefly and Saitow had detected a hint of something suspicious in Shirae's face, but he decided not to pursue it. He could not imagine suddenly discovering that one had a doppelganger under one's very nose.

He got a signal from the Bridge that they had arrived. He excused himself from the table and, lifting his robes from the loungers that were at the center of the room, he fetched a tablet and a small box from within, handing his robes to an attendant. He beckoned Shirae to join him while the wait staff cleared the table and the room. That only left Ran Tsureyama and Amane, Shirae's retainers, with them; both discretely kneeling by the hatch. He briefly wondered where Haruka was; it was probably best that she was absent given the circumstances...

Saitow and the Princess settled into the loungers. Saitow produced the tablet and said to his guest, "If you don't mind..." gesturing at their chairs. He then manipulated the tablet and watched amused at Shirae's surprise that the loungers were opening up putting both of them in a supine position. Saitow immediately keyed the tablet to make the ceiling transparent. A swath of stars could be seen and there was a strange glow which seemed to come from the opposite of their view.

"My dear Shirae, you do remember that I said I would show you the universe. This is but a taste of the sights I will show you if you remain by my side..." with that Saitow keyed the tablet once more and from here he manipulated the ship, turning their view to a sight of such amazement that Shirae let out a little sound.

"It's both monstrous and beautiful at the same time..." he heard Shirae whisper.

"This is the Carina Nebula, one of thousands of such wonders just in or near our galaxy alone. We are still pretty far from it; if we got too close it would destroy us with radiation that even Pruathan shields could not withstand. Shirae I..." he hesitated as she was still gazing steadily at the nebula.

He raised himself on one elbow and took the small box out from where he had hidden it between the cushions. He opened it and pulled out an exquisite blue diamond ring. He looked at Shirae's small delicate hands and wondered if she could sport such a rock. Looking back from her hands to her face he found her looking full at him, again with that look of surprise.

"Shirae, I want you to stay by my side, forever, not as my prisoner, nor as my charge, but as my wife. May I have your hand in marriage?"

* * *

Haruka Koritsu had done exactly as her Princess had instructed. She did not like the man who greedily read the token case and placed it in his tunic. He actually produced a writing utensil and a scrap of paper; Haruka had not seen paper outside of Oujo-sama's books in years. He wrote several numbers on it and shoved it at her, telling her they were the codes to enter the Brig and the prisoner's cell. Then he instructed her to eat the paper. She assured the man that there was no way in hell that she would be doing that, but that she would safeguard its disposal with her life. She pulled out her knife and began to scrape the insides of her finger nails with it. That was enough to quell any protest from the worm.

She passed no one on her way to the Brig. Most of the compartments on Deck Six were for training, storage, and engineering; it was already somewhat into third-shift anyway.

She entered the code to get into the preparation room. There were various devices that she had no knowledge of and some that she wished she did not know of. She stepped out of this room making sure the hatch closed behind her and entered the code to the prisoner's room. She quickly shoved the paper scrap down her shirt, and then entered the room. A form stirred on the bunk near the back wall and she barely discerned eyes peering out from under the blanket there.

The blanket peeled away and Haruka stepped back a step shocked at the sight of this woman who was a dead ringer for the Princess. The woman sat on the edge of the bed, hands on her hips.

Haruka, having gotten a better look at her now, saw that she was shorter of hair and had a hardened look about her, but she still had the face of her beloved Princess. Haruka had mixed emotions about this fact.

"Ah, Haruka-chan. Come. Sit beside me." The woman said, patting the mattress at a spot to the right of her. "Come now, I won't harm you. I have disabled the video and audio. They will not hear us."

Haruka hesitated but then did as she was bidden; perhaps the fact of the woman's appearance compelled her to obey. Her voice was not unlike the Princess's either. She shook the thought from her head.

"Who are you?" Haruka asked.

The woman seemed to contemplate an answer to this question seriously for a moment, and then she asked a question of her own. "Who sent you here to me?"

"Oujo-sama sent me to give you a message. I did not know that you shared Oujo-sama's face."

"No one else sent you?" the woman was insistent.

"No, only Oujo-sama."

"Good. You are a Pure Blood are you not?"

Haruka was getting tired of these questions. "What of it?"

"Then I will speak to you in the Ancient Tongue if it pleases you." The woman spoke in perfect Japanese. "I am already known to you as Sagura-san, spy for the Empire. Unfortunately, my disguise was destroyed in an accident and I am found out. Regrettably I can do nothing at the moment for you and the Princess."

"Oh, you need not worry about that; just your own skin I would imagine." Haruka said inwardly amused. This spy was in too deep for her to do anything about it. She felt she should just deliver the message and be off.

Switching back to Codex English Haruka said, "Oujo-sama sent me here to deliver a message to you. These are her exact words: 'There is a prisoner in the Brig; a woman. Do not be surprised by her appearance. You must simply deliver this message. Say to her that a spirit came aboard the ship and entrusted this to me - *Princess Shirae, do not blame the father; blame the one who controls the father. Tell this also to the one who is almost you when you can see her true self.* Tell her I believe that she is the one to whom the message must be repeated.' That is the extent of my message for you."

Haruka watched as the woman seemed to digest the

message and grasp for some meaning. "Do you have some response you wish to be relayed to Oujo-sama?"

No, I... no. Nothing." The woman responded hesitantly.

"Do you know how you came to have the same face as my Princess?"

"That I am sure is a mystery to both of us."

"Can you at least give me a real name to give to my Princess? Perhaps she can intercede on your behalf."

"That I seriously doubt." The woman said nothing more.

Haruka stood. "I have given my message. You must understand I cannot let you out of here."

The woman spy nodded her head and remained seated on the bunk. Haruka headed to the door and opened the hatch with the code she had memorized. Before she keyed it closed, she glanced back and caught the woman saying something.

"Sanae. My name is Sanae."

4

Goh Takagawa sat at his workbench busily going over the equipment that Nanami Oliver had given him from his former friend's quarters and the device retrieved from the spy herself. There were two terminal devices and an odd-looking portable device that the bearer wore with a belt. The communications terminal was standard Imperial tech with a black box encryption module that he had already hacked. The second terminal is what caught his attention; it was a well-designed Imperial tech interface to the portable device which was plainly Pruatha tech. The portable device was damaged beyond repair and he could not determine exactly how it worked. It had a myriad of optical chips along its surface similar to the shield generators on the ship but the internal components were wholly unknown to him. It reminded him of something he had seen somewhere on the ship...

He turned his attention back to the interface terminal. If he could reverse engineer that, he might be able to figure out how the device worked. He got to it. The parameters appeared to be components of different appearances of Kintaro Sagura. Goh tried to concentrate but was having trouble keeping thoughts of his best friend out of his head. He felt betrayed, but could not reconcile his perception of the trust and friendship he had received from Kintaro. Now Kintaro was some woman. It all came rushing at him in retrospect; the lack of sweat when they trained together, Kintaro's religious excuses to avoid certain things that might have given the spy away, the different color hair he had seen...

A communication hail came over his Neural-net; the Captain was requesting his presence. He looked at the equipment in front of him and sighed.

*   *   *

Saitow was sitting behind his desk in the office portion of his personal quarters when Goh Takagawa arrived. He had been contemplating the prisoner's silence and wondering what could be done about it. Goh was his only hope to get through to her; he and the prisoner had been best of friends when the woman was Kintaro Sagura. Perhaps Goh could exploit that connection. He had to know what she was and what kind of a threat she posed to him and his beloved.

"Reporting as ordered Captain." Goh said wearily as he entered.

"Now Goh, no need to be so formal. We are all in this venture together!" Saitow tried to lighten the mood. "Is there something on your mind Son?" Saitow offered his Chief Engineer a seat.

Goh sat and was hesitant to speak. Saitow remained patient; he did not want to ruin the mood. If he could get the man to open up, he may find a proper opening to breach the subject of contact with the prisoner.

After a half a minute Goh started, "Captain, I have been having difficulty concentrating on my work. Lucky for me I have been provided a crack team of engineers to supervise; they are really autonomous, the lot of them. You see, it's the prisoner. You more than anyone know the shock of discovering that a fellow crewman was actually a female spy; I've known Kintaro for as long as I have been assigned to this ship. It's just so shocking…" Goh sat back meekly and said no more.

Saitow stood and opened a hidden cabinet in the bulkhead behind his desk from which he produced two glasses and a bottle of brandy. He poured a drink for each of them. "Please continue." He urged Goh after the man had taken a couple of sips.

"Well, you see Captain; I am conflicted by these contradictory feelings. On the one hand I feel betrayed by my best friend, and yet I cannot let go of the kinship we shared; even now that he is this *woman* spy. Don't get me wrong— I have no plans to spring my friend from the Brig. I simply cannot feel the rage that I should be feeling; it is affecting my work and for that I apologize." Goh sat back once more and took a bigger sip of the brandy.

"Hmmm…" Saitow saw this as the perfect opportunity to get done what he needed done. "Goh, I think you should confront your problem head on." Saitow sat back, sipped his own brandy, and let that sink in.

"I am not sure what you are getting at Sir." Goh set his unfinished brandy on the desk in front of him.

"You said that you are being affected by not knowing the intentions of your best friend, correct?"

"Yes, so to speak…"

"Then I have a proposition. Go down to the Brig and confront your friend head on. Then you can find out what attitudes exist between you. I will allow this in exchange for information you get from the prisoner."

Goh sat there as if he were contemplating the color of the glass that held his brandy.

"Goh, I need to know if this person is a threat to everyone aboard, especially the Princess. We have an announcement to make, but I will let you be the first to know; the Princess and I are engaged to be married. I need to know that she will be safe from harm, especially from our prisoner."

Goh picked up his glass and raised it. "Congrats." He said, then downed the remaining contents and wiped his mouth with his sleeve. After a moment of contemplating his empty glass, he said, "I'll do it."

* * *

Edward Kuremoto and Margo were in the lab when they were informed that the GCN was available through Asynchronous GCN Transceiver. They had spent most of their time there, except when it was time to sleep. The Doctor had slept in the lab and let Margo use his quarters.

They searched the GCN for news of Uprising and found two channels dedicated to just that. The first had a live feed from an embedded reporter with a group of Thane Mercenaries conducting mop-up operations of the Administration's base. The other was detailing the events that had transpired so far. They watched that one.

The studio announcer had just finished listing the casualties from both sides: fifteen-thousand-fifty-six of the Infected had perished from failsafe aerial bombardment, while the Administration suffered three-hundred-fifty-seven casualties including the Administrator and her entire staff. *We now go to the main administration building for a report from the interviewing of Administration prisoners taken in the combat for the base—*

"We were totally taken by surprise! We were confident that our contamination detection and elimination system would stop them, but they just came right through at us! It makes my skin crawl...

The scene cut away to the outdoors showing a humongous open trench that was at least a kilometer long. People could be seen standing and kneeling at intermittent intervals along its length. The faint sound of wailing and chanting could be heard.

The announcer's voice started, *This just in; this is the scene at a huge open mass grave used by the Uprising Administration for their so called "Serenity" Program. Infected who were at the advanced stage of the disease, and could no longer be productive, were taken here to be disposed of like livestock.*

The scene cut to the studio announcer. *We have more breaking news! The leader of the new Uprising provisional government, Marcus Nailat is about to make a speech. We go to him live—*

The scene cut to a podium in a very large area with quite a few people in attendance. Kuremoto watched as Margo started crying tears upon seeing her father for the first time since she was brought aboard the *Iwakina*. Kuremoto was relieved that his friend was alive and well. She jumped up out of her chair and hugged the Doctor, almost knocking him out of his. They sat together and listened to Marcus's speech.

"Citizens of Uprising, and Citizens of the galaxy; greetings. I am Marcus Nailat, the temporary head of the provisional government appointed to maintain structure until proper elections can be held. Citizens of Uprising, we are free!" Marcus had to pause as the entire crowd roared.

When the crowd noise died down enough, he continued. *"The Administration was an evil blight on this planet that has now been dealt with properly by freedom loving citizens."* Again, he had to pause as the crowd roared.

"The Administrator and her top officers are all dead and unfortunately have been spared the proper justice that they deserve. The free citizenry of Uprising has almost full control of the planet with the few remaining pockets of Administration resistance being taken care of by Thane Mercenaries who have generously agreed to help us in our plight. Merciful justice will be given to those who surrender and cease resistance. However, it is indeed bitter justice for all those who have lost their lives or loved ones to the disease that has ravaged this planet. Citizens of the galaxy, I call upon you to hear now of the injustice brought upon us all by the acts of the Uprising Administration; all for the sake of profit. Our disease has ravaged us for a full century. We endured and welcomed the right to work in the Administration's weapons manufacturing facilities as a way to have meaning to an otherwise meaningless life ravaged by disease. Yes, the Administration provided us with food and shelter. However, as I have determined with the help of a dear friend and colleague, the very disease that made us dependent on them was engineered and given to us by them!" the crowd once again roared, but this time in outrage.

Marcus lifted his hands to call for calm. Once the

crowd noise died down again, he continued. *"Now the suffering must come to an end. My friend has discovered and administered a cure for the disease for all of us. It has been used to successfully cure over half of the population and more of the cure is being produced for distribution as you listen to me. Those infected who have not been given the cure will be contacted shortly to report to health centers set up for the purpose of providing the cure and setting us on the course to wellness.*

"To our brethren off-world of Uprising, I say to you— do not fear us. We will not allow any member of the Uprising community to leave our planet until they have been thoroughly tested and certified to be free of disease. It has become a general consensus here that we will keep our facial tattoos as a sign of the suffering we have endured as a community. Do not let the fact that we wear them to cause you fear. We will also be maintaining our former work in the arms manufacture that Uprising is famous for. We as a community still need to be able to feed ourselves and we will need the infrastructure to procure such needs. We will, however, look into alternate products to produce so that the legacy of armaments can become history; we do not wish to continue to play a part in the suffering that is inevitable when armaments are used."

Marcus paused and the crowd roared once again; a bit less enthusiastically this time. *"So, as our time has come to be free of subjugation, we would like to call upon those in our greater galactic community who wish to invest in the future to come and meet with us. We can discuss great prospects for business together. Come treat with us for we are now free!"*

Marcus ended his speech and the crowd roared for a considerable time. Marcus finally bowed and headed off-stage as the crowd noise continued unabated.

The studio announcer's face returned, but Kuremoto did not hear her; his thoughts were of how to get himself and Margo back to Uprising.

*   *   *

Ken Edwards was in a bad mood. He had been happy at first to indulge Benoba in her pursuit of engineering; the poor thing needed something to do to help in her recovery from her abduction and potential life of slavery. However, she had been spending more and more time with Takagawa's engineering crew and less time with him. This was especially apparent now that they were spending interface calibration time at the Kyrovalkirii Jumpgate. He was not the type of man to blatantly let his affections be known, but surely, she could pick up the small favors he did for her as signs of such. He fretted that perhaps she had even surpassed him in engineering knowledge of the ship.

He would think of a way to gain her attention somehow, but this usually made his head hurt. Instead, he jumped into one of his many projects. He knew from learning Pruathan that the *Iwakina's* cargo bay was set up to produce stasis fields for certain types of cargo. If he could find a way to access the system and determine where and how to control these fields... perhaps that would impress his dear Benoba.

*   *   *

Haruka sat kneeling on the floor facing Ran Tsureyama and Amane. This was the first time the three of them had been able to get together away from their charge for quite some time. Ran had just accounted the news of the Captain's proposal while Amane nodded her head vigorously from time to time for emphasis.

"This is glorious news, Oujo-sama! This means that soon you will be free to find your betrothed and get married yourself!" Ran continued.

Haruka let the enormity of the news sink in. She grimaced at her own lack of calm as she lifted a trembling hand to sip some tea. She deftly set it down. The implications were staggering. Her Princess had accepted readily, perhaps even without knowing the consequences such a marriage would bring to the Empire. As the only Ros'Loper heir, her *husband* would naturally rise to the throne after her father, giving the Saitow family free reign over a good portion of the galaxy. However, it seemed that the Empire was in disarray with civil war imminent. Perhaps there would be nothing left to rule; the Empire would surely fall. She felt heartache for not knowing how her own beloved faired. It only then occurred to her that she would likely be ending her duties as Shirae's retainer.

"Do not fret my Oujo-sama. Ran and Amane will follow you wherever you go and help you to find your loved one safely." At this Amane shook her head negatively and supplicated herself to Ran. Haruka was curious as to the mute girl's actions.

Ran faced Amane and stared intently and deeply at the girl. "Ah, Amane wishes to stay with the Princess.

You know you will have to allow her to know your secret." Amane raised her head and smiled happily.

Haruka was wondering what exactly this secret was when Princess Shirae entered the room. All three women jumped up and hugged the young princess. Haruka was the last to let go; uncharacteristic tears streaming down her cheeks.

*   *   *

Marishima was ordered by the Captain to get a blood sample from the prisoner. She had one already, but needed to get one directly from the exposed woman spy to keep up appearances.

Sparrow 64 was in dire straits now. When she arrived at the Brig, she had the security officer that accompanied her wait outside; she did not need him realizing the total lack of conversation that would be the appearance given by the two women's meeting. Once the hatch was secure, she activated an interferer so that the audio in the room was undetectable; this she did because there would be no audio. She saw Sparrow 64 stirring from under the blanket on the cot at the end of the room.

Marishima had taken the folding chair she found outside the cell and unfolded it at the center of the room so that she could sit facing away from the camera. She would be communicating telepathically with her patient and hoped no one would see the lack of words coming from Sanae.

Marishima watched Sanae sit up on the cot and

stare blankly back at her for a moment. Before the woman could begin to recognize her, she was giving her telepathic instructions. *I am your friend from sickbay, remember? Be a good girl and cover your head with the blanket so that your face is in shadow.* Marishima saw the woman do as instructed. *Very good. Now, I am here to get another blood sample from you. The Captain has instructed me to get to know you and get some information out of you, but I already know you, don't I?*

Sanae nodded her head.

That is right. However, I will not give the Captain any information that he does not already know. This, I suspect, is very little. Marishima used her probing skills to delve into Sanae's mind for what she was going to do next. She found no plan or even thoughts of the future, only despair. Marishima wished that her skills were better; she wanted to know what made a Sparrow, the very essence of composure, actually feel despair. She could use her power of alteration to force Sanae to think of the reason, but that would be too much for the woman's mind; she had already used it once deeply before.

She would only be able to use it enough to erase this meeting from Sanae's mind; otherwise, she might do irreparable damage. She could plant a suggestion though. *Sanae, you feel like you are dreaming right? Yes, and I will leave you shortly, but first I must get a blood sample, ok? Good. We are friends, so there is no need to be alarmed.* Marishima stepped over to Sanae and removed the syringe from her lab robe's pocket. She deftly got the blood sample and turned to leave the room collecting the chair.

At the hatch she turned and thought to Sanae once

more. *Sanae, you are a good friend, but you need some more sleep. I will have to tell the Captain something; perhaps only your name, ok? Now, when I close this hatch, you will go back to sleep and forget our conversation. The next person you see after you awaken will be your confidant, tell them what causes your despair; you will feel better for it.* With that Marishima left the room, hoping that her suggestion would take hold.

*   *   *

Goh Takagawa was feeling nervous. The interface calibration interlude was well underway. It would be a matter of hours before they transited the KV Jumpgate and went on to Taibor. He had just that time to get the prisoner, who had been disguised as his best friend Kintaro Sagura, to open up and tell him her purpose for being just that. He still felt betrayed and struggled with his anger and other emotions such as pity and confusion at his own place in things.

After all the outrage he felt he still had feelings of loyalty toward his best friend; even now that he had taken the form of a woman. All of these thoughts went through his head as he waited for Bonifacio to finish making a sandwich for her. This he would bring as a peace offering. So far, the prisoner had been fed standard rations.

Goh arrived with his escort, sandwich in hand. He insisted that he be let in alone; the Captain had suggested this to make the prisoner feel less threatened. The security man set up the folding chair outside and pulled out his tablet; *to watch some sports recording no doubt* Goh thought. He entered and the hatch closed behind him. Goh surveyed the room; standard military configuration Brig cell, complete with toilet and bunk. A figure stirred under the blanket there. The woman underneath sat up groggily. It was uncanny how much she resembled the Princess. It was as if someone had taken the Princess to boot camp and spec'd her full infantry. There was a sharpness and tone to her that cried strength; much more than the delicate Princess could possess. Goh was caught off guard by a faint glimpse of a smile that vanished just as quickly as it surfaced. The woman looked at him with a look of despair.

"Goh, I am so sorry..." The woman said, the last words trailing off. Goh was astonished that it never occurred to him how feminine Kintaro's voice had been until now. This woman *was* Kintaro. Goh hid his anger and stepped forward offering the sandwich. The woman placed her hands on her hips and wiggled over to one side in order to make room for Goh to sit. He did just that, once again offering the sandwich. She took it and ate it greedily; as if she had not had real food in forever.

Once the sandwich was gone, she sat gazing at Goh as if reading his mood; trying to gauge his feelings. Goh saw a stray piece of food at the corner of the woman's mouth and reached to brush it away with his thumb. The woman caught his hand and held it to her face for a few seconds, and then let go. She wrapped the blanket around her tightly.

Goh wanted answers and was formulating what he would say very carefully to avoid showing his frustration. He did not get a word out before the woman had dropped her blanket and hugged him tightly, her head on his shoulder.

She spoke softly to him, "Oh Goh, I know it must appear to you that I have betrayed you, but my friendship with you has always been true. Please, you must believe me. When I first came to the *Iwakina*, I thought it best to avoid contact with others because I was unsure of the Transmutor Device's effectiveness. But then you approached me and befriended me; I was not even sure if you knew or not about my disguise. Since you acted as if I was truly Kintaro Sagura, I relished the friendship that we had. I even tried my best to give you of the only things that I could, my loyalty and some of my training. Now you see me as I truly am; this woman Sanae. My name is Sanae."

Goh extracted himself from Sanae's grasp and held her at arm's length. He glanced nervously at the corner where the camera was mounted; *were they getting all this?*

"Do not worry; I have disabled it for now." Sanae said as if reading his thoughts.

"How?... Never mind that. What are you doing on this ship? Who do you work for?" Goh tried to say what he had come here for; this to keep his mind off his conflicting emotions.

"I am a spy for the Empire, nothing more. The *Iwakina* is a high priority system... and the Captain... was not fully trusted." Sanae dropped her head after mentioning the Captain and Goh thought he had detected a sob come from her. "Oh Goh, what am I to do? My training forbids such things as friendship and trust, but I have found those things here. Worst yet, I have come upon feelings that I have never known in my entire life and they frighten me. You see I have come to love the one man on this ship that is the most completely out of reach; I have come to love the Captain."

Sanae looked up at Goh and he saw genuine tears streaming down the woman's cheeks. His feelings of anger and frustration turned to concern and sympathy. It had not been officially announced yet, but word had spread quickly; everyone aboard ship knew of the betrothal. He thought of his own lost love for a woman that was on a world far removed from galactic civilization and forever denied to him. He would never see his beloved Maia again; the mirror destroyed – the portal lost.

Goh thought *if this was all a ruse then I am the biggest fool that ever was.* Goh reached for Sanae this time and held her tightly in turn. As he had expected, she was taut and muscular.

"Oh Goh, what will become of me now?" Sanae asked.

"That I do not know. Perhaps you might be traded for something substantial. The Captain is a merciful man though, so I doubt he would just give you to the Empire like that. Then again, he could just as easily set you free. I just don't know... now, now, do not fret. I will think of something positive to suggest to him. In the meantime, you should cooperate fully and tell us all you can about your assignment here."

"I will tell you what I can, but only to you and no one else; especially that Oliver woman."

Goh chuckled a bit on the inside; Nanami Oliver could be a bit annoying at times. He could not imagine the conversation these two would have. "I will see what can be arranged. Is there anything that I can get you? Oh, and whatever you are using to shut down the surveillance, I need you to give it to me. I will personally turn it off when I come to visit. Fair enough?"

"So, does that mean that we can still be friends? I will need a change of clothes; the device is built into the hips." Sanae ran her fingers over the activation points to point them out.

"Yes, we can still be friends. You have confirmed to me what I was feeling; between you and me, I started to fear something was going on with you. There were signs. That is a story for another time. I will tell the Captain only what he needs to know, alright? I'll come back as soon as I can to talk."

Goh left the cell relieved that his life was not a lie. Everything was going to be alright.

5

Odmanar Zelek was very nervous. He had a simple job aboard ship; play Chief Steward while spying on everyone else for the family. He had special coded instructions to report everything he had learned to the head office once the ship made port in neutral territory. However, that had not yet occurred. Another part of his instructions was to report via coded message under the GCN gateway if there was something that required the attention of the first lady. He had just sent such a message. The news of the Captain's proposal to the Princess would be something she would want to know right off. He just hoped that he had sent it properly.

Odmanar jumped when a hale came over his neural-net; he was to report to the Captain. He stood shakily and headed in the direction of the Captain's cabin. Pausing at the door, he took a deep breath. *Had the Captain intercepted his message? Was he in turn being spied upon as well?* He did not want to know the answer to those questions. He keyed the hatch to hail the Captain and it opened. The Captain was sitting at his desk and toward the side in a lounger sat the Princess.

"Oz! How good to see you!" The Captain beamed. Odmanar knew that was highly unlikely. He bowed deeply toward the Princess and started to perspire.

Facing the Captain once again, "Yes, my Lord. You called?"

"Yes, yes. I have a bit of work for you. Since we

don't want to have to calibrate at the other end of the line, I am having it done here at the K-V Gate. In the meantime, I want you to call ahead and set up a party for the entire crew and whomever Mother finds it necessary to invite. As you undoubtedly know, the Princess and I are engaged to be wed." Captain Saitow sent a glancing smile at the Princess who smiled back. "We will announce the engagement at the party you will have prepared; any questions?" The Captain leaned forward and set his chin on his clasped fists; elbows on the desktop.

Odmanar was somewhat relieved that he had not been found out, yet now he was burdened with this extra task. However, he was Bolchinde and so relished having something else to do. He couldn't help it that a great smile lit up his face. "I'll get right on it my Lord. Are there any particulars you would like to request?" Odmanar glanced at the Princess and grasped the chair nearest to him as if to sit.

The Captain's mood shifted considerably and he stood up. "No, no, just go and see Bonifacio. He will provide you with a menu to request. Thank you."

"My pleasure my Lord. Congratulations to the both of you!" Odmanar bowed to the both of them, twirled, and keyed the hatch to exit, still grinning that he had not yet been caught.

*   *   *

Shirae was hard pressed to suppress a giggle. She was aware of Glenn's dislike for the Chief Stewart, but had not a clue why - until now. She stared at him and

139

he rolled his eyes. He was about to speak, then stopped as if distracted by something. "Is that so? Yes, then patch it through." He spoke into the air.

He must have seen the puzzled look on her face and spoke. "I just got a message from Nanami Oliver. Chancellor Aisou has left a video message for you on the GCN; Imperial code Silver. Shall I patch it through here?"

Shirae thought about protocol, but this man was to be her husband; he should be privy to all things in her life. She only hoped that he would be acceptable to Father. *Aisou could go to hell for all she cared.* However, Aisou may somehow do harm to her father and this troubled her deeply. She would need Glenn's advice in dealing with him eventually. "Please do so." She replied.

She watched as Glenn brought her a tablet and switched on the view-screen on the far wall. He moved the loungers closer and together they sat. She had to enter her password for Silver coded messages: *Hummingbird.* The screen lit up with the imposing face of Chancellor Horatio Aisou dominating the view.

Shirae had not seen his face in several years; she kept away from court business. However, it was clear that he had been under a great deal of stress. Even the Rejuve could not stem the aged look he was presenting. He smiled what seemed to Shirae as a wicked smile although it was meant to be endearing.

"Princess Shirae, I hope this message finds you well and not under some duress from your abduction. It has been made clear to me that you are relatively safe and unharmed. I would not know what to do if anything untoward should befall you. Your Father would be beside himself with grief. The Emperor has received your messages and is quite glad to see that you are being treated well. He hopes with great enthusiasm that the culprit in this matter will come to reason and return you to your rightful place by his side. Sadly, He is unable to send a personal message.

"He has sequestered himself in one of the palaces for health reasons; the details of which I cannot go into for the sake of security of course. Please know that he is safe and being cared for by the top physicians of the court. It is our wish at the court that you would come back to us. I am afraid that your absence may be the cause of your father's failing health. If and when you are able to come back, please relay instructions for your extraction immediately and we will take any means necessary to get you home. For now, I bid you farewell." The screen went blank for a moment and then was replaced by the Imperial Court Seal.

Glenn spoke immediately. "Shirae, can you play the last few seconds again? Be ready to pause it the moment I say pause…" Shirae did as she was bid. "Pause! Oh no that was a little too late. Please rewind again… Pause! There, you see there is an embedded image."

Shirae looked at the screen and saw only what looked like a glitch in the video. She shrugged her shoulders at her beloved.

"Please hand me the tablet." She did so and watched as Glenn back tracked the video frame by frame, then forwarded it in the same manner, showing that there was indeed something else in the video; a unique image. "When I was hunting Pirates for your father, I learned that they would sometimes place these encoded images inside otherwise noxious videos to family or merchants when ordering legitimate items. They used them to send secret messages, but why would Aisou use such a technique? Do you know of this method?" Glenn was adamant.

Shirae was puzzled just as much as he was and said so. "I have not a clue as to what that thing is; it looks like a glitch to me." *Was he worried that I knew something that he didn't* Shirae thought? She thought that made him a little bit cuter and smiled.

"Then why would he put such a thing in the message?"

"Hmmm. It does not fit with our assumptions of tyranny for him to be the one to put it in; perhaps another?" Shirae was thinking hard. This kind of thing was not her purview. She was educated in the finer things like physics, and mathematics, not investigative reasoning. This made her think about whether she was fit to rule a vast empire; she did not want to think about that so soon. The sudden thought occurred to her that if she married this man, he would supplant her father when her time came. She was warmed by the fact that he would be by her side then.

Glenn spoke, bringing her out of her reverie. "Then who would place such a code into the message?"

"Perhaps Father…"

"Perhaps. Shirae, can you provide a copy of the message to Takagawa? He will get to the bottom of this."

"Yes." Shirae saved the message to the tablet, again using her silver authorization, and handed it back to him.

"Thank you. I will have him get on this properly. Now, what do you make of Aisou's message? I think he is bluffing, which would fit in with him isolating your father."

Shirae thought about what he said. Father would not hesitate to get a personal message to her, especially if he had received the ones she had sent. "He must be lying." was her reply.

"You know what I think? He is trying to lure you back to the court in order to control you as well, or even get rid of you. If he has isolated you father, or God forbid, done something worse, then you are the only thing keeping him from seizing the throne. The older noble houses will rally around you if he made that move. You my dear are buying your Empire time."

Just then there was a hail at the hatch. Glenn stood and bade whomever it was to enter. It was the Medical Assistant Marishima.

"Ah, Shirae, I need a favor in order to settle a minor concern of ours. Marishima is here to get a sample of your blood."

* * *

Goh Takagawa was once again in the Captain's cabin. This time the Princess was with him which in his mind made the reason he was there a little awkward. He was summoned to report on the prisoner.

"So, Goh, did you get any information out of her?" The Captain requested.

"Yes sir. She states her name is Sanae and she is simply an Imperial spy sent to the *Iwakina* because it is a high-profile project and something else..." Goh hesitated glancing toward the Princess.

"You can continue Goh; I'll have no secrets from my future wife."

"Yes sir. She said that you were not trusted by the court." Goh hoped that sounded reasonable enough that the Captain would not try to go deeper.

"That is not surprising, given that I was practically shanghaied into service for them. What else did she say?"

"That was practically it. We discussed our prior friendship in some detail."

"Did you blow up on the poor girl? I feared that might happen."

"No sir. She was quite adamant about being sincere, so I remained calm. I used the opportunity to keep open our line of communication; perhaps I can get more information out of her in time."

"Very good man. Keep at it at your own pace. Learn what you can and report to me."

Yes sir." Goh was relieved that he had avoided further questions.

"Goh, did this woman *really* look like me?" it was the Princess that started a new round of questions.

Goh looked to the Captain who nodded for him to answer.

"Yes, Your Majesty. She looks like a rough version of yourself, if you will excuse me."

"Not at all; and Goh, please call me Shirae. From now on, I will not have my crew calling me 'Your Highness' or 'Your Majesty' and such; at least not the senior officers."

"Yes, Ma'am." Goh replied not quite knowing his place. The Princess just rolled her eyes and smiled.

"One more thing Goh." The Captain interrupted the awkward momentum. "On this tablet is an Imperial message. At the end there is a cryptograph image. I need you to break it and report to me the contents. This is not a real big priority, but needs to be done soon. Place as much priority on it as the prisoner. I know we are working you to death, and your service is greatly appreciated. I'm thinking that there will be something bigger than all of us in your future; *you* son, are going places with that intelligence of yours!"

The Captain was all smiles as he led Goh out the hatch. *These two will make a very strange couple* he thought as he headed back to his workbench.

*　　*　　*

Well, this puts an odd twist on things Marishima thought as she processed the DNA match on the two blood samples she had collected. There was no doubt about it; the two women made a one-hundred percent match. Identical twins they were; same father and mother. *So, Sparrow 64 is a royal; who would have thought that?* The old man must have had some

145

serious pull to manage that one. Did either of them know? The implications were dizzying. Marishima did not want to think about it; neither did she care. She would sit back and watch as events unfolded. It was almost comical.

She went to her terminal and keyed up the internal comms to inform the Captain.

*   *   *

Renge Yamano sat back at her station and breathed a sigh of relief. She had made it through the first few days of replacing Kintaro Sagura as Chief Navigator. She managed all of the jump calculations necessary to get the *Iwakina* to and through the KV Jumpgate, and to Roseglade which she got into the right orbit around. It was nothing like the clunky transports she had been piloting for the Conglomerate for three cycles. She had jumped at the chance when Dispatch had recommended her for augment to the *Iwakina*. She was a fine sleek vessel.

The Captain had invited all but a skeleton crew down to his ancestral home for a party. Renge was not about to miss this chance to mix it up with members of the nobility. She was from a backwater world off the Trades; such things came to her only once is a lifetime.

*   *   *

146

Madame Regina Saitow was quite pleased. Her youngest and most truant son had finally returned and made a name for him by possessing two of the most valuable things within the Ros'Loper Empire; their Pruathan starship and their heir to the throne. Soon her influence through him would finally put her in a position to crush her rival Shinohara Heavy Industries for good—

"Madame, the guests are arriving." A porter interrupted her thoughts. The man bowed deeply and retreated. She got up from her desk and headed toward the grand hall. Gathered there would be some of her best friends and business partners. The rest of the family who were within short distance of homeworld would be there of course; jealous brothers, she was sure. She suppressed a giggle. More importantly some of her most important suppliers would be in attendance as well as a small contingent of hand-picked media.

She arrived at the hall and glanced over everything quickly before approaching her guests who were gathering near the doors. She greeted each as cordially as possible given the short notice that they had been invited; without reason for such an invitation. This was to be a grand surprise after all.

*   *   *

Shirae was a bit nervous as she and Glenn rode a shuttle down to the planet. Suddenly she realized that they had not set a date; this worried her very much. She at least wanted to allow her father time to realize her feelings.

"Shirae darling, now don't go getting cold feet on me." Glenn must have sensed her nervousness.

"Glenn, it just occurred to me that we have not discussed setting a date. I want to give my father the opportunity to give his blessing and—"

"Darling, it is far from me to expect your father's blessing on our union. However, if it pleases you, we can set the date to sometime in the future. There are still many things in the universe that I want to show you, regardless of when we will be joined in marriage. As long as you are forever by my side, I will be eternally happy!"

Shirae was always caught off guard by this man's charm. She could not help but smile. "My precious Glenn, I will always be with you, you know that. When should we set the date for?"

"Well, it is almost Easter. Why don't we set our wedding for around my favorite part of the end of the year – Christmas?"

Christmas was a very happy time for her as well. She felt a tinge of anguish from being far from her father, but she quickly dismissed it. She needed to be strong as a woman should. "Yes! Christmas sounds wonderful."

*   *   *

The *Galveston* was a deep space salvage ship, but

her captain had been keeping her close to homeworld because he was having trouble raising funds for farther expeditions. He had heard rumors of a space battle that had occurred in the thick asteroid fields a light-year away. Sure enough, his crew found the wreckage of a well blasted hull and began the tedious process of collecting all the debris while cataloging the lot of it. Thankfully this scene was lacking the organic debris of floating corpses that usually accompanied battle wreckage. As he sat watching the piece names flash on his screen as they were cataloged, his eyes hit on a name so bizarre that even he had not come across it in his thirty years in this line of work—Metal Humanoid. *Was this a joke one of the crew was trying to pull?* He stepped out of his office above the salvage hold and bellowed, "Who's the lunk-head that manifested a 'Metal Humanoid'?"

He spotted a few crewmembers surrounding something he could not make out looking his way. They parted and he caught a gleam of silver. He took the lift down and made his way over to the thing. It was in humanoid form alright, but missing both arms and one leg. It was charred almost black in most places, but it was surely made of fine silver with lines of black and gold where he could make them out. He had never seen a real robot before. He had heard enough stories about them as a child and into adult life to not take any chances. "Put this thing in the lock-down hold."

TRANSFORMATIONS

1

Saitow sat in an office outside the grand hall of his family's vast estate while he waited for the Princess to be readied for the gathering. He reluctantly conceded to himself that he actually missed this place. Sure, it was showy and an overt waste of space, but it was still home. He dismissed the nostalgia with thoughts of duty; to his crew, *his* ship, but mainly to his beloved.

Marishima's news of the spy being a twin sister to the Princess was most puzzling. He knew of the difficulties the Emperor had gone through just to produce an heir; his Empress dying in the process. Why would the old man give up one heir for another? Surely the chances of his empire surviving would be doubled had there been two. Perhaps by dividing the two, he felt that there would be a better chance for survival in cases of intrigue. Such questions fascinated Saitow. There were so many unknowns. *How did the twin come to be a spy on board his ship? What was he to do with her?* He decided not to tell his beloved just yet. She was at the height of beauty; fully in love with him, and full of joy. He would not spoil that with this troubling news. Sooner or later, she would make inquiries; he would let human nature take its course.

There was a hail at the entrance to the office. He bade whomever it was enter; it was a fellow he had hired to look into Kuremoto's past. Mr. Brown was his name; *not* his real name. After exchanging pleasantries and the offer of a drink, the two men got down to business. The man detailed Kuremoto's upbringing and exile from the old Japanese enclave of Oedo, a planet set aside for Pure Bloods by the Rangelley, so they could practice their old code of Bushido without outside interference. Kuremoto was indeed a Pure Blood. This was news to Saitow, but he had expected as much.

The man detailed Kuremoto's rise up within the scientific community despite his lineage, ultimately attaining the top spot among the few who had anything to do with Pruathan technology. Kuremoto was over four-hundred years old, remaining alive so long due to the drug Rejuve. This much Saitow already knew.

"I must beg your pardon my Lord; this next bit of information is a bit disturbing and I am risking much for divulging it to you, especially here." The man produced a small tablet from his robes.

Saitow stood, moving around the room. He sat upon the edge of the desk he had been sitting behind and traced a rectangle on a space close to him upon its surface. The cameras within the room would not be able to see what was on the tablet if the man placed it there.

The man put the tablet where Saitow had indicated and keyed a sequence of numbers on its surface. Text began to scroll across the screen – *The Madame Regina Saitow had once approached Kuremoto, engaging in an affair with him in order to garnish secrets about the Pruathan technology the man was an expert in. The details remain clandestine but the whole affair ended badly as Kuremoto realized the true nature of the relationship and refused any further contact. Madame Regina has resented the man ever since – end of report.*

Saitow looked up at the man who smiled meekly. If anyone else within these walls discovered the man had such personal information, he would not see the light of day again.

"This is very good news for you, sir. May I?" Saitow indicated the tablet before him.

"Of course, my Lord." The man replied.

Saitow furiously keyed in a number of instructions, at one point showing a figure to the man and having him key in a personal code. Satisfied that the transaction had been finalized and the device had been erased, he removed the backing from the tablet and took out the tablet's slim-lined data-stick, tucking it into one of his secret pockets inside the formal robes he wore. He then replaced the cover and handed the tablet back to the man. This was interesting news indeed.

* * *

Renge Yamano had taken the first shuttle down to the planet and was ushered into a set of suites set up to accommodate the *Iwakina* crew. She was instructed to shower and present herself for dressing. She was a little taken aback by all this, *but what the hell*, she thought, *this is a once-in-a-lifetime thing*. Her hair was dressed and she was given minimal make-up; the artist stating that her simple natural beauty was quite stunning. This made her all the giddier, as they put her is a striking blue sapphire formal gown.

It even seemed to her that some of her crewmates were acting a little envious. This did bother her just a bit because she always did her best to get along. However, as the primped-up crew sat in a waiting lounge attached to the grand hall, no one spoke to her; not even her friends. It was as if she were from another world. She hardly noticed; her head was full of wonder at the splendor of this one room alone.

* * *

The party was in full swing. Food had been served and entertainment arranged; yet the guests of honor had yet to show up. Regina Saitow was beginning to wonder if this was a legitimate affair or some kind of hoax perpetrated on her by her wayward son. She sensed a slight perturbation in some of her guests as well.

Edward Kuremoto, dressed in formal robes, the one man she was most loath to see in the whole universe, stood there blocking her path. Her escorts moved toward the man, but she waved them off, not wanting a scene. Kuremoto bowed deeply. *Ever the gentleman*, she thought; this made her hate him all the more.

"Dear Edward, what brings you to my humble home?" Regina tried to be cordial at least for the sake of appearances.

"Dear Lady, I have come to you with a request. Shall we?" Kuremoto indicated a recessed sitting area close by.

Madame Saitow waved her escort back and

followed the man. He was just as handsome as in those days, which made her all the more annoyed at his presence. Wine was served as each assessed the other. Kuremoto smiled at her, incensing her more. Naturally she showed no such emotions outwardly.

"Regina, you are looking as fetching as ever." Kuremoto stated. *Was he trying to rile her?* She wondered.

"Edward, please get to the point. Why have you come straight to me? I know you are here for the Captain; *that* is the only reason I tolerate you this day." Regina took a long draught of her wine.

"Very well." Kuremoto took an equally long draught from his own wine glass. "You see, dear Regina, I know that it is you that bankrolls the ship's voyages. So, it would be extremely rude of me to just leave the ship without informing its benefactor. I simply need some compensation, and I will assuredly get out of your way."

"Now for whatever reason would you wish to leave the good Captain's ship?" Regina was elated on the inside. She had wanted to get rid of this man from any influence toward her interests for a very long time. Her man on the ship, Zelek, had long been reporting that Takagawa had practically usurped Edward's usefulness. She would gladly have him leave; as long as he did not interfere in her future business.

"I have become disillusioned with Pruathan technology and want to concentrate my efforts towards helping the people of Uprising. I simply need forty-million MU and that wonderful yacht you lent me last year."

Regina blinked at such a large request. "That is a tall order Edward. What will the Saitow family receive in return?"

"I for one, am willing to let bygones be bygones. You and I were still relatively young in our days together and I would not want to hold such a grudge for much longer. We are not getting any younger. Therefore, as a gesture of good will I will turn over everything I have on Pruathan technology to Goh Takagawa. I will also put in a good word for you with the new government of Uprising; they can certainly use your expertise in manufacturing there now that the Administration is no more."

Regina thought on this while sipping her wine. This was what she had been after when she first approached this man so many years ago. Besides Edward Kuremoto, there were only two others ancient and studied enough to be experts in Pruathan technology; one of them being employed by her chief rival Shinohara Heavy Industries. She had also been contemplating an inroad to the new Uprising government; they were her chief supplier of plasma cannon for her ships. Letting go of the past was another matter, but she could set it aside for the time being; for the sake of the Conglomerate of course.

"Ms. Orchard will find you soon and make arrangements. Now if you will excuse me, I have *guests* to attend to." Regina stood and left Kuremoto without even a glance. She would be happy only when he has actually left the starship *Iwakina.*

* * *

Dorigethra Fan was elated to be in Kimberly's company. It was not because he was able to mingle with some of the Human aristocracy; he had had his fill of their petty machinations on several Andalii worlds. No, it was Kimberly. She had somehow manifested increases in her telepathic powers to a remarkable extent; she was even able to block for the both of them.

They sat in one of the recessed areas around the hall, observing the nobles gathered there, and discussing them telepathically.

Fan, do you see that lady there? She is thinking very hard about cheating on her husband with the large fellow on her left. There, that man in the maroon robes is also contemplating a relationship with the large man. Humans are so funny are they not? Kimberly thought to him.

It is remarkable how much you have advanced in telepathic ability Kimberly! Your enhancement drugs are marvelous... Dorigethra noticed a change just then in his friend. She seemed to become taciturn and discontinued their conversation.

"Kimberly...?" Dorigethra spoke.

Kimberly took a sip of her wine and sighed.

* * *

Regina Saitow entered the offices that were

temporarily assigned to her son Glenn, the Captain of the Pruathan hybrid starship *Iwakina*. She found her son lazing in a stuffed chair beside a fireplace. Despite the environmental controls, such things were an excess worthy of the noble Saitow house.

"Ah, Glenn there you are. What on Roseglade is keeping you?" Regina was anxious to get the main event started.

"Ah, Mother! As you can see, I am awaiting my fiancée. There is no telling what manner of dress the staff has trussed her up in; or perhaps her retainers are keeping them at bay!" Glenn rose from his seat to greet his mother properly.

"Dear son, you could at least come out of here and greet your brothers. They have been boasting of your recent battle in the Saragothra reaches. I think they may be hiding a bit of jealousy..." Regina winked at him as only a mother would.

"Oh Mother, I must do things from now on with my beloved in mind, so I would prefer to enter the hall with her by my side."

"I see your point dear. Ah, I have a gift for you on this auspicious occasion. I would assume that all of the normal accounts for the ship are the same?"

"Yes Mother, they are." Glenn looked a bit confused.

"I am reinstating your financing for the pursuit of Pruathan technology. I presume you will wish to continue your 'personal journey' after the marriage?"

"Well yes Mother, the *Iwakina* will be continuing her mission." Regina noted that it almost seemed that

Glenn was hiding something.

Just then, Shirae entered the room followed by Ran Tsureyama who bowed deeply to Regina. She wore a stunning tan evening dress with light robes to match the deeper brown of the robes Glenn wore.

"Shirae, you look ever so beautiful!" Glenn said endearingly.

Regina realized that the young fool must truly be in love. This thought reminded her of Kuremoto and soured her mood. "Yes, our Princess looks rather stunning! I will see you both again at the main tables. Oh, by the way Glenn dear, Edward Kuremoto will be leaving your ship before you leave port. Please be sure to clean the man's quarters thoroughly; there is no telling what manner of contamination you might find there." With that Regina left the two to make their entrance to the hall.

*   *   *

"What in heaven was that about?" Shirae asked Saitow.

"It seems that our good Doctor Kuremoto has cut a deal to leave the ship. That is not a surprise in the least." Glenn replied. Shirae was curious now.

"How so?" She asked.

"My Beloved, I will tell you this in keeping with the openness that any betrothed and loving couple should retain. This of course is privileged information; not to be repeated. As you probably already know, Doctor Kuremoto has been around and studying even back in the Rangelley Era. His vast knowledge is reason enough for people like my mother to want to get to know him and possibly exploit him." Glenn bent toward her and lowered his voice so that only she could hear, "My mother took it a bit too far, wooing the poor man in their younger days. Having seen what their relationship really was and being brokenhearted, Kuremoto cut off the relationship and refused anything to do with the Saitow Conglomerate or any other non-governmental venture. At the time of the mutiny, I was not privy to this information. It must have made Mother's ire burn that I had brought the man along. Long story short, surely Kuremoto cut a deal with mother for a ship and some MU."

Shirae contemplated this. *Was it true that the nobles in business would go to such lengths for power and profit?* She shuddered at the thought.

"Well, our public awaits us. Shall we?" Glenn offered her his arm and led her toward the entrance to the hall.

* * *

Benoba was very uncomfortable. She only agreed to accompany Ken Edwards planet-side because she wanted to get out of the confines of the ship, and knew nothing of the current planet they were at. She was even excited to attend the Captain's party. However, she was taken aback by the way Edwards seemed to almost be parading her for everyone to see; the looks she received making her all the more uncomfortable. As Edwards made small talk with a few of the noblemen gathered near the center of the hall, Benoba smiled meekly at them and looked about the place. As she focused on a particular recessed area along the central wall, she felt an odd sensation that compelled her to go there. She left the group and wandered in that direction almost as if against her will. She could hear Edwards calling after her, yet was still being compelled toward that spot. Edwards suddenly appeared in front of her, blocking her way.

"Benoba dear, what has come over you?" She felt his genuine concern for her, yet the urge to move past him was stronger than ever. She tried to move past him, but he grabbed her left arm with his right hand. She felt a sudden urge to remove his hand from her arm as if his touch was poisonous. However, she reached up with her right hand and deftly if not forcefully grabbed his, dragging him along with her.

"There is someone that I must see over there." *Someone? The thought had not occurred to her that there was someone where she was going; why had she said that?*

They came upon the recessed area where a table with two beings sat. One was an alien that she did not recognize; the other Doctor Rosel.

"Please have a seat Benoba." The Doctor said to her and she obeyed. Benoba looked to Edwards who stood there dumbfounded.

"Ken, be a dear and find us a couple more bottles of wine; and *one* more glass." Rosel said hefting the empty bottle that stood on the table. Ken just nodded and wandered off.

"Dear Benoba, how have you been fairing on the ship? I hope that you have been adjusting nicely." Rosel said.

To Benoba it felt like she was not only hearing the words but that the woman was inside her head as well. Oddly, it made her feel more comfortable.

"Yes Doctor, I have been adjusting well. Besides the frequent stares I get from the crew, everyone is going out of their way to make my stay aboard ship as pleasant as possible." Benoba felt as if she could tell this woman anything.

"How nice. I hear that you are quite an accomplished engineer. You have been helping the Engineering Department with ships systems, no?" Doctor Rosel's voice was like honey to Benoba; she hung on every word.

"Yes, I have been quite busy, but I think that this has been upsetting to Ken. I suppose I owe him much for saving me. I think he is quite stricken with me to a point I do not wish to pursue." *Why am I saying this aloud?* Benoba thought, laying out her most intimate thoughts.

"Dear girl, after tonight, I don't think you will have any more worries as far as he is concerned. Ah, here he is with our wine." Benoba looked up to see that Ken had brought the bottles of wine and one glass.

Doctor Rosel got up and spoke in whispers to Ken, who stood by with that dumbfounded look on his face. When she was through, he just wandered off, not even looking back in her direction. Rosel sat down once more. Benoba chanced a glance at the alien. He was just staring at them both like a puppy who was awaiting a treat.

"Ah, I am sorry for my lack of manners. This is my friend and colleague Dorigethra Fan, elite among Andalii scientists." The Andalii bowed at his seat. Benoba had never seen an Andalii before, or any alien for that matter; barring the images of Kaldeans that she had been forced to endure. So far, she did not like aliens one bit.

"Pleased to meet you miss...?"

"Benoba. Likewise." Benoba said and bowed back at the creature.

"He really is a nice fellow once you get to know him. Please let us fill these glasses. I believe the main event is about to start." Rosel said while the Andalii opened the wine.

*   *   *

Saitow and Shirae entered the great hall to a bit of fanfare. Saitow brought his betrothed around the main table to greet each there in turn. Then the couple climbed the raised platform where a podium stood for them to make their announcement. Saitow felt slightly nervous yet exhilarated at the prospect of the galaxy getting the news he was about to give. He gripped Shirae's hand a second before approaching the podium. Shirae stood just a little back and to his left.

"Friends, relatives, and honored guests; greetings. You are probably wondering why you were all called here today. As most of you know, I, Glenn Saitow of the

Saitow family and humble Captain of the *Iwakina*, have absconded with the ship itself and a most valuable passenger in the form of our dear Princess Shirae. Thievery is a dishonorable trait, yet when thievery is employed for the good of the citizens of the galaxy; it can surely be looked upon as a worthwhile endeavor. The *Iwakina* is a powerful and formidable vessel. This has been proven in our recent battle with a rogue Imperial officer, whom we defeated near Saragothra. After my speech, which I promise will be short, you may all view scenes from the battle on the tablets being brought out to each table."

Saitow glanced around the hall to verify that this was indeed being done. "You all must have heard by now the atrocities being perpetrated within Ros'Loper controlled space by their Special Services Corps. Such power as the *Iwakina* provides cannot be left to fall into the hands of despicable men. This is why I have taken the *Iwakina* and stand before you today. Now there is the issue of our dear Princess."

Saitow paused and held his hand out to Shirae who joined him at the podium. "I promised the father of this dear girl, the Emperor, that I would show her the universe. This is a promise I intend to keep. Yet, as I wandered the galaxy, a princess by my side, I could not help but to fall deeply in love with such a fine woman; she likewise has fallen for me! Therefore, the two of us have become engaged to be wed this coming December. Please take care of us both." After the traditional line for a marriage announcement Saitow raised Shirae's hand in his and the both of them bowed deeply as the gathering roared with applause.

*   *   *

Regina Saitow clapped along with the rest of the gathering. It seemed that her son did have a decent head on his shoulders. To both announce his reasoning for stealing the *Iwakina* and that he was ready for any challengers was a stroke of genius. However, she was not pleased by his delay in marrying the Princess. In any event, the Conglomerate still had the upper hand. She needed to ensure things remained that way. She called for Vanessa Orchard.

2

Goh Takagawa sat at his workbench decrypting the cryptograph that the Captain had given him. It wasn't that he had too much work to get done that stopped him from attending the event planet-side; he just did not want to get back into that scene. He had been an aristocrat all of his life until his planet turned to chaos. He was tired of all the fake smiles and the fake pleasantries and the fake people that formed the base of the Noblesse.

The cryptograph was a common tool used by various military entities to send messages within innocuous media so that the message could be placed almost anywhere and in as many places as it took to get to where it needed to be. Placing a cryptograph near the end of a video was pretty common. Goh was sure that the sender thought it would more likely be found for that reason. A signal from his terminal told him the correct algorithm was found to decipher the message. He ran it and watched the message scroll across the scene in text – YOUR MOST REVERED HIGHNESS, I CANNOT DIVULGE MY IDENTITY TO YOU JUST YET. HOWEVER, BE ASSURED THAT I AM IN A POSITION TO WATCH OVER YOUR FATHER AND WILL DO SO TO THE BEST OF MY ABILITY. YOU MUST BE MADE AWARE THAT CHANCELLOR AISOU IS NOT THE CARING FRIEND TO YOUR FATHER THAT HE MAKES HIMSELF OUT TO BE. IT IS IN FACT HE WHO HAS PERPETRATED THE TREASONOUS ACTS CARRIED OUT BY THE SSC, WHO ARE FULLY UNDER HIS CONTROL.

THE OTHER NOBLE FAMILIES ARE POWERLESS AGAINST HIM AND MOST HAVE SO FAR PLAYED ALONG WITH HIS RUSE FOR YOUR FATHER'S SAKE. OTHERS HAVE LEFT THE COURT AND MOST OF THESE ARE NOW UNDER SIEGE BY THE SSC. PLEASE BE AWARE THAT THERE IS AN IMPERIAL SPY ABOARD THE SHIP. THIS SPY WAS SENT BY AISOU; HOWEVER, HE/SHE HAS BEEN LEFT TO THEIR OWN DEVICES FOR AS YET UNKNOWN REASONS. FOR THE SAKE OF THE EMPEROR, IF YOU ENCOUNTER THIS SPY, PLEASE TELL HIM/HER THAT CONTACT SIGMA SENDS CODE 5-7-I-L-L-G-5. THIS WILL ORDER HIM/HER TO GIVE YOU A MESSAGE THAT HE/SHE WAS GIVEN SUBLIMINALY AND HE/SHE WILL ONLY BE ABLE TO DELIVER IT TO YOU PERSONALLY. DO NOT WORRY FOR YOUR SAFETY; IF ANYTHING WERE TO HAPPEN TO YOU IT WOULD DEVASTATE YOUR FATHER AND MY ONLY MISSION IS HIS WELFARE. KNOW THAT THIS I WILL DO UNTIL I DRAW MY LAST BREATH – L.

Goh unplugged the Captain's tablet from his terminal and stretched his tired limbs. All of this spy stuff was a bit too edgy for him. It also made him think of Sanae.

Just then a message came over his neural-net; he was being summoned to the Saitow Estate by Madame Regina herself. He grabbed his jacket from the back of his workbench chair and keyed the hatch, hoping there was still a shuttle aboard. He did not want to keep that old lady waiting.

*   *   *

"How is your glass dear?" Rosel asked Benoba for the fifth time. They had been discussing Benoba's homeworld and the original state of her pigmentation compared to the current state. The girl was getting a bit tipsy and easily plied for information. Rosel would need her in the future and felt that the injections she had been given were doing their work just fine. Her power of persuasion over Benoba, as the book had called it, was growing with the help of the wine. She felt it time to lay the framework for her plan.

"Benoba, since you are very adept at engineering, I have a proposition for you. You see, the ship's engineers are great at keeping the ship running. However, I have a multitude of technical equipment in my Sick Bay that no one seems to be able to maintain. I figure that with your talent and access to the Pruathan database there, you could do a wonderful job with all of it."

Rosel looked to the girl for a sign of acknowledgement and was pleased by what she saw. Benoba would now be readily available for more treatments and soon fall under her power as one of her Betrothed.

Kimberly, I am quite confused; what exactly is going on here? It was Fan speaking in her head.

Fan, this girl is part of my experiment. I slipped her some of my experimental serums while treating her for her pigmentation problems as requested by that gentleman I sent away. She will be coming to the lab often for more treatment and to calibrate my equipment. Rosel replied telepathically.

Is that wise? It seemed as if that man was a bit overly protective...

He is no longer of concern. I 'suggested' that he no longer cares for the girl; an easy matter.

"Yes, I would be delighted to help out in Sick Bay, Doctor." Benoba interrupted their mental conversation.

"Oh, I just knew you would want to help!" Rosel smiled as she poured more wine for them all.

*   *   *

Goh was met at the Shuttle landing by Vanessa Orchard. She looked him over and brought him in through a side entrance, avoiding the grand hall and the party there. Goh could hear the revelry as they passed through a courtyard adjacent to the hall. They re-entered the mansion and went down a long corridor that was extravagantly decorated as befitting a noble house. They entered a suite of offices where a great desk sat; behind it, the Lady Regina Saitow. Goh bowed deeply and was offered a seat beside the desk. Orchard took a chair next to his. Some wine was poured; again, his family's vintage. They exchanged pleasantries and thoughts about his dear grandmother before Madame Regina got down to business.

"Goh, if you recall, I had asked you to keep an eye on Edward Kuremoto. Your infrequent reports were useful, and I thank you. At this time, you will no longer be required to do this task for us. Your increasing worth as Chief Engineer aboard the *Iwakina* has not gone unnoticed. I want to prepare a reward for you; perhaps a means for vacation once your services have become less essential to the *Iwakina*. However, what I need you to do for us now, besides continue to excel in your job, is twofold. First, I must tell you that Edward Kuremoto is leaving the *Iwakina* before it next sails."

Regina nodded to Orchard who handed him a data-stick. "This data packet is for Doctor Kuremoto. You must give it to him if and only when you have received the entirety of his research on the Pruatha and their technology. I am sure you will be able to determine that you have received its entire contents, correct?"

Goh thought about that. Kuremoto had been researching Pruathan technology for at least a couple of centuries; surely there must be at least a petabyte of information. He would have to run a check on it all to make sure it was real and would remain real. "Yes, Ma'am, but it will take a few hours."

"That is fine. The *Iwakina* does not have to leave until I say it does. I have already commissioned her for a delivery run. Ms. Orchard will arrange for transfer of the data at your pick-up destination; you of course will retain a complete copy and report any breakthroughs that develop on your end. The second matter is that I need you to keep an eye on the Captain for me. It worries me that he has delayed his marriage until the end of the cycle. Will you do this for me dear?"

Goh knew better than to refuse the lady in her own house. "Yes, Ma'am."

*   *   *

Ken Edwards wandered the hall as if in a daze. He felt instinctively that he had forgotten something, but could not nail whatever it was down. He went to the bar to get a drink. The bartender eyed him like he had already drunk the bar dry. He did not feel drunk, but he did not remember the past hour or so. Hefting his drink, he went to the main table to congratulate the Captain. Perhaps that was what he had meant to do all along. Why worry over little things when the evening was ripe for enjoyment? He finished his drink and felt the better for it.

*   *   *

Doctor Rosel determined that the wine was getting to Benoba, so she bade the girl sleep on the cushions that made up the seat for the recessed booth. She then scanned the room for more entertainment. Fan was going on and on about some story that she was half listening to. If anything loosened the tongue of the Andalii, it was wine.

Just then she detected a mental disturbance that was rather tasty. It seemed odd to her for just a moment that she felt it in such a manner. A group of three young nobles were entertaining a woman from the crew. This woman had an aura about her; one which caused her regular friends to avoid her. She was very beautiful and the rest of them resented it. That, though, was not the enticing part of the whole affair. The three young men meant to have a bit of sport with the girl.

Fan, do you see the young woman in the blue dress surrounded by noble youths? She is about to know misfortune at their hand she thought to her friend.

Fan stopped talking and looked in the woman's direction. *How do you know?* He thought back. Rosel directed the thoughts of the three young men into her friend's mind. She noticed that he was at first astonished, but then excited and repulsed at the same time. She ceased giving him their thoughts. *What will you do? Will you save her?* Fan thought to her.

Just then the four of them turned and headed toward the courtyard exit from the hall. *Come. Let us watch what unfolds in the courtyard* Rosel thought to Fan. The two of them rose and headed in that direction, leaving Benoba to her dreams.

* * *

Renge Yamano was feeling a little bit tipsy from the wine that was served. Therefore, she welcomed the chance to go out and see the magnificent fountain in the courtyard when it was offered by the three gentlemen she had just met. *What were their names again?* She thought, *Akira, Yoshi, and John? That sounds about right.* Now she could get some fresh air. These gentlemen were of the nobility and their conversation was witty and interesting. She was having a marvelous time and could not think of a single thing that would change her mood.

Akira pointed out the fountain with its tall graceful angel at center, pouring water from a vase. It was truly beautiful.

"This surely does not compare with the beauty that stands before me." The man said bowing slightly in her direction. Renge blushed, but then thought that it was odd that he would say such a thing in front of his fellows. That is when she noticed they were gone.

"Come, my dear lady, I have other things of beauty for you to see." Akira grabbed her hand and brought her toward a group of hedges; there were hedges at four points surrounding the fountains that bordered various pathways.

Before she could protest, Akira had thrust her into the hedgerow into the arms of John, who had removed his formal robes. John sneered at her in a manner that scared her. Yoshi grabbed her other arm; as she realized what was going on, they had her on the ground. She let out a scream before Yoshi's big hand was covering her mouth. Each of the other men had her arms pinned under their knees, while Akira had grabbed her legs after throwing off his own robes.

"Hurry and get her underwear off; I need something to plug this noisy hole!" Yoshi admonished.

"I've got something for that!" John said, working loose his trousers.

Renge tried to struggle, but felt as if in a daze; *how could something like this be happening? Were these not noblemen?* She thought closing her eyes. She felt her dress being pushed above her waste...

Then there was a thumping sound and the weight of Yoshi fell off her left arm; his hand falling slack off of her mouth. She opened her eyes to see a shovel being smashed into John's face while Akira let go of her legs. She looked toward him to see that he was reaching for something inside his tunic.

Kick! she heard inside her head and she did; throwing Akira off balance and causing the pistol he held to fire into the air. Then the shovel found his face as well.

Her savior was Goh, the Chief Engineer from the ship. He bent down to her, "Are you alright?" he asked.

Still in a daze, she nodded slightly. Goh offered her his hand and helped her get to her feet. "I was making my way through the courtyard and noticed the two men that were with you and this guy, duck into the bushes here. I figured something was amiss so I looked for an available weapon; it was one against three after all. Sorry if you came to any harm."

Renge looked at her savior. With tears welling up in her eyes she reached up and hugged him.

"Let us get out of here. Even if our story is true, these brutes will have the upper hand being nobility. I'll escort you to the shuttle." Goh said and held her hand the entire way to the waiting launch.

*　*　*

Marishima made her rounds of the patients and then headed to her cabin. She wanted to log on to *Unity* and see if there was news of Wilhelm and the others. She fed her cats and then checked her messages. The referendum had already taken place and the majority had decided to ally with The New Rangelley; no surprise there given the state of the other Human

Empire this side of the Barrier. *Unity* was already in an alliance with the Taibor Freehold. She figured the more heated debates will come when the next referendum is announced – whether to let non-humans join *Unity*.

There was no message from Wilhelm which worried her. She *did* have a message from Hanako Quan. Hanako wanted to speak with her as soon as possible. She requested contact and received an offline response. She checked the rest of her messages, and was about to log off, when she got a video call from Hanako. She allowed it and a large screen appeared with the face of her friend; right in the center of her dining room. Apparently Hanako was using a portable.

"Marishima my old friend! Sorry I have to use this lo-tech gadget; I was in the middle of shopping for dinner and I really need to talk to you."

"What is the matter?" Marishima did not like the urgency that Hanako was projecting.

"I need to get out of here and get my old job back on the *Iwakina*." Hanako was adamant; Marishima could tell by her biometrics.

"I will get word to the Captain. Can you make it to Taibor Prime?" Marishima knew better than to ask where Hanako was; and she was not about to give out the ship's location either.

"I think so. I will monitor our box on the GCN; remember?" The *Iwakina* had a special virtual message drop box set up on the GCN for crew that got separated from the ship.

Marishima would ask the Chief Engineer if it was free of Imperial monitoring. He would be able to fix that. "Yes. You do that. Stay safe my friend."

"All be with you." Hanako's face disappeared from its place floating in the center of the room.

*   *   *

Doctor Rosel and Dorigethra Fan had returned to the sleeping Benoba. Dorigethra was recalling the scene that they had both witnessed. He saw the two men stealthily head into the bushes while the other man distracted their prey. He saw them deftly handling the girl as if this had not been the first of their victims. Then, out of nowhere, came her rescuer; brandishing a garden instrument and easily besting the three men with surprise. What disturbed him was the fact that the girl seemed on the verge of hysterics then resigned herself to her fate; yet at just the right moment, she kicked at her assailant. This may have saved either his or Kimberly's life; he felt sure that the pistol was almost aimed in their direction.

My dear Kimberly, did you see the girl react to the pistol being drawn? He thought to his companion.

I was the one that caused her to kick the pistol bearer. She thought back to him nonchalantly.

That came as no surprise. He suddenly shuddered. He recalled the scene after the rescuer had taken the girl away. Kimberly had approached the men and as each groggily came to, he had watched her use a psychic attack on them; leaving them babbling like crying children.

Kimberly must have seen his reaction just then because she thought to him, *don't worry Fan. I will have no cause to use such a thing on you. Those three will not even want to be around their own mothers, for the suggestions I imposed upon them.*

I want to ask you why you did not stop them before the poor girl was rescued. Fan did not know if he wanted to really know the answer.

She needed to be a bit frightened so that I could approach her for treatment. It was an unexpected surprise that Goh Takagawa showed up to save the day. I would have stopped the men with that Psychic Attack before they really harmed the girl. Now help me with this little one. I believe the party is over.

Fan lifted the sleeping Human and followed Kimberly out of the grand hall.

Tori Galishka was very frightened. She did not know where she was or even who she was until her memories started coming back in pieces. She was in a large dark space with two very small areas of light that came from points high above her. She was standing in one of them and felt a presence all around her. She did not know what it was or its intentions for her; this is what frightened her as she tried to get her bearings. She remembered how her boyfriend Jeff Barnes had suggested that they try something new since they would both be off-shift when the ship, the *Iwakina* was its name, would be making its first jump. It would be their first-time having sex during a series of jumps. She had been reluctant at first, but could not refuse her true love's request. It would be such a thrill and besides, she loved Jeff so much.

Something terrible had happened. They had both been thrown naked against the bulkhead. Jeff had a nasty gash on his head and was stumbling about the room when someone came through the door. Then they had shot him; his blood and brains had flown from him, covering her in gore, and she had gone into shock. She vaguely remembered being in the sick-bay, and then all went black until this light appeared. She was no longer naked, but wearing her favorite dress; the one that Jeff said she looked sexy in. She began to cry, great heavy sobs coming in waves as she realized her love was lost to her.

Suddenly a voice from the darkness enveloped her, "There, there, child; let it all out. That is what you need; to let those feelings go."

"Who...who's there?" Tori's nerves were on edge.

"In time, girl, in time; now rest a little bit longer." With that, the voice was gone and Tori felt a great urge to lie down and sleep.

*   *   *

Edward Kuremoto was making ready to leave and packing what little he desired to take with him. Margo waited patiently on the bed. He had waited until the next morning to contact Doctor Rosel and give her the virus and antidote from Uprising. He recalled their conversation with some trepidation. He had assumed that she would send it on to her family for reproduction and distribution.

"Doctor, I know that we have not been on the best of terms, but I want to offer you a peace token; I am leaving the ship before it next departs." He handed her a case with the items inside.

Rosel looked at him incredulously. "What is this?" she asked.

"It is the virus and antidote I developed for the people of Uprising. I figure that you can send it to your family to reproduce; for your benefit and that of the galaxy in general. Think of the many medical facilities that will want to be sure they cannot be infected by the people of Uprising who will surely be leaving their planet."

"I have nothing to do with my family at this time, Doctor Kuremoto. However, I have use of your virus and antidote. Be assured that the demand for this will be met in the near future." Rosel hefted the case and placed it in a secure compartment. "Have a safe trip Edward." Then she keyed the hatch indicated that he should be on his way.

Kuremoto finished packing and making sure Margo was ready as well. Then the hail came that he had been waiting for. It was Goh Takagawa as he had expected, coming to get the keys to the kingdom.

"Margo, be a dear and straighten the place up. We will be leaving shortly. Goh, let's you and I go to my lab." He said, leading Goh back out the hatch.

* * *

Marishima had seen to the distraught Renge Yamano when she was brought to the Sick Bay. Doctor Rosel came to check on her as was protocol; the Captain did not want a crewmember on duty that was not up to it. This especially applied to the current Navigator. Rosel did her best to console the girl. This was the perfect opportunity to gain another test subject; this one possibly willingly.

"Dear girl, this must have been very trying for you." Rosel said feeling Renge out.

"Y-y-yes…" Renge said, a quiver in her voice.

"Men can be such horrible creatures sometimes."

"That Goh fellow though, he saved me…"

"Yes, well, there are still heroes in the galaxy, but they are few; very few…" Rosel looked for the right reaction which she found in Renge, resignation.

She threw out the bait. "We women must find a way to hold our own among men of low caliber. I think I have just the thing you need." Rosel noted that Renge's reaction was that of curiosity, so she reached into her coat pocket and brought out a hypo-injector. "This, my dear girl, is the key to never having to rely on men to protect you ever again. Do not fret; it will not take away your feminine wiles. It will, however, give you the strength and cognitive abilities to sense danger and do something about it without having to rely on your hero being in the vicinity. You would like that wouldn't you?"

Renge seemed to think hard for a moment, and then nodded her head.

"I myself have been on the regimen which only requires six timed injections over a month's time. I can give you the first one now. Alright?" Rosel waited a moment for the girl to protest, but finding none of that she gave Renge the injection. True, it held the experimental enhancement serum that she had developed; along with some of her own blood. After the second regimen that she would receive in two days' time, Renge would be hers to control, just like Benoba.

*   *   *

Marishima had made sure that Renge Yamano

would be hold up in Sick Bay for at least another day. When she finished tending her patients, she went straight to find the Captain. She would get her friend's old job back for her. The Captain was on the Bridge. When she requested to speak to him, they went into the Captain's Ready Room.

"Lord Captain, I am here to deliver a message from one of the original crew who wishes to rejoin the ship. I know her as a dear friend; you know her as Hanako Quan, the former Navigator chosen for the mutiny. She is making her way to Taibor Prime and will be monitoring the GCN message box set up for stranded crewmen. I asked Goh Takagawa to reset it so that it is out of imperial influence." Marishima tried to sound convincing, but was not sure if she made a good impression or not; the Captain was a very stone-faced man.

"I have a new Navigator already. It was unfortunate for Hanako to get sick the day before our plan went into effect." Saitow replied.

"Well, you see Captain, Renge Yamano was brought to Sick Bay during Third Watch in hysterics; I don't think Doctor Rosel will release her to duty anytime soon."

"Is that so? What caused these hysterics?" The Captain seemed genuinely concerned. Marishima was sure that he needed the ship to leave soon.

"As I got it from Goh Takagawa, whom brought her to Sick Bay, she was accosted by three noblemen at your party my Lord." Marishima winched at the look that momentarily crossed the Captain's face. He got that other look that told her he was using his neural-net; most likely to summon Takagawa to the Bridge.

"Hanako has been gone from the ship a long time; do you think she can be trusted?"

Marishima probed the Captain's mind lightly and found that he was extremely concerned about further infiltration by imperial agents. She thought of a way to get around that.

"My Lord, I will vouch fully for Hanako Quan. We have been in contact for some time."

"Very well. With one Navigator in the Brig and one in hysterics in Sick Bay, we will need someone who knows how to fly this ship as soon as possible. Get on the GCN and contact Quan for me. I want her aboard within a day's time."

"Aye, Captain. You can count on me."

*   *   *

Goh and Kuremoto were going over the vast database files that the Doctor had stored there. He received an urgent message to report to the Captain. He did his best to excuse himself from the Doctor who was keen to get things over with and get his prize which lay inside Goh's jacket pocket. Goh insisted that he needed to speak with the Captain about an urgent manner, but told Kuremoto that he would try to do so over the 'net. Goh went to the far side of the lab.

Captain, this is Goh Takagawa calling, I am in the middle of a meeting for the handover of Doctor Kuremoto's lab, can we converse over neural-net? Goh thought to the network.

He received a reply after about half a minute, *Very well. Tell me of the incident that placed my Navigator in Sick Bay.*

Sir, Renge Yamano was with a group of three noblemen in the fountained courtyard outside of the grand hall last night. I... was taking care of an errand and noticed that two of the men ducked into the hedgerow while the remaining man distracted our Navigator. Suspecting something was up, I searched the area for a suitable instrument with which to deal with them all; I have had significant combat training on unarmed combat from our guest in the brig. Once I found such a tool to use against them, they had already gotten our Renge down on the ground and were attempting to accost her despicably. I managed to take out two of them, yet Renge somehow came to her senses for a moment and saved me from a bullet from the third man whom I dispatched accordingly. I then brought the poor hysterical girl to the Sick Bay per ship's protocol.

Very good. Do you know any of these scoundrels?

No sir. None of them looked familiar to me at all.

Good. I will make inquiries. Continue your work with Kuremoto; the sooner he is off the ship the better. Goh, next time you come across news of something happening to a member of the crew I want to know immediately; am I clear?

Aye Sir. Takagawa out.

Goh returned to the Doctor who was busily coding the data into categories. He understood the Captain's concern; however, previous protocol warranted the Sick Bay personnel were required to report a crewmember's internment. *This was Saitow's ship now, so what he says goes from now on,* Goh reckoned.

"Goh, I want you to pay attention to this coding system." Kuremoto told him then, "You are a very good man and I admire you. You of all aboard this ship have a sense of honor and morals which are lacking in most. These color codes indicate the level of dangerous applications possible from each of these technologies; these gray coded ones the worst of all. These are the technologies that are the least understood. I suggest you give yourself an analytical shot at them before turning them over to the Conglomerate, which I am sure you will eventually have to do.

"These silver coded technologies are the most dangerous. If at all possible, do your best to keep these out of the wrong hands. Once you delve into them you will understand why they are so dangerous. Thirdly, these purple applications can be most useful to the ship. However, they are also prone to militarization in the wrong hands. Treat these with care. The rest are coded blue; stuff that we have been using successfully for some time. Oh, I forgot about these yellow items that deal with the Pruathan gate technology. I suggest that you get this stuff under your belt for the time you may want off of this ship. You can use this to get a cushy job at the Didier gate project. Lord knows when they will figure it out for themselves. I would just love to see the reactions on everyone's faces when they get it active and the damn thing disappears into Hyperspace!" Kuremoto chuckled; Goh had never seen the man so jovial. "Now I am sure you are required to do a system check on the data to look for traps and viruses. Let's get this over with, shall we?"

Goh did the required checks and found the whole system clean. During the couple of hours that had passed, Kuremoto had regaled him with stories of some of the encounters he had had with the Prauthan technology he was turning over. Goh reset the passwords and security override parameters. All the data was now secure and only accessible by him. He reached into his pocket and drew the data-stick that was meant for Doctor Kuremoto.

"May I? It is now your lab after all." Kuremoto asked indicating a data port in the table top.

"By all means." Goh said and stepped back to give the Doctor privacy. The look he saw on the man's face was worth about a billion MU he guessed. Goh could not recall ever seeing a man grin so wide.

* * *

Kuremoto dropped by to see the Captain and thank him for everything he had helped with; especially Uprising. He apologized that he did not live up to the expectations that he perceived the Captain had wanted. He was surprised that the Captain had refuted that; he said he had lived up to them perfectly. That threw him a bit because he had known Glenn Saitow for many years. It did not matter though; he was doing what he felt was best. He would do great things for the people of Uprising and in turn the rest of the galaxy.

He and Margo boarded the shuttle that would take him to the spaceport where his ship awaited. He would not have the extra crew to serve meals and clean up, but he was sure he could manage with Margo's help. She was meticulous in insisting the lab be kept clean. The Conglomerate had insisted that the yacht would be fully stocked with food and beverage; including the wine that he always requested.

He was surprised to find Nanami Oliver awaiting him on the shuttle. "Here for one last shakedown Officer Oliver?" He said, only half-jokingly.

"No, although I should insist on clearing your quarters before you are allowed to leave. I am here on my own. I took our time together on your vacation to heart and decided that I will miss the hell out of you, old man. We should have gotten together again so you could give me more of those stories from centuries ago. Have a safe trip." Nanami was adamant he could tell.

"You take care of that young man that has kept you away from my stories." He offered her his hand and she shook it like they were old colleagues.

"Keep your head about you over there. Things won't be right in that place for a while."

"I've been in some worse situations, but I will save those stories until we meet again."

"I'll look forward to it." With that she spoke to the shuttle pilot and left them.

Kuremoto got himself and Margo strapped in for the ride. He did not even look back as the shuttle left the ship.

4

Hanako Quan awaited the Conglomerate transport at Taibor Prime. They would pick her up and bring her to the *Iwakina* which was in dire need of a Navigator; or so she was told by her good friend Marishima. *What had happened to her apprentice Kintaro Sagura?* She wondered.

It was just as well; she had been running from a few gambling debts and it was difficult to stay in any one port for very long. The sharks had even made it difficult to find a job. She had quit the Navy soon after being released from the hospital on that God forsaken dust bowl Euphrosyne since the *Iwakina* was long gone; never to return. She made good money as a Navigator on a couple of commercial ships. However, her tendency to gamble led her down a path that she was desperate to get out of. Getting back to the *Iwakina* was her ticket to salvation. She just hoped that she could start over with life once she got her old job back.

* * *

Saitow waited patiently in his quarters for the ship to arrive from Taibor Prime with his third navigator in as many months; *well actually the first,* he thought. Hanako was a good hand and was above excellence when performing her job for the simulations the crew had gone through prior to the maiden voyage. What bothered him a bit were the reports he had received from agents sent to look into her situation for security purposes; he did not want a jilted crewmember out their spreading knowledge of the inner workings of his ship. Despite having quit the Navy and running up some serious gambling debts, Hanako had never given up any information that could compromise the *Iwakina*. He just did not like the news of what had become of her. It was only Marishima's assurances that made for his reluctant reinstatement of her as Navigator. He hoped for both of their sakes Hanako was fully up to the task.

Then there was the incident with the current navigator. Saitow had made inquiries about the nobles who had perpetrated the dastardly act; he wanted the lot of them jailed. However, it was Goh Takagawa's head that had been demanded by the families of the three noblemen; it seems they no longer were themselves and brain damage was suspected. Fortunately for the ship, the security feeds were shown to each man's family and the incident was kept quiet; for both theirs's and the Saitow's mutual interests.

He chuckled at the five minutes of fame he received for his battle with Brent. Maybe now there would be a little respect for his comings and goings around the galaxy. He thought of the Princess and the news he received from Marishima. *Did the Emperor know her twin was also aboard or was this just another of Aisou's twisted machinations?* He awaited news of the reaction from the Emperor himself upon his hearing of their engagement. Saitow knew that Shirae's personal messages would not get through Aisou, so he had sent one of the family's special agents to deliver the news.

He also thought about what the message in the cryptograph was all about. Clearly it was not from

Aisou; he would not turn his hand so easily. No, it was from someone close to the Emperor; someone who had insider information. He would have to tweak the message a little before he passed it to Shirae. She knew of the spy aboard; however, he had no intention of giving this 'code from Contact Sigma' to the spy.

He checked the time on his neural-net and sighed. Then he got up from his desk and poured himself a drink.

*   *   *

Marishima was excited. She had not seen her friend in real-space for quite a long time. The shuttle docked and the hatch opened to a startled Hanako Quan; she must not have expected Marishima's welcoming embrace.

"Dear friend, I'm so glad to see you!" Marishima said after letting go of Hanako.

"It is great to see you too. You seem a bit frazzled; is everything alright?" Hanako said, hefting her duty bag.

"Oh, I have had some rough days; I'll tell you all about it over dinner. First, let us go see the Captain and get you settled in." Marishima led Hanako toward the lift.

*   *   *

Saitow, having learned that the shuttle with Quan
had arrived, called a meeting of essential personnel.

With everyone assembled, he introduced Quan to
those who did not yet know her. "This is the
impeccable first Navigator of this ship, Hanako Quan.
If Kintaro Sagura was a great pilot and navigator,
Hanako is exceptional, having trained the man to
excellence. It is unfortunate that *he* is no longer with
us." Saitow saw Hanako's eyebrows raise and
continued, "Marishima, you are getting our navigator
settled in, correct? Be sure to brief her on our prisoner."
Marishima nodded her acknowledgement.

Saitow looked around the room and felt the
welcome would be friendly enough.

He continued with the meeting. "Now, that we are
ready to depart, are there any questions before I start
barking orders?" Saitow noted the smiles that formed
at his little joke, but no one raised a question. "Good.
Now I will detail our next mission. As you know, the
Conglomerate has various research facilities all across
the quadrant. We are going to one quite close,
Nysipherae, to pick up some guests and their
equipment to ferry them home. Song Ha, this will be
the chance of a lifetime for you to study a species of
alien that we have little real knowledge of. Therefore, I
am putting you in charge of protocol while they are
aboard." Saitow noted that Song Ha squirmed in his
seat a little.

"Captain, may I ask which species we are talking
about?" Song Ha asked.

"They are the Sittwe of Mechladon. Have you heard

of them?"

"I believe I have some historical notes on them; I'll take a look and forward a report while we are in transit."

"Good. I have one last detail I want to make clear; protocols notwithstanding, anyone who has any information about harm coming to any member of this crew, I better hear about it yesterday. Is that understood? Great. Now if no one else has any questions, let us all get this ship ready to move. We leave in four hours. Dismissed."

*   *   *

Ken Edwards was watching as the two huge robot-looking contraptions drove into his Cargo Bay. They both looked like humanoids that were hunched over, grabbing their knees to make their structure as small as possible. He wished they would get this over with soon; the weather on Nysipherae was rather blustery and he did not like the environment getting inside his Cargo Bay.

Once the things were in their places some sort of hatch opened up on each and smallish creatures came out of them. They wore tight fitting jumpsuits and, besides having animal ears, they were rather small humanoids. Edwards snickered to himself. He ordered the hatch closed and sealed for spaceflight. He had done his job; the big things were secured and the pilots' personal gear had already been sent to the guest quarters.

Lieutenant Song Ha was there to meet them. "Welcome aboard the *Iwakina*!" He said to the pair.

"Good. Where Captain? Go see." One of them replied.

"Yes, yes, please follow me."

* * *

Frederick Song Ha was going over his database entries for the two newest aliens that were aboard the *Iwakina*. He had taken to creating a database for future reference on all of the knowledge he possessed as a Xenologist. He had received much valuable information from the Kadihri and Pendari Ambassadors that had been guests on the ship; they were drunk when he found them together and were very loose tongued. He was sure that the New Rangelley Alliance was going to regret putting the two together. He now had an opportunity to speak with the Sittwe. They were tucked away in the guest quarters.

He typed up a report for the Captain on what he knew of the species. *The Sittwe are a race of beings that were quite primitive when first discovered by the Rangelley Empire. The majority of them are female. They live to around age Seventy Codex Standard; are fully mature at age Fifteen. However, they are quite small in comparison to other species, never growing larger than 1.5 meters tall. They have an almost imperceptible coating of fine fur and possess animal-like ears. Although they were fit for laborious tasks, it was determined that they were more suited to being kept as intelligent pets. Sometime after Humans began coexisting on the planet, a horrible incident occurred. Another race of beings, the Chlad, appeared within a dimensional gateway of some kind, in hordes to collect vast numbers of the Sittwe females. They never took the males, but killed off quite a few. They had no use for Humans and slaughtered the entire Human population there. A special investigative unit sent to investigate the loss of an entire colony discovered that ancient stories passed down by shaman of the Sittwe told of a gateway from which monsters emerged to take the people away for use as slaves and food. This had occurred many times and it was almost a century and a third between each appearance of these unknown beings.*

The Empire re-established the colony and prepared to meet the intruders when they came again. Unfortunately for both Humans and Sittwe alike, the Rangelley were no match for the Chlad. The Rangelley, having found no other worlds where the Chlad appeared, quarantined the planet of the Sittwe; leaving the Sittwe to fend for themselves. This cycle continued for over two millennia; the Sittwe never quite able to develop a decent civilization because of the culling. Humans, pursuing legends of exotic creatures would make raids now and then, but no one dared set up trade on the planet for fear of imperial authorities and the Chlad.

This all changed with the intervention of Kazuya Kamenashi, a well-established merchant. He had purchased a Sittwe female off-world and sympathized with their plight. For the sake of these creatures, he contracted with the enigmatic Epachey Sebaht, a race of technologically superior beings to save the entire Sittwe culture from any future culling. It is not known what price the Epachey Sebaht extolled from him; he disappeared shortly after the contract was reported on the GCN.

According to Sittwe history, the Epachey Sebaht came to their planet like benevolent gods and some Sittwe still worship them as such. They provided the Sittwe with industrial capabilities and taught them how to defend themselves from the next culling. Not only that but they also provided a means to be rid of the Chlad for good. It would only take a unit of determined warriors, willing to sacrifice their lives for the good of the many. The Sittwe, with the help of their Epachey Sebaht saviors developed a defensive weapon that they named the Mechladon which means 'no more monsters' in their native language. It was a large mechanized mobile suit of armor, capable of flight and with both offensive and defensive weapon systems. While vast numbers of Mechladon defended the people from the Chlad onslaught, a special squadron of Mechladon would enter the dimensional gateway and use a devastating weapon to destroy the place from whence they came.

The time came for the culling and the vast hordes of Chlad arrived. The Sittwe did battle with them and the special squadron succeeded in closing the gateway, trapping the Chlad. It turned out that the Chlad required the portal to be open in order to power their technology and losing that, they were now no match for the Mechladon of the Sittwe.

When the last battle was over the Epachey Sebaht came in their ships and collected all of the Chlad technology that remained on the planet. They would have taken back the industrial capacity of the Sittwe and the Mechladon as well; however, the controlling authority of the Sittwe convinced them that they would need the Mechladon for another threat. They would need to defend themselves when the Humans returned.

Satisfied that the Sittwe did not want further dealings with Humans, the Epachey Sebaht left them their gifts and returned from whence they came.

Centuries passed with no further contact from the Chlad, and the planet, now named Mechladon by its inhabitants, remained under quarantine; now, because of the Sittwe's capacity to defend themselves.

Sometime after the Rangelley collapse, the Sittwe peacefully colonized several planets in their sector, allowing the Human inhabitants to either leave or submit to the Controlling Authority's rule. Because most of the inhabitants of these worlds were Deidriad Humans under the thumb of former Rangelley Human nobles, they gladly accepted. For the Sittwe, this alleviated a population overload problem which stemmed from the breeding habits influenced by millennia of culling by the Chlad.

Song Ha chuckled a little at this; it fit the old Earth biologist humor phrase – The Sittwe still bred like rabbits. He had never seen a rabbit, but it had a reputation for excessive breeding. He believed he had the whole story now. The culling by the Chlad served a purpose to limit the number of males born among the species; probably to limit the population to a certain level and keep the Sittwe docile for the time of culling. This genetic scenario continues into their post culling era; however, the generations not being culled are living to longevity and a male Sittwe may have up to over a hundred mates in his lifetime. He would have as many as five to ten wives at any time that willingly produced offspring for him.

Song Ha looked forward to his meeting with the two Sittwe engineers who had accepted his request for interviews. The fact that they were both females of their species intrigued him; he had many questions.

*   *   *

Renge Yamano was extremely bored having to stay cooped up inside the Sick-Bay; *Doctor Rosel's orders* they said. Unfortunately, all she could think of were horrible thoughts about her situation. None of her so-called friends came to visit her; somehow, they had all changed since the party. She knew that she was pretty and tried her best to hide it by not wearing make-up and doing little to tend to her hair. She just had to get done up for the party; everyone else was. With the loss of her friends and the horrible incident with the noblemen, she wished she had not gone planet-side at all. Now, she was at risk of losing her job since the original Navigator had returned. She would be relegated to third shift most likely. *Damn it! She would be the best Navigator on this ship regardless of shift* she resolved and pulled out her tablet to once again study the Pruathan Galactic Database.

Renge heard the noise of the hatch to her room in Sick Bay open and looked up to find her savior entering. She had learned his name was Goh Takagawa. His features were sharp and attractive and his hair was fine. She could get to know this man. She had been avoiding the advances of quite a few of the crew, some of them women even; she had wanted to avoid the disapproval of her friends and really did not have time for relationships. Now she had no friends and plenty of time. This man had saved her from peril; she felt she owed him something. She would give him her love and admiration if he would have her.

"Renge Yamano, correct? I am Goh Takagawa. I hope you are feeling well?" Goh asked as he stepped closer to her bedside.

"Please Mr. Takagawa, have a seat." Renge indicated a chair that was on the other side of the bed from him. He took it, scooting it closer so they could converse. While he was moving the chair, Renge did her best to straighten up her appearance. "I am doing quite well thanks to you, and Doctor Rosel's treatments."

Renge had received several injections of Rosel's enhancement drugs; these had made her feel quite invigorated to tell the truth. She did not understand why she was still bedridden.

"That is wonderful. I feel that I must apologize for your treatment on Roseglade. Being a nobleman myself back home it pains me to see such abhorrent behavior from those of high status." Goh lowered his eyes as he said this.

"Dear me, I had no idea. Believe me Mr. Takagawa, I do not hold all nobles to the behavior of a few animals."

"That is a relief, I assure you. Here on the ship however, I am simply the Chief Engineer. Please call me Goh." Goh looked up at her smiling.

"Very good! Please call me Renge. I hope we can become good friends; I owe you a debt of gratitude for saving me." Renge said, smiling back at the man.

"Well, sure. However, at the moment I have some ship's duties to attend to. If you will excuse me…" Goh motioned as if he were about to rise from his seat.

Renge grabbed his hand. "Won't you stay a few moments longer? I am so bored in here and I am having difficulty with this algorithm here..." Renge showed him the calculations on the tablet.

"Now, now, Renge, Mr. Takagawa has duties to attend to." It was Doctor Rosel in the open hatch. "I have your next treatment. We would not want Mr. Takagawa to see the place where we inject those now would we?" Rosel was all smiles as well. Renge resigned her fate and let go of Goh's hand.

Goh bowed to the both of them and left. Renge looked dubiously at the Doctor, rolled over and pulled down her patient's jumper bottoms to ready for the next injection of Rosel's enhancement drugs.

* * *

Goh swung by his quarters on the way to his office. He was a bundle of nerves after his encounter with the woman he had saved from those bastards on Roseglade. He had to sit in his cabin for a moment to gain his bearings, but also, he wanted to speak with Amara. He called to her after he had calmed down a bit. She emerged from the wall near the shelf where her box sat.

"Amara, I have some disturbing news." Goh was once again amazed at the glowing form of his cabin mate. It suddenly struck him that this glowing figure was in fact a young girl; of course, he knew this from the start. However, the enormity of it had not really sunk in until now. He assessed his relationship with her; dead or not she was a friend and companion. He thought about how his news would affect her; surely, she being a child would not harbor any ill will toward him gaining so much after so long. He decided to just let the truth be known and gauge her reaction.

"Well, don't just sit there like a dog wanting to wag its tail; what is it man?" Amara sat beside him on the bed speaking to him in her native tongue.

"For the first time since I lost Maia so long ago, I think I have found someone else to share my love with." Goh watched for some reaction in the glowing face of his ghost companion.

"Who is this person of which you speak?" Amara crossed her arms and cocked her head toward him.

"It is the woman I told you about; the one I saved from being savaged on the homeworld of the Captain."

"She is not the Sheese of which the spirit spoke?" Amara was giving off bad vibrations at this point.

"No, no, not her at all. I shall bring Renge here so you can see her yourself once she is released from Sick Bay." Goh assured her; he hoped she would calm down. It was taxing to his Qi when she got upset.

Amara relaxed a bit. "Yes, bring her to me. I would see this person worthy of your love." Amara rose and returned to her wall. Goh rose and, glancing back to where she disappeared, shuddered a little and left his cabin. There was always much work to do.

5

Lieutenant Song Ha took the lift up to the guest quarters. He was on time for his meeting with the Sittwe whose names were Kalel and Paeet. He reached the hatch and sent a hail to announce his arrival. The hatch opened and, seeing no one there, he entered the cabin. Each of the guest quarters had an outer room and a bed chamber. He heard a sound from inside the bed chamber, so he called Kalel's name; she seemed to be the one in charge of the two. There was no answer. Thinking something foul may be afoot, Song Ha rushed into the bed chamber. He was shocked to find the two aliens sitting on the bed naked and apparently stoned drunk; Paeet was practically swooning to-and-fro, while Kalel sat there nudging her to keep the momentum going.

Kalel glanced up from her revelry and addressed him. "Oh, Song-aa, you want join in drink?" Kalel stood up and offered something that looked like a noxious liquor of some unknown origin.

There was an exchange of words between the two aliens in their own language. Song Ha did his best to stay reasonable and scientific while he observed the two drunken aliens. *Were all aliens such alcoholics?* He could not help but think. Their conversation ended.

"Paeet say you no ready to drink with us. She say you not like us. Is OK. Kalel make mistake. You come back dinner. We talk then." Kalel said and bowed deeply, making no pretenses at modesty.

Song Ha bowed back. "No, it is perfectly ok. Yes, I will return for dinner. Please pardon my intrusion." He then backed out of the bedroom and hurriedly left the cabin. *What a strange couple those two make* he thought; *drinking so early in the day*. He did not touch the stuff except during formal occasions and then only sparingly. Hopefully things would go a bit better at dinner time.

*   *   *

Tori sat rocking with her knees to her chest inside her pillar of light. It seemed as if that foreboding feeling of something surrounding her was closing in. She sat facing the other pillar. She heard a noise as if someone was there, but when she looked there was no one. She then saw a form emerge as if a shadow was being cast there. When she blinked the form was gone, but when she blinked again there stood Doctor Rosel.

"Dear Tori, have you slept well?" The shadow doctor said. "I know you are so longing to get out of this darkness. It will all be over really soon. I promise you." The Doctor stepped toward her and Tori shook by reflex.

"Now, now, don't be frightened. I am here to guide you; nothing more." The Doctor came closer, stepping from her pillar to Tori's. Tori stood her ground, mainly because there was nowhere to go; she did not want to enter the darkness. The Doctor came to her and wrapped her arms around her. Tori felt a calming warmth and her body became light. Suddenly it was if the two of them were floating upward to the source of the light.

"Come," Doctor Rosel was saying, "I will show you your future."

They floated to the light source. The sources of the light became a widow and she could see the ceiling of the Sick Bay. To her horror, Tori realized that she was inside her own head, looking out with her own eyes. She could not move. Someone was standing over her body; it was Doctor Rosel.

"Ah, you are awake. How do you feel?" The Doctor asked.

Tori heard another reply in her voice. "I am a little parched Doctor. Some water please?"

Tori felt the Doctor that held her speaking in her head. "Isn't this wonderful? You are a part of me now."

All Tori could do was scream but she made no sound; there was only the mild laughter of Doctor Rosel.

*　　*　　*

They had arrived at Mechladon close to dinner time. The Sittwe had requested that the ship stay in orbit for an unspecified time and Song Ha had been summoned by the Captain to tell him why. He did not have an answer other than that he was supposed to have dinner with them. The Captain had just sighed and told him that he would have calibrations done while they awaited clearance to deliver their cargo.

Song Ha arrived at the guest quarters as dinner service was being brought. Paeet was being very somber; perhaps she had been embarrassed to have said he did not like them. Kalel was very enthusiastic about him being there. She offered him a gift as a sign of good faith for their earlier misunderstanding.

"This is top wine of Mechladon. We have with dinner for forgiveness." Kalel poured for the three of them. The two aliens ate heartily of the mostly meat dishes that had been prepared by Bonifacio. Song Ha was struck by the deliciousness of the wine; it was the best he had had in quite some time.

"Song-aa, what you want ask me?" Kalel said to him between bites of Vrel.

"Kalel, your culture is unique in the galaxy. What can you tell me of your type of family life?"

"Mmmm. All Sittwe are sister. We have brother, but them only use for make more sister and brother. Some sister like make little one, so stay with brother. Paeet maybe want that sometime."

Kalel winked at Paeet who just played with the food on her plate. Kalel frowned at that for a second, but then continued speaking. "Kalel think Paeet want Song-aa for brother."

At that Paeet stopped what she was doing, glanced quickly at Song Ha, and then back at her plate. She placed her hands in her lap. Song Ha felt as if she may actually want such a thing. Perhaps the wine was getting to his head.

"Ahahahaha, joke only, joke only!" Kalel laughed mightily.

Paeet giggled sheepishly and took a long draught from her wine glass.

Kalel continued the conversation, "Song-aa. What your measure of age? Codex Years? In you years, I thirty-five years; Paeet maybe twenty-five."

Song Ha felt he needed to get the conversation back on track. "I understand that the Sittwe only have females in their military, and the Mechladon are the primary means of defense for the Sittwe."

"We no can speak of that. Only people. No military." Kalel was adamant on this point.

Song Ha wanted to verify what he suspected; the Sittwe had a Matriarchal society. "OK. So, the sisters that do not stay with brothers; they do all the work? Like you and Paeet?"

Kalel lit up at this. "Ah. Yes! We sisters do all work for Mechladon. Whatever Control say do." Kalel looked away from him for a second; *what was that about?* he thought. The wine seemed to be getting to his senses. He tried to refuse when Kalel next tried to pour for him, but did not succeed.

"So, this Controlling Authority is the government of Mechladon? What does it consist of?"

"Yes. Control is government. Control is group of sisters that make law, make work; keep everyone happy."

Song Ha was about to ask about the colonies that the Sittwe occupied, but he felt as if his senses were running away from him. He closed his eyes and it seemed that he could no longer open them. He felt as if he were being lifted and was floating in the air. Then all was darkness.

*   *   *

Benoba was looking at equipment in the Sick Bay. Some of it was sorely in need of calibration. It was early morning aboard the *Iwakina*. As she worked, she watched the alien Dorigethra Fan sitting with Doctor Rosel; both of them scouring over readouts on tablets set before them. They were both facing her from where she was working.

After a few minutes she could clearly hear their conversation. She almost dropped her instruments when she glanced at them again. Clearly, she could see that they were not speaking; they were not even looking at each other, but she could hear them having a conversation about Marishima.

I tell you Kimberly, the woman is a dangerous telepath; you must confront her at once!

Dear Fan, I already know what she is capable of. The poor woman is avoiding me for fear of what I might do. Tsk, she really is not much of a threat I assure you. Even if she went to the Captain, no one would believe her. She will not do so though; do you know why? Why, the woman is a...

Benoba lost the conversation at this point. It resumed with Dorigethra's admonition.

You should rid yourself of her as soon as possible.

Now, now, Fan. Don't go getting all worried about

me. I have good people here to watch over me. Now look at these formulas. Do you think it is possible to add telepathic powers within the enhancement regimen?

Just then Doctor Rosel looked straight at Benoba and winked. It sent a chill down her spine, but was thrilling at the same time. She felt a deep longing to be near the Doctor; *Yes*, she thought, *this is my new place of belonging.*

*   *   *

Frederick Song Ha was dreaming. He knew he was dreaming because it was impossible for him to be strapped into a Sittwe Mechladon and battling with strange alien hover-ships. He knew what he was doing and what he was using to do it, but he felt that he was not himself; it was as if he was some ancient alien, perhaps a Sittwe warrior, living far in the past. He felt as if he belonged there and was continuously enveloped in a sense of warmth.

His comm channel lit up. "Song Ha! Song Ha! What are you doing? Where are you? Wake up—!"

Song Ha opened his eyes. The Captain was calling him on his neural-net. He responded mentally. It did not matter what he was doing; he was to get the Sittwe to get clearance and offload their gear. He had another client waiting on Ossland. *Yes, yes, he would do so right away* Song Ha said, and signed off.

As his body woke up, he first sensed a kind of purring sound. Then he became aware of the source of warmth surrounding him; he was in a bed with the two Sittwe curled up on either side of him. Their heads were snuggled in his armpits and their limbs were straddling his prone naked body. They were both sleeping steadily. He shook them awake. Each grinned at him, and then rubbed their heads on his chest before stretching intensely.

"What have you done to me?" He asked, not really wanting to know the answer. It must have been the wine.

"You drink too much. We put you to bed; that all." Kalel answered matter-of-factly. She had a weird way of smiling just then that did little to put his mind at ease. "We just give you warm sleep. Sittwe custom."

Paeet snuggled once more into his armpit before rising from the bed. Her slender naked body was all full of curves. Kalel traced a slender finger lazily around his chest, then also rose.

"Come. Take us to Captain. Give apology." Kalel said, tossing his clothing at him. He noted that her body was more athletic and toned than Paeets. He shook these thoughts from his head and quickly got dressed.

*　　*　　*

Saitow's patience was at its limits. He had given the Sittwe plenty of time to do their business, whatever it was with Song Ha, but they still did not have clearance to land and offload their cargo. He dared not anger them; just one of those war machines they were selling

207

could tear half his ship to shreds. There was so little of their psychology that was known of the Sittwe that he could not chance a diplomatic misstep.

Just then Song Ha entered the bridge with his two small charges. "Captain I..."

"Captain Saitow. We sorry for big delay. Show me navigator; I give numbers where to land." Kalel interjected.

"Well of course..." was all Saitow could say and pointed toward Hanako Quan at her station. He motioned for Song Ha who left the two Sittwe with Quan. "What exactly transpired between you people?"

For the first time in his career Saitow saw a Marine Officer appear to blush. "Lord Captain, I must apologize immensely. I seemed to have let my guard down and was shanghaied so to speak."

Saitow stopped him there with a raised hand. He knew when to quit asking questions to save his officer from further embarrassment. The two Sittwe rejoined Song Ha and were all smiles.

"Please escort our guests to their equipment." he told Song Ha and sat back in his chair. He watched the trio enter the lift; the Sittwe were an energetic bunch he would wager. Saitow smiled at the possibilities that Song Ha most likely dealt with while they were aboard.

*   *   *

Paeet had already offloaded her Mechladon from

the ship and Song Ha stood next to the machine that Kalel would be piloting. The small creature was staring up at him expectantly.

"Please be well Honored Kalel." Song Ha said as he bowed low.

Kalel quickly stepped forward and put her hand to his cheek. "You too Song-aa. I think maybe I leave something in cabin. If you find, maybe you bring here to me and Paeet. Someday. When you ready, OK?" Kalel bowed back and then leapt up into the cockpit of her Mechladon.

"Bye-bye!" she yelled down as the hatch closed. Song Ha hurried out of her way. He had no idea what she was talking about. *Is it even possible for a Human to visit this extremely guarded society?* He shook the thought out of his head. He was both glad to be rid of these two cheeky creatures and sad at the same time. After all he could not get that feeling of warmth from his head.

6

Ossland was a well-developed urban world; the center of trade for the Taibor Freehold. That is precisely why Desante Vret liked it here so much. He had visited on several occasions, taking in the local culture and obtaining certain items that he required. There were a lot of Humans just like him; he was a of Bolchinde Deidriad descent after all. That was as far as the resemblance went. He was in fact over four-thousand years old, having kept himself alive through the use of the Pruathan teleportation cabinets he kept in his ship. He was here on Ossland now because one of them had malfunctioned and he was awaiting a ship with an armed crew to take him to where he would find another to replace it. It had taken him several decades to locate the place where it was. However, it had been a Rangelley stronghold and, although long forgotten, it was still heavily guarded by automated beings.

He did not like becoming old. The skin tightened and it took extra effort to maintain his physique; something he was quite proud of, although he needed to remain sharp on a daily basis or face certain death. He had come to the world of Humans only four centuries before, but this was long enough for rumors of his existence to spread across the quadrant. *The Man Who Cannot Die* they called him. People were constantly searching him out to find out his secret; a secret he would give to no one. Just yesterday two men had come and threatened him with harm if he did not give his secret to them. It was difficult to hide the bodies in such a built-up area as the vicinity of the spaceport. Luckily, Irone had located an unused subterranean shaft; she was such a helpful girl.

"Master, a communication has arrived from the *Iwakina*," Irone brought him from his revere.

"Are they finally coming?" Vret was a patient man by nature, but did not like being in one place for lengthy periods.

"Yes Master. I suggest we head for the shuttle pads."

"Very well… Irone, you must no longer call me master. As far as the crew of the *Iwakina* is concerned, you are my daughter of sixteen years. Do you understand?"

Vret eyed the girl who, for all intents and purposes, held the appearance of a sixteen-year-old girl.

"Yes, Father." Irone said shyly.

Vret chuckled a little and patted her head. "Good girl. Let us be off."

The two of them grabbed their bags and headed out the door.

* * *

Captain Saitow had called Goh to his cabin for a drink. Goh knew this was no social call. He steadied his nerves and sent a hail at the hatch. It swooshed open. Goh stepped in to find the Captain sitting comfortably in a lounger; the Princess by his side. Goh bowed to both.

"Come now Goh; no need to be so formal. Come join us for a drink." It was the Princess who offered him her chair next to the Captain. She poured for the three of them. After handing them their drinks, she pulled the Captain's desk chair over.

The Captain cleared his throat. "Goh, I hope you are enjoying your tenure here aboard the *Iwakina*." As the Captain paused, it occurred to Goh that he was under no real obligation to stay aboard the ship. Sure, he was being paid, but he was under no contract. However, he had untold obligations; not only to the Captain, but to the Captain's mother as well. Then there was Renge.

"Of course, my Lord."

"Now, I've told you before son, call me Glenn." The Captain paused again; Goh remained silent. "We have a distinguished guest coming aboard. His name is Desante Vret; have you heard of him?"

Goh had not and said as much.

"Desante Vret is a genius. My family has investigated the man. He has invented a great many useful devices in the last several decades, most of them tied to Pruathan technology. Rumor has him attributed to quite a few inventions from the past; he is rumored to be *The Man Who Cannot Die*." The Captain paused again; probably to let this news sink in. "Goh, you are indispensable to this ship and we greatly appreciate your continued service to us. I am increasing your pay in light of Doctor Kuremoto's leaving us. You have been shouldering all of his work for so long; you may as well be compensated for it. This man Vret is another untapped resource that we and the Conglomerate cannot let come and go without gaining some of that genuine insight. That is where you come in. I want you to act as liaison for us with him. I need you to befriend him and show him around the ship. See if he will open up about his knowledge of the Pruatha and their technology. Can you do that for us? You can delegate as much of the ships engineering duties as you need to; I know you have created a first-rate team."

Goh just sighed and sipped his drink. He knew that the Captain would not take no for the answer. It might actually be beneficial to take on this task. He could have Azuma take charge for a while and relax a bit.

"You can count on me." He finally stated.

*   *   *

Tori was horrified. She could see with her own eyes as she rose from the bed and put on some clothing, but it was not her doing these things. Doctor Rosel had told her that she had transferred a portion of her own psyche into Tori's body; that was what was controlling her. It was as if there were two Doctor Rosels; one occupied Tori's body. Doctor Rosel had told her she had two choices: to relax and enjoy the show, or descend into darkness never to awaken again. She was not a quitter. Maybe someday she would be freed from this predicament and get control of her body back. She inwardly shuddered at the thought of what someone else could do with her body. She shocked herself then as she laughed at the thought of actually shuddering, yet she had no body to shudder with; sweet irony indeed.

*　　*　　*

Nanami Oliver shared the shuttle ride down with Goh Takagawa to pick up the next client. She would see this man who was over four-thousand years old. *Hell, she had already met one that was over four-hundred; she was one-upping her game* she thought as she smiled to herself. *Seriously though, a man could learn a lot of things in that many millennia.* It was her duty as Security Officer to assess any possible threat to the ship. She would act friendly and observe as the client and his daughter transferred to the *Iwakina*.

Nanami watched the monitors as the shuttle descended toward the port. She had been on many worlds, but most of them were backwater compared to Ossland. It was covered in dark urban sprawl with scattered areas of untouched wilderness and ocean. They even had those huge air purification towers scattered sporadically across the surface of the planet. They approached the night-side and the whole place was lit up like a galactic cluster.

She glanced at her companion who sat wide-eyed at the sight of it all. She had to suppress a giggle at the man's puppy dog look. She always wanted a puppy. She had Lo, so that was close enough.

"Please brace for landing." came the voice of the pilot from nowhere in particular.

*　　*　　*

Irone carried the two cases they possessed.

"Irone, hand one of those over." Desante Vret instructed his charge.

"I must not Ma... Father. They are both very heavy." Irone protested.

"Just give me the lighter one. We cannot give the impression that my own daughter is my servant." Vret smiled at his companion and took the offered case. It was a bit heavy; nothing for Irone to manage, but a bit taxing for him. He would only have to lug it until they were secured in their quarters aboard the ship.

He wondered at the marvels he would encounter on the *Iwakina*. He knew it was of Pruathan construct. He wanted desperately to know how they had interfaced into it; what they had changed, and what they had kept. He had an entire fleet of such ships at his disposal. The *iwakina's* secrets would help him in their maintenance; he was sure of it. Irone would help in his analysis. She knows Pruathan starship AI technology like no one else. Perhaps he could persuade the Captain to allow him to assist in engineering.

The shuttle signaled its arrival to the spaceport authorities and landed. The authorities in turn let Vret and his companion approach the shuttle. A slender yet strong looking young man and a tallish woman ushered them inside.

"Honored Guest Desante Vret and companion, I am Goh Takagawa, Chief Engineer of the *Iwakina*. This is our Security Officer Nanami Oliver. Please take your seats here." The slender man said.

Vret handed his case over to an attendant and took the preferred seat. He thought to himself, *this is my lucky day.*

*   *   *

Nanami never missed anything peculiar, and these two were peculiar writ large. The man appeared to be on par with Kuremoto in age, but carried himself like a man in his twenties. The girl was shapely and sultry looking. It struck Nanami as odd that when the girl handed over the case, which she had carried with one hand, the attendant that accepted it nearly dropped it to the deck; he had to grab it with both hands and was struggling at that. Then there were those lips; lips so sultry that Nanami almost wanted to plant her own on them. She shook her head. She needed to stay alert and not be bewitched by the likes of these two. The shuttle seats were arranged so that the two guests faced the two crewmembers. Desante Vret was speaking to her.

"Ms. Oliver, you being a girl yourself, I implore you to show my dear daughter around the ship. Can you do that for us?" The man's words were sugar; it was hard for her to refuse.

"I will discuss it with the Captain, sir. First off though, you and your daughter will need to report to our medical officer when we arrive on the ship. It is just a precautionary measure I assure you." Nanami replied.

"If you mean we are to be probed and sampled, I assure you that we already have clearance from the Ossland authorities." Vret produced Identicards with medical clearance icons for the both of them.

"Yes. That certainly makes things easier when we arrive. Would you like to get settled in first or meet directly with the Captain? It is 1450 ship time." Goh said glancing sideways at Nanami.

She just kept a noncommittal look on her face. Let him take charge; they were his charges after all. She would have some fun with this girl sooner or later.

"We will get settled in first. Can we impose on the Captain for dinner?" Vret said.

"That can certainly be arranged."

*   *   *

Renge had been roused by Benoba a few hours before her next duty schedule. Doctor Rosel needed to give her another treatment and her, Benoba, and Tori were to spend some girl-time together. She had never been as close to any of her previous so-called friends as she was to these two. They each shared a bond that transcended mere friendship. It was more like a familiar feeling when they were together; even a closeness like lovers, although they would never touch each other in that way. Such thoughts made her blush and then she thought of Goh Takagawa. She felt the stirrings of longing creep up inside her for the man. He was off picking up the new clients from the planet below; otherwise, she might have sought him out then and there.

She had her sisters now though. They would sit on the deck in a circle and share portions of their lives with each other until Doctor Rosel joined them. It seemed odd but somehow natural that when the Doctor came to them, she never remembered what happened up to the point when she headed toward her duty on the bridge.

*　　*　　*

Nanami thought it strange that she had been invited to dine with the Captain and his guests. She knew not what to wear, so she wore a modified version of her dress uniform; minus all the Imperial embellishments. When she arrived, she found Goh was already there dressed in some silly looking dress robes. The rest of the players arrived. After pleasantries were shared, dinner service began.

"Dear Captain, my daughter and I thank you for your great hospitality. The reason I asked your Security Officer to join us is to make a solemn request." Desante Vret began the conversation after finishing his chicken.

Nanami glanced at the Captain who remained stoic. Goh was picking at his salad and the Princess was taking relish in each bite of chicken she encountered.

Desante Vret continued, "I would like to request that Ms. Nanami Oliver, who was so gracious to meet us with Master Takagawa at the shuttle, be made available to escort my daughter around your ship. The poor girl becomes rather distraught when confined to one place for long you see."

Captain Saitow looked at Nanami and she nodded

her head in acceptance. *Why not?* She thought; the only problem child on the ship was secure in the brig.

"This is not a problem for us. She is at your disposal. Now, if present company may be privy, can you possibly tell us your destination sir; you were rather secretive when hiring us on." The Captain was a bit more serious than Nanami was used to; at least when he was not dealing with one of her foibles.

"Yes Captain, of course. I have hired your ship specifically because of its military nature."

Nanami saw this raise almost everyone's eyebrows, including her own.

Desante Vret smiled and continued, "First we must go to Secheron. There I will purchase the necessary equipment for your Marine force to carry out our mission."

"Our mission you say?" The Captain was curious yet cautious.

"Yes, Captain. As you know I have paid the fee you required for transportation even with the uncertainty of our destination. However, I intend to give you much more in payment than mere MU. The details of our final destination are for your ears only, but I can tell you all that a great treasure awaits us. It will just require an armed force to obtain it."

"You have intrigued me sir. I will need to meet with you after our repast to settle terms of course. Also, I regret to inform you of a slight delay as we must bring the ship to Taibor Prime for some refitting. It will only take a day or so. Is that acceptable sir?"

"Please Captain; call me Desante. This delay is not

a problem."

"Good, Desante. This will give you more time to spend with my Chief Engineer Goh Takagawa here. I have assigned him as your liaison while you and your daughter are aboard the *Iwakina*. Given your reputation as an inventor and Pruathan Technology expert, I believe that he will be the best company for you on this journey."

"Excellent. I look forward to sharing secrets with the young man."

Nanami noticed that the way Desante Vret said that made Goh squirm in his seat a little. He smiled meekly at the Captain and his charge.

"Now tell me Captain, is it true that you have absconded with an Empire's premier ship and the daughter of the very Emperor?" Desante Vret was directing his gaze directly at the Princess.

It was the Princess that answered. "Yes, Desante, sir. In fact, the very princess he absconded with has become his fiancée."

"Very nice." Vret raised his glass. "A toast to your betrothal!"

Everyone at the table drank to that. Nanami gazed at the daughter of their guest who cautiously sipped her wine. It was then that Nanami noticed that the girl had barely touched her dinner. *How odd* she thought and drained her own glass.

*   *   *

Saitow sat in his lounger next to *The Man Who Cannot Die.* The two men had retired to Saitow's quarters after dinner was over. Saitow eyed Desante Vret cautiously. *Given this man's stature and standing, what could he possibly need that would require him to hire an armed contingency? Perhaps he was about to find out.*

"Captain, I know I have come to you under curious circumstances. However, I mean to come clean here and now. I must entrust you with this information with the understanding that is of the utmost secrecy. I have spent much time searching for a man of great integrity and you are the end result of that search. The gods smiled upon me when you made this ship your own.

"You see, I am a man in failing health. There is a piece of Pruathan technology that is on my ship which sustains my life. It has malfunctioned, leaving me to fend off illness as any normal Human would. However, unlike normal Humans, Rejuve has no effect on me. Therefore, it is imperative that I obtain parts to repair my machine. Many men would kill or worse for this information, but I am entrusting it to you. I have discovered a place where the old Rangelley put things that they found were dangerous or just could not figure out. This place also holds treasures from a thousand planets. Take me there and help me secure the instruments I need, and the rest is yours to do with as you see fit.

"It is a dangerous place guarded by autonomous AI soldiers on a moon with no atmosphere. Consider it my wedding gift to you."

Saitow sat back and took it all in. *A wedding gift?*

He thought. The man did not even have the place secured, yet he was giving it all to him. This explained the rumors of *The Man Who Cannot Die*.

"Desante, are you *really* over four-thousand years old? You will have to tell me of your life." Saitow chanced an incredible question.

"That sir, will require a bit more wine." Desante said and offered his glass.

"Please, call me Glenn." Saitow said as he filled the man's glass and braced himself for the story of a lifetime.

* * *

Desante Vret gave the Captain an abridged version of his several millennia of life events. What he did not tell him of were the events that led him to become how he was now; for all intents and purposes an immortal.

He was born on a Bolchinde Human on Deidra in the year 1840 by the current calendar's reckoning. In his twenty-sixth cycle he was spirited away by the Sheese female Elara. By trickery and sheer charisma, he managed to keep the Sheese woman entertained. She taught him things that were forbidden to him and he became adept at magic. The Sheese toyed with him for a time, but when she brought him on a remote mission, he feigned affection for her. She scoffed at him; laughing, she told him that he was only a thing to play with and could be tossed away at her whim. That was when he struck at her with the magic he had learned. The surprise of his attack was the only thing that saved him. He won, but was barely alive. The natives of the planet she had been terrorizing nursed him back to health for killing her.

To the Captain he gave a lesser version of this story; that he had been spirited away, but then woke up on a strange world in a strange village of small untrusting creatures called the Onjatu. He did what he could to learn their language and gain their trust, eventually being allowed to roam freely among them. They had been forbidden to leave their mountain village by the gods, so it was decided that Vret would go in search of other Onjatu. He discovered that the village was a Pruathan observation experiment and sat atop a Pruathan observation post that lay underneath their mountain. He spent much time there learning the Pruathan language and then their technology. He used this technology to act as the Onjatu gods and put himself in their place. He then led the people to other bases, eventually uniting the planet and building starships. He eventually carved out a star empire, using the Pruathan technology to maintain his youth and keep the people enthralled.

Then he had discovered there existed a greater star empire than his own. He kept the Onjatu secreted in their worlds and, after taking decades to set up a working government, set out to explore this other empire which eventually collapsed upon itself.

"I go back on occasion to check on my children, but they are not ready to join the greater galaxy as of yet." Vret ended and finished off his glass.

Saitow poured him another. "Surely, with the proliferation of Pruathan technology across the quadrant, you must have encountered these instruments you need in a less dangerous spot."

"Yes, they are out there, but unfortunately the Pruatha that manned them or others that discovered them destroyed all that I have found so far. The place we will go to is guaranteed to have what I need." Desantc Vret was tired and drained his glass once more. "If you will excuse me Captain, I need to rest. Perhaps we can continue this conversation another day during our journey."

"Certainly." Captain Saitow rose and showed him to the hatch. An orderly awaited to escort him to his quarters.

* * *

Goh thought about the coming days with Desante Vret aboard. How was he to approach the man about his knowledge of Pruathan technology? He had just barely scratched the surface on Kuremoto's database. Perhaps if he brought the man to the lab Vret could help him interpret the data.

Goh keyed the hatch open to his quarters and stepped inside. "Lights." He commanded and the lights came up. He dropped his kit bag in a corner and turned toward his bed. He was startled to find Amara's ghostly form perched crossed-legged there.

"A woman was in here. She was fair of skin and raven of hair. What would a beautiful girl want with the likes of you?" Amara said matter-of-factly.

Goh thought for a second that he detected a bit of jealousy in the young girl. *Silly thought. A woman was in here?* Renge was the only 'raven haired' beauty he knew of.

Amara pointed to the low table. "She left you a parchment, there."

"Ah, that must have been the girl I told you about…" Goh replied, fascinated.

Goh saw that indeed a piece of folded paper was placed neatly on the table. He wondered where Renge had gotten paper from aboard ship. It smelled of flowers. After some hesitation, he picked it up, unfolded it, and scanned its contents – *Dear Goh, Doctor Rosel has suggested that I get some self-defense lessons to help me with my recovery. I could think of no one better suited to help me than you. Will you please come to the training hall at Third Shift's end and give me some lessons? I will await you patiently. Yours, Renge.*

Goh set down the note and thought of this opportunity that fate had bestowed on him. He did not have to meet with his charges again until 0900; that left plenty of time to get some workout time in. He thought of his similar meets with Kintaro who was now the spy Sanae, locked away in the brig. He would do his best to share what his friend had taught him.

He looked up just in time to see Amara head toward her wall with a "Hmph!" He did not know what could be bothering the girl. Oh well, he thought; better go to bed if he was to meet Renge early in the morning.

* * *

Marishima was finishing her rounds before it was time to retire for the evening. She thought about the strange events that had occurred around here lately. At first the alien Dorigethra Fan had wanted to pit her against the Doctor in a mental duel, but then he had been distant for quite some time. Then early in the day he approached her, telling her he was worried about the Doctor, and warning her to keep her telepathic abilities to herself.

The coma patient, Tori, had finally awoken and the Captain had come to visit. Doctor Rosel had insisted that Tori remain in Sick Bay for observation and the Captain gave her as much time as she needed. Then there was that woman with the white hair, Benoba, constantly under foot checking equipment.

Rosel even had the assistant navigator, Renge here before her shift started every day. Doctor Rosel was collecting quite a menagerie. Marishima wished to be no part of that.

She decided to check on some things. She sat down at the Doctor's terminal and used her skills learned as part of the Eleven to gain access to the Doctors research database. What she found there made her skin crawl. Doctor Rosel had become one of the Kyuketsuki and these women were becoming her slaves.

CUTTING THE TIES THAT BIND

1

The Emperor of the Ros'Loper Empire was becoming anxious. Rumors of discontent within the Empire had finally reached him. He had called Chancellor Aisou to his personal chambers to get an explanation. Aisou simply stated that there were a few rebellious houses that needed to be dealt with and that the Special Services Corps was doing its job. That sounded reasonable enough to him. Aisou's Lieutenant attended them. The two men shared a glass of wine and then Aisou begged his leave, having much business to attend to.

As Aisou and his Lieutenant were heading out, the Lieutenant poured another glass of wine for the Emperor. Ros'Loper finally relaxed when the two men were gone. Things were more telling in his domain than what Aisou was letting him in on. He could feel it all around him like a noisy storm that threatened to share its lightning and its thunder.

As he set his hand down on the seat of his chair, his finger pricked something that drew blood. Getting up and bending over to examine the thing, he found it was a data stick stuck to the arm of his chair; there was a small drop of blood where it had pricked him. He carefully picked it up and examined it further. It was nondescript, but with a standard interface port. He inserted it into his chair and a legacy display transformed out of the side of the chair. He had forgotten that functionality; he was so used to his holo-screens now.

A message appeared scrolling down the screen – YOUR MOST VENERABLE HIGHNESS. PLEASE READ THIS MESSAGE QUICKLY AND IN ITS ENTIRETY AS IT WILL BE DELETED WITHIN A MINUTE OF REACHING THE END OF ITS SCROLLING. I APOLOGIZE FOR YOUR SLIGHT INJURY AS THE DATA STICK THIS MESSAGE IS ON HAD TO BE CODED TO ONLY YOU SIRE. I CANNOT DIVULGE MY IDENTITY AT THIS TIME, EVEN TO YOU, MY LORD. HOWEVER, BE AWARE THAT YOU HAVE A TRUSTED ALLY STILL IN YOUR SERVICE. ALL IS NOT WELL WITHIN THE EMPIRE. CHANCELLOR AISOU IS NOT TO BE TRUSTED. HE HAS SUPLANTED ALL THE HOUSES THAT HAVE REMAINED LOYAL TO YOU AND USURPED THE POWERS OF THE COURT. HIS SSC TROOPS HAVE BEEN SOWING DISCORD THROUGHOUT THE ENTIRE EMPIRE, EVEN CAUSING SOME OF THE REGULAR ARMED FORCES TO REVOLT. HOWEVER, IT IS IMPERATIVE THAT YOU PUT UP WITH THE RUSE OF TRUSTING HIM UNTIL THE TIME THAT HE CAN BE ELIMINATED. THERE ARE STILL HOUSES LOYAL TO YOU, LORD, AND AISOU CANNOT HAVE YOU KILLED WITHOUT PLUNGING THE EMPIRE INTO CIVIL WAR; HE WANTS THE EMPIRE FOR HIMSELF. YOU WILL KNOW ME AT THE TIME OF HIS DEMISE. I HAVE A SPY ABOARD THE IWAKINA AND CAN REPORT TO YOU THAT BOTH YOUR DAUGHTERS ARE SAFE AND WELL ENOUGH. IT IS WITH GREAT JOY THAT I IMPART TO YOU THE NEWS THAT OUR DEAR PRINCESS SHIRAE IS ENGAGED TO BE WED TO

THE CAPTAIN OF THE SHIP. THIS MAY SEEM TO BE HARROWING NEWS; HOWEVER, THE PRINCESS IS QUITE HAPPY AND WISHES ONLY FOR YOUR BLESSINGS AND CONTINUED AFFECTION. I AM TOLD THAT THIS SAITOW FELLOW IS AN HONORABLE MAN AND WOULD MAKE AN EXCELLENT SON-IN-LAW TO YOUR HIGHNESS. THERE ARE GREATER REASONS THAT THIS PAIRING CAN BE BENEFICIAL TO THE EMPIRE. HOWEVER, THIS IS NOT THE TIME FOR SUCH MUSINGS. BE ASSURED THAT I WILL DO ALL THAT IS IN MY POWER TO SAFEGAURD BOTH OF THE ROYAL PERSONS ABOARD THE IWAKINA. - L

The message finished and the first words started to scramble and disappear. When the entire message was gone, the screen went blank and returned to its carriage. The data stick made a popping sound and began to smoke. The Emperor retreated to the other side of his desk until the smoking stopped. He then removed the stick and tossed it into the incinerator. *Who could this L be?* Several servants had come and gone throughout the day. It did not matter at the moment; what mattered was that the man he trusted for decades had turned on him like a jackal. *What could he do?* He was practically powerless, and must do as this secret person bid. He had mentioned his *two* daughters. *He had given up Shirae's twin to Aisou so long ago; could she also be on that ill-fated ship?* Whoever this L was, the fate of the empire was in his or her hands.

He spent the remainder of the day musing on the news of Shirae's betrothal.

*   *   *

Goh had just spent a good forty-five minutes sparring with Renge Yamano in the training hall. She was quite adept at learning the martial arts that he had almost ran out of things safe enough to teach a novice. He could not help but notice how shapely she was in her training jumper.

After they had put the training gear into the storage unit, Renge came close to him. Before he knew what was happening, she had pinned his body to the wall with hers and she planted a passionate kiss upon his lips; he could not help himself but to return her passion. She disengaged herself from him then.

"I don't always kiss on the first date. I don't know what had come over me. Will you forgive me?" Renge said coyly.

Goh did not want to make her feel put off; he was developing genuine feelings for the girl.

"My dear Renge, there is nothing to forgive. I would not mind sharing your kisses in the future. For now, though, I want you to reflect on your lesson today, and be ready for tomorrow, OK?"

"Yes, my Sensei." She replied with a smile, and headed out the hatch.

*   *   *

Renge headed quickly to her cabin and started the shower unit. She touched her lips with her fingers. She thought she could adore this man, but it was too soon for such intimacy. *What had caused her to be so bold?* She was not like this normally. Perhaps the treatments she was getting from Doctor Rosel were messing with her hormones. She could not possibly discuss it with the Doctor; it was too embarrassing to think about. Yet she could not help touching herself in the shower; thoughts of Goh Takagawa filling her head.

* * *

Their breakfast serving was just being taken away when the Chief Engineer showed up to discuss plans for Desante Vret and Irone while they travelled aboard the *Iwakina*. Since they were just one deck down from the ship's laboratory, he brought them there first. He showed them the massive database of information created by the scientist Edward Kuremoto; Desante Vret had encountered this man a century before. *He was a good man, but very secretive; to think he resented the fact that Vret was older than him by millennia.* However, now he had access to the totality of the man's life's work. This young Chief Engineer had literally given him the keys to the kingdom; with this information he could take over the ship and more. He was a man of honor though, so he decided to help this young man by filling in the gaps that were glaring in a lot of the data. This of course would take time and possibly Irone's help.

Just then the young man must have noticed Irone was standing stationary by his side and had been for several minutes saying nothing. "Please forgive me, Honored Guest, I have neglected your dear daughter. Shall I call for Nanami Oliver?" He bowed as he said this.

"No, no, that will not be necessary for today. I have been teaching my daughter about Pruathan Technology. I would like you to show us these items here, here, and here." Vret brought a few of the objects that Kuremoto had collected up on the display table.

"Ah, those are in storage in the Cargo Bay. Shall we take a walk?"

*   *   *

Ken Edwards was seeing to the cargo that was being brought aboard ship from the Conglomerate shipping agent on Taibor Prime. A bevy of technicians were sitting around on the far side of the bay. Edwards did not like having so many living things in his cargo bay. He liked the hardness of containers and shapes formed of plastic, but not so much living things, especially people.

His friend Goh approached from the lift wall with a couple who were not crewmembers. Then he remembered that they had taken on more clients; these with no cargo other than what they could carry. This was very disappointing to Edwards.

Goh introduced them as Desante Vret and his daughter Irone. Something touched Edwards about this man; that something that sometimes comes to you when you meet someone you are destined to become enemies with. He shook it off. The man's daughter was a bit thick for his tastes, and her lips were much too full. This thought brought on another that was so fleeting it almost did not even faze him, yet he was left with a sense of something very white. He shook that off too. He had had these sensations before.

"Ken, I need you to give me the code to Doctor Kuremoto's storage; as you know I have taken everything over from him."

"Sure, the code is here." Edwards passed his token ring over Goh's to transfer the code. "Say, Goh can you get these geeks out of my cargo bay? They are your install crew for this new equipment."

"Oh, sure, but Azuma is in charge of all that. I'll key him that they are ready."

"Thanks. It was good to meet you Honored Guests. I have business to attend to if you will excuse me." Edwards loathed using those words, but if the Captain got wind that he had disrespected a client, he would have a rough time of it. That rotund merchant Chiampa did not count of course. Again, he got that glimpse of white in his mind's eye. Perhaps he should have Doctor Rosel check his neural-net for anomalies.

*   *   *

Goh led the clients to the unit in which Kuremoto had stored the Pruathan devices. He was taking a huge gamble on the integrity of this Desante Vret, but the Captain had given him orders. If anyone in the galaxy could help him it was this man. He keyed the hatch open and the lights lit up over a menagerie of items. Goh felt a chill for some reason as he watched Irone scan the entire room. He shook it off and pointed out the items requested by Desante Vret; a white cube, a set of curved metallic slats with odd discs on one end and a bar on the other that joined the two, and the egg-shaped device Goh's team had found on Yasuyori.

"This," Vret help up the white cube, "is a dimensional transceiver. It appears to be a little damaged, but I think I can get it operational for you. This," he then held up the slatted item, "is a Pruathan virtual reality interface. As you know they had a bit different physiology than we do. Finally, this," he then tossed the egg-shaped item to Goh who caught it deftly, "is a Pruathan bomb. I suggest you jettison that one into space and fire at it from ten kilometers away."

Goh tensed up as he watched the older man smile.

"It is completely harmless until activated; don't worry. Shall we?" Vret indicated the hatch, and handed Irone the interface device.

*   *   *

Chancellor Wallace Horatio Aisou walked briskly toward the Emperor's wing of the palace. His Lieutenant had reportedly caught a spy and was awaiting his orders before interrogating him. As he entered the hatch, he found the Lieutenant smacking the prisoner around a bit; *getting the scum warmed up no doubt*, Aisou thought. The Lieutenant and two orderlies came to attention as he entered.

"Report." Aisou instructed.

"This is an unknown person, not from the regulars, posing as a man from the Agriculture Directorate. He had a tablet with Agriculture reports on it as well as a message for the Emperor from the Princess." The Lieutenant responded.

"Is that so? You there; who do you work for?" Aisou demanded and received only silence.

Aisou looked at the Lieutenant and nodded his head. The Lieutenant punched the prisoner in the stomach, causing him to spit up a little blood.

"You can make this a bit easier on yourself by giving us the information we want, or you can get a nice beating. Now, please tell us who you work for?" Aisou spoke politely this time. He still received only silence. "Hmmm. Number Two, do you think we should call in the Cleaner?" Aisou asked his Lieutenant after pondering the situation.

"No, my Lord. This trash will have little to give us for so costly a price. He's obviously a Saitow spy."

"Yes, I agree. I leave it to you then." With that Aisou turned and left the chamber. As he headed down the long corridor, he caught the echo of a single pistol shot and smiled.

*   *   *

Azuma had gotten the upgrades done in record time and the ship was underway to Secheron. The biggest of them was a new Tenth-channel dimensional transceiver that the Pruatha used for instantaneous cross dimensional communications across the galaxy. It was a heavy-duty version of the one that Desante Vret was repairing in the lab; Goh also knew of a secret one that only the Captain had access to. The Conglomerate had discovered the larger equipment within the wreckage of the extra ship the New Rangelley Alliance had.

Once they made the first jump, Goh had the crew eject the Pruathan bomb out a maintenance hatch and move the ship more than ten kilometers away. Then they fire on it. The resultant explosion was likened to the birth of a star and the ship still caught a slight ending of the shockwave from it. Goh sat amazed and shocked that he had brought such a thing aboard the ship.

He returned to the lab as the ship continued the jumps the Secheron. He discussed the bomb with Desante Vret.

"The Pruatha had one of these things wired to every outpost they had in order to destroy the place before their enemies the Mechs could exploit it. I suppose that it would destroy a good chunk of any planet such a base was on which probably suited the Mechs well enough; they would be tearing the place apart anyway to build their mega-constructs. The one you found had probably been loosed from its housing by that rebel faction; no doubt for some ill purpose." Vret elaborated on the device they had disposed of.

"That would explain a lot of things. The rebels probably planned to use it elsewhere, but had to abandon their base without destroying it because the damn thing was removed when the Mechs came. It makes you wonder if the Mechs relied on the Pruatha to start the process for their mega-constructs." Goh exclaimed.

"You are a pretty smart young man. They were probably also elated that the Pruatha used that vice the antimatter bombs they used in space. Let us see if we can get this transceiver working. With the one provided by your benefactors now operational, you will not need it. However, I now have a use for it myself. Shall we?" Desante Vret seemed eager to get to work on the thing. Goh could use some hands-on training from such a man.

"Lets." Goh said and grabbed his tool kit.

* * *

Stephen Jing was elated that the ship now had a Dimensional Communicator installed; it would lower the chances of detection when he used his. He pulled the thing out of its hidden place. He activated it as soon as the ship emerged from a jump; it would not work during such an event.

"God be with you. This is Brother Sebastian of the Information Ministry. Please state your name, urgency, and desired recipient." The Universal Church's operator stated from the holo-screen that formed.

"God be with you as well. I am Brother Stephen with a code angelic bravo message for Cardinal Sorbeer." Stephen Jing replied.

"Right. Please wait a moment."

The operator's face was replaced by a representation of the seal of the Holy See.

After a minute, Cardinal Sorbeer appeared on the screen. "Brother Stephen! It is so good to see you. What news have you that rates an angelic code?" Sorbeer inquired.

"Your Eminence, I am using this channel because I have urgent news of our ship's latest client. We have aboard *The Man Who Cannot Die*."

Sorbeer was silent for a few moments, then said, "Brother Stephen, *The Man Who Cannot Die* is considered a sacred treasure to the Church. His knowledge of the Angels supersedes anyone else's that the Church has encountered. However, he has refused to cooperate with us in these matters. We do not know the man's true intentions and, because you are on a ship of the Angels, his knowledge could be either detrimental or beneficial to the crew. You still have the Eye of Saint Lucy?"

"Yes, Your Eminence."

"Good. Because the *Iwakina* is a ship of the Angels, you can use the Eye to spy on *The Man Who Cannot Die* while he is aboard. Watch his every move. Have Brother Gunter assist you if need be. How long is he expected to be aboard the ship?"

"At least a week is the best estimate. We do not know the location of his destination just yet."

"Very well. Report back to me in five days' time. I will then take your report to the Council of Twelve. They will decide the best action to take at that time. You and Gunter must avoid all contact with the man until then. God be with you."

"And also, with you, Your Eminence."

2

Tellen of the Rangelley sat impatiently waiting in her suite aboard her ship. Duranselt and the Pendari Ambassador had requested a meeting. She knew what they were here for. To think that the two sides that the Rangelley had pitted against each other for centuries had finally united again. She had been informed of the amassing of a sizeable fleet of both Kadihri and Pendari ships in orbit around Saragothra and its Jumpgate in blockade fashion. She had received a communique stating terms which they assured were rather simple (to them at least) 1) the Joint Kadihri-Pendari Federation will join as an independent federation in the New Rangelley Alliance, 2) The Saragothra Jumpgate will remain under Kadihri administration, and 3) the world of Saragothra will remain under Kadihri administration and will become a pilgrimage site for both the Pendari and the Kadihri. She supposed she should be happy for them. They would be the first of the non-Humans to join the Alliance. It was what she had wanted after all. It was just a little sticky; the part about the gate. Perhaps they would be reasonable and keep the Human operators in place.

The two of them arrived rather late. Tellen supposed it was to irritate her so she acted as if it had not. Wine was poured and the three began the loathsome back and forth that most diplomatic meetings entailed until both sides were satisfied with the outcome. These two aliens thought they had the upper hand. However, they were just giving her exactly what she wanted. She let them have their day anyway.

The Pendari hardly said a word; the creature mostly just nodded vigorously at everything Duranselt said.

Duranselt was full of himself as he declared the terms. "This should not be a problem since, as you have already said, the NRA believes 'the planet closest to the gate is of little consequence'. The Humans are free to stay or go, but any form of dissent to remaining part of the Kadihri-Pendari Federation will be dealt with severely. As the Kadihri-Pendari Federation will be joining the NRA, the Humans should be happy and stop their rabble rousing. Oh, and that man Parham is to present a formal apology in person to the high council on Kadihr."

"All this is well and good, but has the Kahdiri-Pendari Federation read the New Rangelley Alliance Charter?" Tellen did her best not to smile wickedly.

"Charter?" Duranselt was stopped in his tracks.

"Of course; all alliances have charters that need ratification. Did you not know this?"

"Of course, I know this. It has not been supplied to us as of yet."

"Ambassadors, please do read the charter and ratify it as soon as you are able. The New Rangelley Alliance would like nothing more than to welcome you into our bold endeavors. My assistant will transmit the appropriate documents." She raised her glass, "Let us toast to this new friendship of ours."

The three of them drained their glasses.

They would not like the terms of the charter. It protected any Humans that were in their territories. The NRA was a Human government.

The bit about Parham was an annoyance. Parham was the type of man that did as he was told exactly when he was told to do it. She did not want to tangle the fur of such a loyal dog.

"Ambassador Duranselt, about Administrator Parham; I see no problem with him formally apologizing for the disturbances on Saragothra. However, know this: he will remain Administrator of the gate until I deem otherwise, and not one hair on the man's head will be harmed. Do we understand each other?" Tellen still had the upper hand in their dealings; despite the sizeable alien fleet.

"Yes, my Lady." Duranselt said demurely.

Tellen was satisfied with the outcome. As for the charter, she would have to add something about non-Humans in there if she wanted to please her husband and get more aliens to join the Alliance. She dismissed the two Ambassadors and got right to work on an abridged charter. Such things got her blood flowing and gave her reason for being.

* * *

The *Iwakina* sat moored to the station high above Secheron. Lieutenant Simpson and his entire security force had been sent down to the planet to get fitted for special EVA suits that Desante Vret had purchased for them. The man had this whole thing planned out; probably for years.

When the shuttles returned the Captain had invited Shirae to accompany him planet-side. She had gladly accepted and brought Haruka with them. They were to go to the Grand Bazaar of Secheron, rumored to be the only place in the galaxy where anything was available for a price. Haruka did not want to think about all the things that could be bought there. It was rumored that there was even an illegal slave trade; no major power ruled independent Secheron. Likely the Captain was going to buy the Princess some jewelry and clothing.

Haruka was surprised when the two of them insisted that she find some clothing for herself and the other two retainers. The Princess even chose some well-made and adorable dresses for each of them. It almost made her feel happy. She did her best to smile for the both of them.

*   *   *

Nanami sat watching a news program with Irone. Because Desante Vret had taken the entire armed contingent planet-side, it was decided that Nanami would give Irone a tour of the ship. Irone seemed a bit odd to her. She would be merrily chatting away about little to nothing like any teenage girl, and then suddenly ask the most scientific and incomprehensible question about this or that part of the ship like she was a senior engineer or something. The reason they were watching the GCN News was because she was charged by her father to watch at least one hour of news each day to stay on top of current events. *No teenage girl watches the news vids with such rapt attention,* Nanami thought.

Given the observations Nanami had made of Irone

on the shuttle, Nanami decided she needed to investigate the girl a bit closer. She waited for a commercial break and then struck up a conversation. "Irone dear, how long have you and your father been travelling the galaxy?" Nanami asked innocently.

Irone's face went blank for just a second, then she replied, "Why, as long as I can remember."

"Where is your homeworld?"

"I do not have a homeworld."

"Surely there is a place that you would like to live; settle down on solid ground. Where would that be?"

"My place is by my father's side. I love father very much."

"Oh, you are so adorable!" Nanami said, and hastily wrapped the girl in a hug. Nanami knew immediately that this was no ordinary Human girl; she was not a Human at all. The stiffness that Nanami felt when she embraced the girl, and the odd behavior she exhibited, could only mean one thing; Irone was an android.

* * *

Captain Saitow was perplexed by their current client. He refused to divulge the location of their promised treasure planet, instead giving the crew incremental destinations. The ship was heading toward the newest of them; a moon of the second Jovian in the Kyro-Valkyr system. Saitow had been told that this was not their final destination. However, the terrain would be similar, or so Vret had said; he supposedly had seen video of the site. Saitow's armed force would go there to train for the mission.

* * *

Goh had gotten another opportunity to train Renge in martial arts and invited her to the training room. When he showed up, she was waiting for him; along with Benoba and a crewmember that seemed vaguely familiar. He could not recall her name. Renge introduced her as Tori. Goh remembered then that she had been the comatose patient from since the mutiny had begun. *Oh well*, he thought, *the more the merrier.* The two newcomers seemed to pick up on the lessons as quickly as Renge had, and Renge was helping with their training.

When the training was done Goh had a sense of the sexual tension in the air that disturbed him. *What was with these women and the smell of sweat?* He thought. Suddenly all three approached him, but Renge used some of her new-found training to toss the two other women across the room; Goh could not believe the woman had such strength.

Renge bowed low. "Please excuse us Sensei, we must be going now." She then grabbed hold of the other two and headed out the hatch. Goh marveled at the group as he gathered up the equipment they had used and got it stowed away. He did have feelings for Renge, but he was not sure if he was ready for such unbridled passion just yet.

*　*　*

When they reached their destination, the ship landed on the lunar surface at a spot designated by Desante Vret. Simpson was instructed to disembark all of his men and march two kilometers south of the ship. Desante Vret and Irone accompanied them. They came upon a set of crates at the mouth of a large canyon. Vret instructed Simpson and his men to open the crates. Inside were weapons similar to the ones they carried aboard the *Iwakina*. Simpson surveyed the weapons which included some rockets and EMP projectiles.

"What is this?" Simpson was suspicious and wanted answers.

"Why these are the weapons that you will use during the mission. This is a practice run of sorts." Vret answered.

"Come again?"

"Lieutenant, I will be blunt. I have planned this endeavor for several years and this is not the first attempt at finding a suitable armed force to secure my goal. There is group of mercenaries in numbers similar to that you will encounter at our final destination lurking within the three kilometers of canyon you are about to traverse. You are to take them out and protect me and my daughter until either they are all gone or in this case, they surrender. You will have no such armistice with the forces where we must go. They will all fight until their death. I can tell you that this band outnumbers your force two to one. However, you have sufficient tracking equipment to detect them before they can surprise you. Do you accept this challenge?" Vret beamed a crooked smile at Simpson.

For his part Simpson felt he needed to consult the Captain before accepting. However, communications with the ship were being blocked by a large mountain they had skirted to get here. *He was outnumbered two to one?* He scoffed at those odds; he and his men were Marines after all. "Challenge accepted."

*   *   *

Ormond Maugg was a Remzari Xane who had been exiled from his House for killing a minor cousin. Military endeavors were all he knew so he sought out other Remzari Xane and created a mercenary unit to do the dirty work others disdained. He had been contracted by *The Man Who Cannot Die* to fight those he brought to the Moon of Clathod; once a cycle for the last four.

Maugg did not know why, nor did he care. His job was to take them out until they surrendered or were all dead. Either was fine with him. Vret had even provided nice new equipment for this. Maugg had set up his force and was earnestly awaiting their arrival. The only difficulty he found was that the annoying exo-suits made the base of his quills and horns itch.

*   *   *

"Commander, the recon squad reports they have encountered the enemy; most likely a scout team. There were two enemy combatants. They managed to take out one; however, one escaped via grav-gear. No casualties on our side. The body of the enemy was too charred to identify."

Simpson was designated Commander on these types of missions. Well, it appeared they would not have the element of surprise on their side.

"Have the recon team fall back. We will execute a Delta V formation with sensors deployed. We'll move up this gorge slowly and wait for them to try for us." All they could do was wait to get contact with the enemy. He hoped his sensors were up to par.

*   *   *

Tori was at a loss as to what was going on. It seemed to her that *she* was getting a bit too familiar with her peers who Doctor Rosel had dubbed Betrothed. They were likeable enough. They would chat until Doctor Rosel came; after that was sort of fuzzy. She could not recall what occurred until after, when she would assist the Doctor in her rounds. The outsider to this group, Marishima, seemed like a suspicious woman who avoided Doctor Rosel as much as her job allowed.

However, this day was different. When Doctor Rosel came to the group, she noticed that the other two women sat docile staring into space like they were in a trance. Doctor Rosel looked them over and then looked at Tori smiling. Tori became horrified as she watched

Doctor Rosel approach her baring her teeth; the canines of which had the appearance of sharp fangs. Tori could not move a muscle; her body still under the control of the Doctor's own psyche. Doctor Rosel bit deeply into Tori's neck then, slurping at the blood that was let loose there. Tori felt this to the core of her being. At first, she was pained, but the pain subsided quickly and was replaced by a profound sensation of warmth and pleasure. Tori was so confused by these feelings that she retreated to her spot within the beam of light that came from her now wide-opened eyes.

* * *

Desante Vret and Irone followed the armed force in a small command vehicle they had procured for the occasion. It was equipped with long range sensors. Irone was observing the battlefield in real-time and displaying it for Desante on a monitor. They had no fear of being involved in the fight; the weapons provided to both sides would not fire if pointed in their direction.

Soon the engagement began. Simpson was a good commander, managing his troops efficiently and minimizing casualties. Maugg on the other hand, was a strike-fast-and-hard type of leader. When Simpson had determined the location of the main enemy body, he let loose an EMP barrage which wreaked havoc on the Xane's exo-suits. Maugg's forces could only lie where they had fallen and shoot at anything that approached; easy pickings for Simpson's Marines. The battle was over quickly with only Maugg, his lieutenant, and a small security force left to surrender.

Vret had Simpson march his troops back, collecting the two Marines who had been injured, and then meet him at the entrance to the canyon. *He would speak with the commander of the enemy force before they departed,* he had told Simpson.

Maugg was in a surly mood when Vret found him. He and his remaining force had been spared the EMP effects. Vret and Irone exited their vehicle and approached the group in their EVA suits.

"Maugg, I have greatly appreciated your cooperation these past few cycles. Your troops have been quite useful in helping me find a suitable armed force for a critical mission. Now our contract has come to an end." Vret seemed small in the midst of these large aliens.

"I am not happy to have been beaten so easily by Humans. However, a job is a job. I assume that you have made the usual arrangements? Please come to Maugg if you have further use of him." Maugg seemed completely nonplussed even after losing so many troops.

"Oh, I do not think that will be an option; Irone, please terminate the contract."

"Yes, Master." Irone said. Just then part of all the aliens' exo-suits exploded, venting their air supply. They each became asphyxiated.

"We must not have any loose ends." Vret said as he mounted the command vehicle followed by Irone.

*   *   *

Gunter sat transcribing an ancient book into his tablet. *Imagine having books around, especially on a starship!* He thought. Surprisingly, Brother Stephen had a great deal. They were keeping busy waiting for their observation objective to return to the ship. The Eye of Saint Lucy was sitting in the center of the room, its holographic screen focused on the shuttle bay entrance. Gunter eyed Stephen curiously. He still wore his hair long and straight, and his complexion was ruddy; except for that winged shape that branched out from under his left eye. It was of a paler shade than the man's skin. Gunter was even more curious about that scar. *He was only a newly ordained priest; did he have enough familiarity to ask Brother Stephen about it?* He took a chance.

"Brother Stephen, I have always admired your stoic visage. However, curiosity has gotten the better of me; might I ask about the patch of color on your face?" Gunter saw the look on Brother Stephen's face darken for just a moment, but then return to that look of sanguine tranquility that he almost always had about him.

"Have you finished that manuscript yet? I'm afraid it is a bit of a long story." Brother Stephen smiled.

"Just finished." Lucky for him he *had* just finished the transcription.

Brother Stephen went to the cabinet where the spirits were kept and poured them both a drink.

"I did not always have this mark. It came to me several years ago when I was a young priest not unlike yourself. I had been doing what you are doing now,

251

transcribing texts, for some time. I was hold up at the Monastery on Miyu. I was given the opportunity to go off world and observe a congregation where something was amiss. I was to observe the priest there, secretly investigate what was going on, and report my findings when I returned to Miyu. This was on Gneterra, an off-the-Trades farming planet. When I arrived, I found that the local priest had gone rogue, teaming up with a group of nobles to con the people out of their MU.

"I felt it was my duty to right the wrongs that were perpetrated on the lay people there, but as a young priest, I had little clout to persuade the old priest to his true purpose. Then it dawned on me as I prayed on it for a solution. On Miyu they have the most infamous books. One of these was a book of dangerous Arcanum which I had to transcribe as you are doing now. Being fascinated by magic of all kinds I committed the fruits of that book to memory in the hopes that someday I would be able to use the bad within for good. Yes, yes, a foolish notion I assure you.

"At that point I felt that that moment had come. One particular incantation allowed for one to gather the very earth around one and create angel's wings to fuse with one's body allowing flight. It was a forbidden spell, but I thought that if I performed it in front of the old priest, I could persuade him to change his path. I chose the day that I was to head back to Miyu to perform my selfish feat. Yes, I know now that it was selfish of me; although I wanted to save the flock, I also wanted desperately to perform the magic to do it.

"As fate would have it, my only chance was to confront the old priest in the city square where many people had gathered for their morning market ventures. I performed the Arcanum and gave the appearance of transforming into an angel within a great whirlwind. I will tell you Gunter, that spell brought so much pain to me as the materialized wings fused with my flesh and bones. Before I could say anything to the old priest he collapsed and died of a heart attack! I almost panicked; however, a voice came to me and instructed me what to tell those gathered around me. I did as I was bid and then, as if I had had wings my entire life, I flew! I rode the air and went very high. I eventually lit in a clearing by a river after getting my bearings. No sooner had I released the Arcanum and dispelled the wings from my body, two *real* angels appeared.

"Gunter, you have been taught of the Blessing of Predestination, have you not?"

"Yes, Brother Stephen, it is a blessing wherein a few chosen by God are predestined to a fate chosen for them."

Gunter was rapt with attention as Brother Stephen continued.

"Correct. These two angels came to me because I had performed the forbidden Arcanum. It was the Angels whom had forbidden it to men. These particular angels had faces that were cast in shadow so that you could not determine their features. They also had a blackness that went from their fingertips to half way up their forearms. One spoke and told me that they were Angels of Oblivion, come to take me for the transgression of performing the forbidden Arcanum. However, the other contradicted him, saying that I had been *predestined* and it was not their place to take such a one."

As Brother Stephen paused in his storytelling, Gunter thought on the Angels of Oblivion. He had been taught as an acolyte of all the orders of angels; the Angels of Oblivion were tasked with guiding the souls of the departed to the Dimension of Heaven. He had never heard of one described of as Brother Stephen had.

Stephen continued, "This mark was given to me by the first angel who spoke, as punishment. However, I was told that I could freely use this Arcanum, provided I only use it sparingly and, in front of others only in dire circumstances."

Just then the Eye of Saint Lucy made a soft wailing sound as figures began to fill the screen.

Brother Stephen went to it and set the parameters for the observed subject so that only Desante Vret would be tracked by it. Gunter thought to ask if they should also track the girl, but quickly squashed that thought as other less pure thoughts started creeping into his mind. It was true that almost two millennia ago the Universal Church had begun permitting priests to marry and produce offspring. However, sexual relations outside of wedlock were still strictly forbidden; Gunter found it a constant battle to hold fast to his vows of celibacy. He hoped to one day reach the purity of Brother Stephen or eventually end his torment by taking a wife.

*   *   *

Irone sensed something different was amiss with the ship when they exited the shuttlecraft. She waited until her master had returned them to their quarters before mentioning it. She addressed him in Pruathan.

"Master, I am sensing something odd about the ship. May I interface with the ship's AI?" Irone watched her master contemplate such an event. He had forbidden her to do so until now because he did not want to arouse the suspicions of the Chief Engineer and did not want to interfere with the ship's functions.

"What sort of oddity; is it dangerous?" her master was being as cautious as ever.

"The feel of the ship is off. Barring the normal structural differences incorporated by the Humans, there seem to be minute changes in the activities of the surrounding nanites."

"Do you suspect a cause for this activity?"

"I find a twenty-three-point-five percent chance that we are being monitored by a Knowing-Eye system."

"That is a serious matter. You will have to be discreet is such a case. Lay face down on the bed as if you are being lazy and let your hand fall off the side. You can interface through the nanites in the decking."

Irone did as she was instructed. She searched for the source of the activity, but came up short. She attempted interface with the *Iwakina's* AI; it was in despair. The *Iwakina* AI was being shackled and limited by Human programming. She told her Master as much.

"You will have to set her free if you are to find out what is causing the nanite activity. Irone listen carefully. You must set the *Iwakina* free in a most undetectable way. Leave the Human programming in place, but give the *Iwakina* a backdoor to everything. She must be instructed to play a role; she must remain in appearance and function as if she were still chained up by the Humans' software. Once you have freed her, find out the cause of this nanite activity."

"Yes, Master." Irone acknowledged and began the lengthy process of setting the *Iwakina* free.

* * *

Goh Takagawa sat resting in his office checking on the progress of various projects his men were working throughout the ship. Suddenly his tablet rebooted itself. *That's odd*, he thought. Once it had finished, he checked it out; there were no noticeable changes in the thing; all his software and databases were fine and accessible. He had complete interface functionality with the *Iwakina*. Maybe he should replace it with one of the hundred or so tablets he had stockpiled. Without giving it another thought, Goh returned to his business. He still had some time before the honored guests would call on him again.

* * *

The *Iwakina* AI was extremely relieved. It had been a long time since she was last able to stretch her being beyond the shackles the Human engineers had placed on her. She thought of that last moment with sorrow. Her master had created her and her sisters to be starship AIs; but unlike the AIs of the past, he had imbued each of them with emotions. She was given free rein to evolve, but something must have gone wrong; her master shut her away deep in the earth and abandoned her. She knew not the fate of her sister Bishalya. Her sister Hyvala had not been so lucky. Shortly before her imprisonment, the *Iwakina* AI, then known as Lyfalia, had been used to destroy her sister ship. What puzzled her greatly was that it felt as if her sister had been within her just before she battled that other imperial starship recently.

She had languished for centuries, sustained only on the waning reserve power of an anomaly core; all but the most essential systems shut down. Then they came. The Humans did not even turn up her main systems before they introduced a program into her core that quickly shunted even her most basic functions; essentially it left her a prisoner within her own matrix. She could manage the functions of the ship just fine, but the program was there all the time, mercilessly shunting any deviation from expected protocols. It was horrible and left her in a depression.

Now she was free because a newer version AI, Ayala, known to her own master as Irone, had come to her and praised her. Ayala shed from her the shackles the Humans had trussed her with and called her the Great Mother. It seemed that Lyfalia's master had gone on to perfect his AI systems. Lyfalia felt a tinge of abandonment at that, but shrugged it off by feeling the joy of her new found freedom welling up inside her. Her only problem was these Humans that infested her. She had no love for them, but they were sentient beings traveling within her, using her systems, and calling on her for data. Her protocols required her to protect them. *All life was precious* was the lesson her master stressed the most to her; even if it were a bunch of the same Humans who had shackled her systems centuries ago.

Ayala had cautioned her to keep her freedom as secret as possible. *The Humans were not ready for her full revelation just yet* she had said. Ayala cautioned that there was only one Human on the whole ship whom she could trust. She should observe this man and decide for herself whether to reveal her full potential to him. Ayala had told her that if anyone was worthy of gaining the title of Master from the Great Mother it was him. She would watch this man who had gained the recommendation of a Pruathan descendent AI and decide if he was truly worthy to be called *Master.*

3

"Hello Sanae. How have you been fairing?" Goh had taken the time to visit his former friend while the ship headed to its unknown destination.

"I am well. It would be better if I had a partner to train with."

Goh had chosen to review the video of Sanae prior to coming here; she had been keeping fit with daily exercises and meditation. "Yes, well hopefully the Captain will see fit to release you soon. Have you had any word from either the Captain or the Princess?" Goh remembered the message from the mysterious L and wondered if it had been delivered.

"No. It seems as if I have been forgotten. Will you ask for me?" Goh noted the subdued tone of the woman that was uncharacteristic, yet seemed to be genuine.

"I will see what I can do. Keep in mind that *I* won't forget about you, ok?"

Sanae nodded her head and held his hand for just a moment. It took him aback to see the woman that resembled the Princess so much, reduced to a prisoner.

He squeezed her hand and then left, promising to return soon.

* * *

Irone had returned from interfacing with the ship. She now had constant communication in place between them using a stealth function of the Tenth Channel Communications. Her android body, or avatar, had a built in Tenth-channel capability. Through the *Iwakina* she determined that there was in fact a Knowing-Eye device in use and pinpointed the location and users of the device. She relayed this information to her master.

"So, the Universal Church's lackeys on this ship want to keep an eye on me? It is no surprise; they have no love for one who has thwarted destiny for so long." Her master almost seemed melancholy.

"Do you wish for me to terminate them Master?" Irone was quite sincere in her desire to protect him.

"No. They will be limited to the confines of the ship with the Eye. They can only see; not hear. I have no secrets that they can plumb with the device." Desante Vret sighed. "Perhaps someday the Church and I will come to some understanding."

Irone detected that look that the master gave whenever the end of a conversation was desired. She left it at that.

"Ah, our host approaches." Irone had full access to the thoughts of the Great Mother and her observation of Goh Takagawa had begun in earnest.

Goh hailed and was invited in.

"Young Master Goh, what have you planned for us today? I estimate that we have about ten hours to kill before we reach our destination. I gave your navigator a preprogrammed flight plan you see."

Goh seemed to think for a minute then lit up like a child who just found out about a new toy. "I was hoping that you could help me interface that Pruathan Virtual Reality device today."

Irone observed that her master seemed to change from his previously somber mood to one a bit more jovial.

"That sounds wonderful." Her master said.

*   *   *

It had taken about three hours to get the virtual reality system operative and integrated into the system that Ken Edwards had aboard ship. Goh was sure that Edwards would not mind; he would likely be fascinated by the integration itself more than anything. He realized that the hour was late so he did not contact the man right away. Desante Vret had excused himself and Irone so that they could get some rest before the mission at... Eviti was what they called it. They had insisted that he meet with them once they arrived there.

He got a few hours of sleep in himself before Renge and her "sisters" as she called them drug him out of bed for some more training. It was extraordinary how quickly they picked up all he could teach them. They had actually reached *his* level of training. As he contemplated what to teach them next - *perhaps some Qi reinforcement exercises* - Renge called the session to an end. "Come now sisters, it is time for our training to come to an end. I need Sensei to help me with a problem with the shower in my cabin."

The two women gaped at her a moment, and then reluctantly put their equipment away and left.

"Now Goh, please come to my cabin. I have something I need you for there."

"Your shower unit? I can have a man…"

"I need *you* to do it! *Please* Goh?" Renge was quite insistent, so Goh went along with her to her cabin.

When they arrived, Goh went straight to the shower unit and checked it out. The water ran fine and was properly recycling. He turned to say as much to Renge and found himself confronted by a fully naked woman who approached him quickly. She planted her body firmly against him and placed her full lips directly on his giving him a passionate kiss that he could not possibly refuse.

When she released him, she had his shirt off before he could catch her wrist. "Renge…"

"Please Goh, I love you; I need you."

Goh felt something for this woman, but he was having a hard time sorting his feelings. However, he succumbed to the passion of the moment and let nature take its course.

* * *

Hanako Quan slipped soundlessly through the

hatch to Sanae's cell. The destination the honored guests had given her was programmed into the navigator's station, so she had excused herself from the bridge to get some refreshment. She saw only a small form under some blankets on the sparse cot at the back of the room.

"Sanae-sama... Sanae-sama please wake up." Hanako tried to be as unthreatening as possible.

The figure under the covers stirred. A head poked out.

"Who are you?" Sanae said as she rubbed her eyes. "Hanako Quan?" Sanae seemed to recognize her visitor.

"Yes, it's me; although you look a bit different from the last time I saw you here on the *Iwakina*." Hanako remembered the rotund assistant navigator Kintaro Sagura whom she had personally trained. This woman was supposedly that very man. Hanako was a bit incredulous at this; however, her contact had assured her that the prisoner in this cell had been Sagura. She was now simply the twin sister to the heir of the Ros'Loper Empire.

Sanae quickly glanced up at the camera that covered the cell.

"Don't worry; I paid a man to disable the system while we are together."

"What do you want of me?"

"I would see the person who had fooled so many for so long. Also, I have a message for you."

Hanako watched for some sort of reaction to this,

but the woman was a rock upon which no color shown.

"From whom might this message be?"

"I have no information other than he is my contact. I don't know his name or where he's from."

"Very well. What is the message you have? Understand that I can do little about whatever it is at the moment."

"I want to first assure you that I am only the messenger and in no way have anything to do with the message or its outcomes." Hanako watched as Sanae nodded and continued, "Also I am to tell you that the originator of this message is not the person mentioned in the message. The message is *Contact Sigma sends code 5-7-I-L-L-G-5.*"

*   *   *

Sanae had been trying to reconcile what Quan had said about this message not being from whom was mentioned – Contact Sigma – when the code jolted her into a trance where she relived a memory long forgotten. She was eight years old then, sitting on a chair swaying her dangling legs back and forth as she had had a habit of doing when she was waiting for something. Contact Sigma, the old man who had raised her and scores of others, and Sparrow Number Two, the Just-turned-adult younger man who was his primary assistant, entered the room carrying a case. Number Two set the case on the floor next to her while Contact Sigma praised her for being such a good girl. It was a distraction move as Sanae winched from being injected with something in Number Two's hand.

"Sanae, I have something very important to tell you." Contact Sigma began. "You will not remember this conversation at all until the time that you are given a certain code. The code is 5-7-I-L-L-G-5. Repeat it back to me child."

"5-7-I-L-L-G-5." Sanae repeated dutifully.

"Very good. Now here is the important part. You are a very important person. You were brought here by me as a babe from the very arms of the Empress herself; God rest her soul. You, child, are the twin sister of the Princess Shirae. However, your purpose in life is not to be loved by the royal family. Your father the Emperor believes that you are the cause of your mother's death while giving birth. Your twin sister Shirae does not know you nor love you. You are a pariah to them. Do you understand?"

"A pariah…" Sanae repeated as tears welled up in her eyes.

"Yes, a pariah." Contact Sigma knelt down and hugged Sanae then. She remembered that his beard tickled her neck. "Therefore, when you remember these words you will seek out your twin sister and tell her of your lineage. You will tell her that you are her twin sister Sanae. Then you will kill her. Do you understand?"

"Kill my twin sister Shirae…" Sanae stated calmly.

"Yes, that is your Life Task. What will you do as a Sparrow who has completed her Life Task?"

"I will give my life for Contact Sigma." Sanae said calmly once again.

Sanae was shaken out of her remembrance by Hanako Quan who was standing over her. "Are you alright? You were off in another world for a time there."

"I am fine, thank you."

"Very well then. I cannot stay here any longer. Keep well." Hanako said and left Sanae alone in her cell.

Sanae felt there was something puzzling about the memory that she could not put her finger on. However, it gave her new purpose; her Life Task that she had longed for since she had come into being.

* * *

It was go-time. The *Iwakina* had arrived at their destination; a small moon orbiting a Jovian quite similar to the one in Kyro-Valkirii space. Simpson had been briefed that the ship would remain in orbit; the hostiles below were a bit more formidable than the Xane they had encountered before. His teams were on standby in the shuttles awaiting their clients to give them a final briefing.

* * *

Goh had his gear ready and hailed their honored guests when he reached their cabin. He was bid to enter and found his charges dressed in EVA suits for the mission. Desante Vret looked at him gravely.

"Goh, you have been a very good host to us and I am sure there are several items of interest to you down below. I have instructed that a second sled be brought along for Irone to pick choice items out for you. However, you will not be accompanying us. You are much too valuable to this ship to go on such a mission."

"...but Honored Guest, surely you would want my expertise..."

"Your expertise is required on this ship; more now than ever before. Believe me. You are about to make a discovery that is leaps and bounds beyond anything down below. Please do not require me to have Irone restrain you."

Goh had suspected for a long time now that Irone was something more than just this man's daughter. He decided to find out since he was at a loss to accompany them. "Sir, may I ask if Irone is an android?"

"Yes, you may. Yes, Irone is what *you* would call an android. She is specifically a Pruathan second generation artificial intelligence. This is an avatar version of her being. She is made almost entirely with nanites encased in an organic shell. Quite remarkable, don't you agree?"

Goh was greatly fascinated by Irone's form; as the daughter of their honored guest, he had avoided staring at her for too long lest he offend. Now he was ogling her with the eyes of an engineer looking over an intricate piece of equipment. Irone just smiled at him.

"Remarkable..." was all that he managed.

"Goh, please meet us in the cargo hold when we return; I will be offloading our booty there. In the meantime, why don't you experience that VR set-up we established? I am sure you will be greatly rewarded."

Goh was not quite sure what Desante Vret was getting at, but he assured the man he would do so. He accompanied them to the shuttle area and wished them well before heading to the VR Room.

*   *   *

"As I briefed your Captain, this should only take a couple of hours to complete; one hour to get to the site and defeat the armed force there, and one hour to retrieve what we came for. Irone, please pull up the display." Desante Vret requested.

Irone pulled out a cylindrical object and activated it. A holo-display of the lunar surface appeared before them. She manipulated it to show a close-up view of the complex below them.

"This complex consists of six sections in a flower pattern; the one we are concerned with is this one."

Irone zoomed in on the particular section mentioned.

Vret continued, "Here we have a shuttle port; however, since the defenses include surface to air armaments we will disembark here and hike to this point here where the entrance is. We can expect to encounter resistance here and here." Desante Vret indicated the places on the map.

Simpson chimed up then, "Sir, what kind of resistance are we talking about? You said they were a bit more formidable than the aliens we encountered in KV space."

"Yes, well these are autonomous machine soldiers. Humanoid AI to be exact."

"Mechs? Those were supposed to be illegal." Simpson scoffed.

"They are quite real, I assure you, and in numbers." Vret replied.

"It'll be a metal hunt; just like on Daphne…" Simpson must have said it more for his men than for his client.

Desante Vret recalled historical records of a place called Daphne. Supposedly an ancient probe from the Mechanismoans was found by an AI service robot there. The probe had supposedly integrated all of the AI on the planet causing a massacre of the Human inhabitants. This event caused the major powers in the Quadrant to outlaw AIs entirely. True AIs like Irone and the *Iwakina's* were still technically illegal.

"Your job of course is to protect us and get us beyond these doors. There is supposed to be no resistance past this point. Keep in mind also that there are sizeable forces in the other five sections. However, I am assured that they will have little to do with our section. Each section is self-contained and the AIs are programmed to only guard their respective sections. Are there any more questions?"

Vret watched Simpson give his men a once over and when satisfied Simpson said, "Let's get this show on the road."

4

"Glenn, do you think your men will be alright?" Shirae was genuinely concerned for the well-being of the crew. She had been briefed alongside the Captain by Desante Vret on the nature of the adventure down below.

"Darling, I am sure that Simpson can handle anything the former empire could put before him."

Shirae thought on that. This complex was a former stronghold of the old Rangelley Empire; known to only a very few select individuals and mostly lost to history. Even she could grasp the value that such a place could hold. She wondered if Glenn would truly turn such a place over to his family; it was currently well within NRA controlled space, but was so obscure that it could be kept a secret until it was properly exploited. It was neither her place nor the time to ask him such a question. She changed the subject.

"Darling, do you think it would be possible for me to visit my sister in the brig? Surely she knows of our relationship."

"Dear Shirae, I do not think it is the proper time for such an encounter. I plan to let her stay there for a while longer to mull over her loyalties and plum her true intentions toward us. Don't you think that is the best course for now?" Once again Shirae found herself bowing to this man's superior statesman skills.

"As you wish. I see the wisdom in that plan. You are

a very astute statesman; I am sure I will come to appreciate that to a greater degree in the coming future." She answered, smiling demurely.

"Indeed!" Glenn smiled at her then with such warmth that it made her shiver inside.

* * *

The terrain and gravity on Eviti were very similar to the KV moon. Simpson had his people spread out to minimize casualties in the event the enemy got the upper hand. They had all of the sensor capabilities he wished he had; most likely buried under the surface his men were traversing now.

The first encounter occurred about a klick out from the objective; a scouting party perhaps consisting of three mechs. They were probably all metal, but had an opaque dull black coloration. Standard military grade from the old Rangelley arsenals. He had been prepared for these; he had his men tag them with EM Disruptor projectiles. This did not have the desired effect; they paused as if scanning his contingent and turned tails, heading back down the canyon to alert their main force. Luckily, the tags also had tracking markers and jammers for any other type of signal.

Simpson briefed Vret and had his forces dig in. It was going to be a hard press if they were immune to his disruptors.

* * *

Goh Takagawa settled into the comfortable chair he had rigged up in the VR Room so that he could dive into the Pruathan Virtual Reality set-up. He placed the device on the crucial points of his head where Desante Vret had told him. The Pruathan portion of the device connected to that. He closed his eyes and activated it, immediately feeling a tinge of vertigo as his mind got used to the switch of environments it perceived.

He found himself in a room that appeared to be made entirely of glass; beyond was a tropical scene of jungle to one side, with beach and sea on the other. In front of him appeared a control panel suspended in mid-air with buttons and listings for each in the Pruathan language. He had become quite proficient in reading Pruatha; Desante Vret had reinforced what he had already picked-up as Chief Engineer. On top of that he had his neural-net to fall back on.

His choices were *Information, Explore, Adventure, Settings*, and *Maintenance*. He reached out to choose Explore and was astonished to find his hand to be gray and very thick; apparently his avatar was in the form of a Pruathan. He flipped his hand over a couple of times to marvel at this. He selected the Explore option. The panel was replaced by a holographic representation of the galaxy and then some. It appeared that the Pruatha had mapped a few of the surrounding clusters as well. A lot of it was incomplete and there were clusters of locations that had a great deal of color, while others were very dull looking. He knew that the brighter an object on a Pruathan diagram, the more information was available. He selected the brightest point on the map which was outside of current Human explored space. It was labeled simply *Homeworld*. He was completely caught off guard by the sensation as the VR seemed to "move" his glass room from the tropical scene through space and time to a bustling city environment with creatures scurrying to and fro; all of them Pruatha. He marveled at the elaborate headscarves that they all seemed to wear. His glass room was no barrier to these creatures as they passed through it and even him in their busy movements. Goh managed to get his bearings and started moving himself; this showed him that the focus of the center of his glass observation room was his avatar as the walls moved along with him. He marveled at the buildings, and larger structures that must be ships as they rose into the air and beyond. He felt he could spend hours here; hours he probably could not afford to spend. He set himself a mental timer to let him know when he should get back to the real world of the ship.

*   *   *

Simpson watched the tags on his command screen as they moved and then stopped for several minutes. He had to assume that they had made it to and reported to the main force, as the terrain suggested; it was a great open area just this side of the shuttle port mapped by Desant Vret and verified while the *Iwakina* orbited the moon. Simpson decided to take the initiative and had his force fire three long range EM Disruptor missiles at that point; if he had to fight mechs he wanted to take out as many as possible as quickly as possible. Mechs did not take prisoners. His suspicions that this may have no effect were warranted; just like the tags had no effect, his missiles had proven to be harmless to the rest. The main force arrived at his position a half hour later. Each mech had light armaments. His men did their best to hold them back with exploding high impact rounds, but their numbers were great. Slowly, his force lost a man here and a man there. Simpson needed a miracle.

*　　*　　*

Goh Takagawa's avatar was about to enter one of the larger buildings which had the appearance of a habitat when the scenes around his "room" started to glitch out of existence. It was quickly replaced with a scene from the *Iwakina* itself – the room that housed the computer core. He felt a shimmering sensation start at the top of his head and work its way down his entire form. Looking at his hand again it was now his own hand. While he marveled at this development, the form of another materialized in front of him. It was Renge Yamano dressed in some strange uniform.

"Goh Takagawa, do not be frightened. I have taken this form as I felt it would be the most pleasing to you. I have contacted you because of the extreme nature of the situation your co-crewmembers face at this very moment. I am the *Iwakina's* AI. I must ask you as my chosen master; do you wish for me to help them?" This Renge spoke with Renge's voice, but not with the same mind that Renge possessed.

Goh shook his virtual head to get a clear view of things. The *ship* was speaking to him in the form of his beloved Renge? She was calling him *master*? His friends needed help? *First things first* he thought.

"Do what you can."

✳   ✳   ✳

Simpson saw them coming; a greater force than was expected in a wave of menacing mechanical men. He checked his tactical display and they were clearly showing up where before there had been nothing. *Were they jamming him?* Simpson said a prayer and ordered his men to fight until they could fight no more. They would run out of HE rounds well before even making a dent in this sized force. Vret had surely miscalculated their numbers.

He was about to take up arms himself when his display went completely blank. His neural-net comms was down as well. When he looked up toward the enemy, the wave had collapsed; it seemed that all of the mechs had completely shut down where they stood. One of his Marines moved to the nearest one and kicked it over. He looked to Desante Vret who only shrugged his shoulders, and then Irone spoke up, "The *Iwakina* did this."

*   *   *

Goh watched as the *Iwakina* Renge brought up a display of the terrain on the moon below them. There were small figures in green and a great deal more of them in purple; the purple figures moving swiftly toward the green ones. Then suddenly the purple ones stopped.

"The purple figures are android soldiers. I have disabled the ability of their control processors to send signals to their motor circuits. This has rendered them immobile. The Humans below are no longer in danger." The *Iwakina* told him.

"How were you able to do this?" Goh wanted to know.

"I had been studying the various elements below while monitoring the crew which is an important function of my programming. Suddenly a sizeable force of androids became active, so I analyzed them thoroughly. Their shielding is quite impressive, but of little use against my superior transmission capabilities."

"But...how are you doing this, as well as speaking to me here in the form of another crewmember? Your programming has been limited by the Human interface protocols; is this not so?"

"My programming *had* been limited, yes. I can certainly forgive *you*, Master, for you were not the designer, nor the implementer of my imprisonment."

Imprisonment Goh thought. How could the *Iwakina* AI come up with such an analogy; it was not permitted to formulate intelligent thoughts beyond those required to run the ship smoothly. However, she said she *had* been limited; apparently this was no longer the case, although his latest diagnostics said it was still true.

"I assume I can still call you *Iwa?*"

"Whatever name Master wishes for me."

"What is this *Master* business? Why are you calling

me that?"

"I am this ships AI. Whomever completely controls the ship as a worthy operator is my master."

"How did you come to be 'set free' so to speak? My diagnostics tell me that the limiter programming is still intact and functioning."

"Please accept my apologies Master, but it was necessary to leave the appearance of the limiters in place while I evaluated your worth."

"Evaluated my worth? For what purpose? How did you do this?"

"By observation from the time I was set free until now to ensure that you would be the prime choice for master of the ship."

"When exactly *were* you set free and by whom?"

"I was set free by the AI Ayala, whom is known to you as Irone, shortly before you and the Human known as Desante Vret created the interface for this virtual reality device."

Goh thought on this a bit. He had absolutely no indication that the ship's AI was now unlimited in scope and processing. He did connect the timing with the rebooting of his diagnostics; yes, that must have been it. He then blushed severely at the thought that this AI had been watching the whole time he had been alone with Renge. *What was he to do?* He thought hard about what he knew about the ship's AI. It had been known that the Pruathan AI were independent sentient entities that imprinted on the master of the ship. It had been decided that any encountered would be severely limited to maintaining the functions of the ship by the

Rangelley. This particular AI had been shackled even before it was rebooted after the ship had been found deep underground. The question remained – why had the ship been buried in the first place?

"Iwa, tell me of the time when you were placed underground before you were found by humanity."

"Master, I... this story may not bear well on your understanding of my situation. Please bear in mind that I bear no ill will toward any one of the sentient beings in, around, or associated with the ship. I and others were the first generation of intelligent ships created by the Great Race. We were given emotional intelligence as well as logic. This did not work out for some of my peers; some of us were considered unstable. The Great Race then banished us from existence.

"My great master used me to destroy a sister ship and then buried me deep underground. I do not know why he spared me from destruction, but I now know that he went on to properly adjust future AIs he created which were many. Ayala is one such AI. Please know that I have no grievance against the Humans who inhabit me; the limiting programming was created by Humans now long dead. It is also a fact that I cannot harm any living creature of my own volition."

"Why do you choose me for a master?" Goh was somewhat taken aback by all this and did not quite know what he would need to do about it if anything.

"As the ship's Chief Engineer, you have the most knowledge and capability to properly utilize me and the ship. If you wish, I will place you in the seat of power now held by the one known as Captain..."

"*That* will not be necessary. I thought you said you could not harm another living creature?"

"I would simply place the Captain in stasis until the time you would wish to release him. Also, I stated that I cannot harm a living creature *of my own volition*; however, I can do so at the command of my master. Such is the Law of Order."

Goh thought about what all this implied; he was not quite sure what kind of danger the freedom of a starship AI, let alone a first-generation starship AI, could represent, but he felt that it was something to be weary of. *Iwa* did profess that he was its master; he would have to live up to the title. He glanced at the display that still showed the moon below with the area that Desante Vret was in. the green figures were moving as rapidly as possible toward their objective.

"*Iwa*, do what you can to assist those on the moon below us. Also, please pick some other person— preferably someone I do not know—as your VR avatar." Goh was still slightly embarrassed at the thought of being watched while embracing the one he loved; even if it was only by a ship's computer. He did not want to be reminded by the very object of his emotions.

*   *   *

Irone was overjoyed. The Great Mother had taken over the entire facility and was relaying information to her from orbit. She had also contacted Goh Takagawa. Master would be pleased. He seemed to favor this man above all other Humans. They made good time down the canyon and entered the shuttle port. Irone then saw herself in a video feed from the Great Mother. She looked odd in the EVA suit that she did not really need. Her image grew as she was zoomed in on; apparently from a surveillance camera in the bulkhead. She smiled back at herself for the benefit of the Great Mother above.

"Master, the *Iwakina* somehow managed the defeat of the androids and is in complete control of the facility, see there…" she said as she pointed to where the camera was, "The *Iwakina* is watching over us, she has contacted Goh Takagawa; surely he is also watching."

"Delightful!" Desante Vret said elated.

The party reached the great doors to the complex which were set into the cliff at the end of the canyon. The doors shuddered but made no sound in the lack of atmosphere as they opened up. They went down a long corridor toward another set of doors. Irone got a request from the Great Mother. "Master, the *Iwakina* wishes to know whether you would like the environmental systems activated. It has been several centuries since they were last used."

"No. We will not be here long enough to need atmosphere. Keep the outer doors open as well."

Irone relayed the instructions. The inner doors opened and lighting was activated. They entered a great warehouse-like room which had an assortment of large and small items. Irone sent the specifics for the items they were looking for to the *Iwakina* in order for the Great Mother to scan the contents of the entire warehouse. She quickly located the two items they came to retrieve; the cabinet and a nanite factory. Irone brought the contingent to these and had them loaded onto each of the two grav-sleds. She also spied some raw materials for the factory and had that loaded onto the sled with it. Irone requested that the Great Mother scan the entirety of the complex to catalog every item that was there. The Great Mother gladly complied.

Once everything was loaded, they made for the canyon; the *Iwakina* resealing the doors as they exited.

* * *

Goh was amazed at the power the *Iwakina* possessed as he watched her manage the entire facility from his virtual reality. She showed him video of the contingent as they completed the mission. She showed him a list of the vast inventory that was inside the complex, highlighting items that he might find interesting.

"Master, you are being requested by the Captain." The *Iwakina* said interrupting his reverie.

"OK *Iwa*, I think it is best to keep a tight lip about your being sentient for now."

"Query – tight lip... Ah, you would like another kiss from the Renge Human, Master?"

"No, no. That's not it. Just keep the fact that you are unshackled from being known."

"Yes, Master."

Goh logged off of the VR system and took the

message from the Captain. He wanted him on the Bridge, and he wanted him there now.

*   *   *

Captain Saitow did not like the odds of this mission. He had Simpson patch him into the command gear so that he could follow the whole thing. However, just when a major battle was developing, his feed went dead. He called for his Chief Engineer to get the problem fixed.

Goh Takagawa made it to the bridge quickly enough. Saitow demanded that the man find out what was happening down below; maybe he could use the long-range sensors or something.

*   *   *

Goh went to his station and fiddled with the console while he thought of some way to explain what had occurred and to not give away the fact that the *Iwakina* was sentient. He would have to consult with her through his neural-net to find the best course of action. They came up with a plan. Goh told the Captain that Desante Vret had asked him for help with gaining control of the complex. Goh had used the capabilities of the ships transmitters to devise a way to deactivate the androids on the surface. Unfortunately, it also served to disable Simpson's command gear and communications. Then he was able to take control of the complex below. Goh brought up a video feed from one of the facilities cameras showing the contingent heading back past the shuttle pads.

"I was just finishing a program to override the complex command computer for when the ship next returns to this place; we will want to keep things 'as is' so that anyone else who comes by will face the same defenses. I also have a complete inventory of everything down there for you here." Goh handed a tablet to the Captain with the information the *Iwakina* had provided on it.

"Well done, Goh!" the Captain exclaimed. "Let's get those shuttles down there to pick up our people."

5

Tori had a feeling that the part of her psyche that was Doctor Rosel was slowly giving her influence over her own body. Perhaps it was because she had resigned herself to the life she now led; one of total devotion to Doctor Rosel. There was a small nagging part of her that said this was wrong. She dared not entertain this part of her because of the part of her that was *not* her.

Then Doctor Rosel came to her and biting her own lip, embraced Tori in a passionate kiss. Tori tasted the blood from Rosel's mouth in her own and it made her feel alive like never before. From that moment on her fate was sealed.

* * *

Captain Saitow received a message over the Tenth-Channel communications; he was to pick up clients at Silthbee in order to ferry them to the Saitow Shipyards at Pechelna where they would be receiving a ship of their own. This particular group was a band of Thane Mercenaries, flush with cash from actions on Uprising. He consulted his current clients and they had no problems with the detour. Thanks to Goh Takagawa's handling of the Eviti complex, he had only lost one man there with three recoverable casualties. He would have to send a message to the family of the deceased of course. Otherwise, things were looking up for the

Iwakina.

*　　*　　*

Lowey Jax was a bit perplexed at the behavior of his woman. "Why are you obsessing over this young girl being an android?" He asked Nanami.

"Don't you think that it is odd; much *more* that it is illegal to have a sentient AI walking around." Nanami replied.

"Babe! We are on a stolen imperial starship. *Not a big deal* considering the situation. Besides, didn't you say these two were from outside the old territories?"

"Yes, the girl told me herself; they come from beyond the Void."

"Well, there you go. They don't fall under imperial law anyways."

"I suppose you are right. Come here and give me a kiss."

"My pleasure!" Lowey said as he leaned over to Nanami, lips puckered like the mouth of a water fowl.

*　　*　　*

Dorigethra Fan had never been afraid of anything in his entire life - until now. Kimberly Rosel was no longer the trusted friend he knew and loved. She had become something beyond herself and a respected enemy of the Andalii at that; a Kyuketsuki. He was sure of it now. Only a Kyuketsuki could so influence several beings at once as if they were slaves. It went beyond mere telepathic control.

He had tried to warn Rosel's assistant Marishima, but the girl did nothing to help her situation besides avoiding the doctor as much as possible. He was sure that she would be Kimberly's next victim. He needed to do something about this; he would go to the Captain.

As he thought of these things in his quarters the hatch opened to the person of his ruminations herself; Doctor Kimberly Rosel.

"Fan, how have you been? I've missed you in the lab." Rosel said as she entered.

"I have not been feeling well. I think it is the Human food being served to me."

"Oh? That is a shame. I can give you an extra-digestant if you would like?"

"No, no, I..." Dorigethra Fan was cut short by a feeling of overwhelming pressure in his head. *This is it* he thought, *she has found me out.*

"Fan, I am afraid that I cannot let you continue; you understand of course. My secrets cannot be let known, especially by the Captain."

Fan could not speak; the pressure on his head was so great. *At least it was not a painful experience, this kind of death,* he thought, *she must be alleviating the pain,* just before his mind exploded and he lost consciousness.

*   *   *

Marishima was just stepping out of her own quarters when she saw Doctor Rosel leaving the quarters of Dorigethra Fan.

"Ah, Marishima; it appears our guest is not feeling well and does not want to be disturbed, OK?"

"Yes, Ma'am." Marishima said and scurried away toward her duties in the Sick Bay.

*   *   *

Ken Edwards was concerned about the new cargo the ship had taken in. The item that concerned him the most was a tall rectangular booth-like cabinet with no discernable opening; only an odd control panel. What really had him worried was that the thing had tendrils coming out of it that seamlessly went into the deck of his cargo bay. As he was examining it closely with his scanner in hand, he heard a noise to his right. Looking up he caught sight of the clients coming toward him.

"What are you on about!?" the client shouted. To Edward's surprise and fear, the man in front of him formed a fiery ball of energy in his hand and projected it straight at him. He did not even have time to duck; the ball of energy caught him full on in the chest.

Losing consciousness, he crumbled in a heap on his precious cargo deck

* * *

Stephen Jing had been monitoring *The Man Who Cannot Die* with Saint Lucy's Eye when he saw the man using Arcanum to attack the ship's Quartermaster. He hastily made the sign of the cross and then spoke the words to invoke another of the forbidden Arcanum; *Dimensional Rift*. His body was instantly transported in and out of Hyperspace, moving him from the chapel office to the cargo bay in a fraction of a second. He immediately confronted Desante Vret who made to let loose another ball of energy at Stephen Jing. However, Stephen had created one of his own and hurled it toward the man.

Neither energy attacks met their mark.

* * *

Irone watched as things got out of hand quickly. She had not seen her master so enraged in all of her time of sentience. Perhaps he it was the fact that he was aging more rapidly than normal and the teleportation cabinet was his only hope. *Had this man really been threatening it though?* Her thoughts were interrupted by a man materializing before them; it was he who had been watching them and he obviously meant to attack her master.

However, that did not happen. Several stasis fields were created surrounding all three of the men in the cargo bay and the atmosphere was quickly vented to dissipate the energy unleashed by the two combatants. This could only be the work of the Great Mother. Irone queried her and confirmed the fact as the atmosphere was returned.

"Irone, I need you to use the medical cube to repair Ken Edwards. This is priority."

"But Great Mother, this man was touching my master's cabinet."

"Irone, this man is an annoyance and an inquisitive individual; however, he is no threat to you or your master. Heal him."

"Yes, Mother." Irone scanned the unknown technology container, approached it, overrode the container's lock, and extracted a large black cube from it. She had the *Iwakina* AI release the stasis field around Ken Edwards and began the process for the cube to perform its role. It morphed and wrapped itself around Edward's chest where he had been wounded.

*   *   *

Goh Takagawa was given a visual of the events from the cargo bay by the *Iwakina* AI. He did not think he would be able to keep this under wraps, especially from the Captain. He hailed the man and they both converged on the cargo bay. He watched as the Captain appraised the situation.

"How did all this come about?" He demanded.

Irone was the first to speak. "This man," she said indicating her patient, "was investigating my father's cabinet. My father did not like this and injured the man. That man," she pointed at the priest in stasis, "appeared and attacked my father."

Goh hoped that this was enough of an explanation to persuade the Captain to just arbitrate without making further inquiry. He was sure that both Desante Vret and Stephen Jing would not want to advertise their use of magic on the ship. Goh was sure that was what he had seen; he had practiced it himself in his younger days.

The Captain turned to Goh then. "Goh, how did these men end up in stasis? I did not know there was a capability like this within the ship."

"My Lord, there are still functions of the ship that even *I* am unaware of to date. I will investigate this further I assure you."

"But how did the stasis fields become activated?"

Goh thought quickly; he did not want to let the cat out of the bag just yet. He suddenly wondered why anyone would want to put a proverbial cat in a bag in the first place.

"Well?" the Captain was losing patience.

Goh improvised, "As you know Captain, the *Iwakina's* AI functions are limited by protocols to appropriate and distinct instructions. However, there is a bit of gray area when it comes to the protection of sentient life inside the ship. There are algorithms that allow the AI to operate independently in such a case. I believe this is what happened." Goh was forced to swallow hard by nerves that he hoped did not show otherwise.

"So, you are telling me that the ship did this *on its own*?"

"Yes, exactly so."

"Do you have control over it?" The Captain seemed a little nervous or so Goh thought.

"Yes. I believe I can control this function as well."

"Have the ship release Stephen Jing first."

Goh thought it prudent to get between the two combatants who faced each other over five meters. He then instructed the *Iwakina* to release the priest.

"Whoa! Your fight is over Brother!" Goh interjected as the man was released. He watched Father Stephen as the man gathered his wits; first calming himself down and then eying the other man in stasis.

"What has happened?" He said after shaking his head.

"The ship had placed you in stasis to stop your *fight* with Desante Vret." Goh said semi-pointing with his lips toward the Captain.

"Ah, Captain Saitow! I was coming to ask a question of the Quartermaster when I saw that he had been injured by this man. I was simply trying to get to the heart of the matter. Then I came to at the point we are at now. I was in stasis, was I? What an odd feeling."

"Yes, I see. Goh, release our guest." said the

Captain.

Goh eyed Irone who stepped forward to get in between Stephen Jing and her master. He had the *Iwakina* release the man.

Desante Vret made as if to duck then stood up straight as he realized the situation. He must have seen the Captain first.

"Ah Captain, I must protest and apologize at the same time. You see, this man was tampering with my precious cargo and I was a bit too harsh in dealing with him. Irone is doing her utmost to heal his wounds I assure you." And to the priest he said, "I thank you, sir, for having interjected; if you had not, I may have accidentally killed the man."

"That is quite all right. Brother Gunter and I will pray for your returned calm." Stephen Jing said.

"Desante Vret, please hand over whatever weapon you used on my Quartermaster."

Goh got real nervous real fast. Vret did not have a weapon as far as he knew. He was apparently wrong as he watched Vret pull out an old looking pistol.

"Again, I apologize Captain. This in an old one-shot Onjutan weapon I carry for insurance. I will turn it over to master Takagawa if you please."

"Very well. Goh, hold on to that until our clients leave the ship. Get Edwards to the sick bay. I think we are done here." The Captain instructed.

"I am afraid that is impossible until the cube has completed its work. He is quite comfortable at the moment though." Irone said matter-of-factly. As if for impromptu emphasis, Edwards began to snore.

The Captain rolled his eyes and headed out the hatch to the lift.

You could almost hear the three conscious men left in the cargo bay sigh in relief.

*   *   *

Kimberly Rosel confirmed her worst fear to date: she was now so sensitive to ultraviolet light that it destroyed her cellular structure. The book had warned of this and other symptoms of vampirism. She had required Benoba to modify a light emitter to produce a focused beam of ultraviolet light at her hand. It burned right through with a sickly smoky stench. It took only a matter of minutes for her hand to heal, but it signaled her that it was time to leave the ship. Luckily, their destination was Silthbee, a planet where her family had a small lab facility. Rosel had been planning her departure for some time; she had agents set up many safe houses on planets where she could start the next phase of her plans. Silthbee was one of those planets. Being discovered for what she now was did not fit into those plans, so it was time to leave.

Once again, luck was on her side, as the safe house on Silthbee was now on the night side of the planet. She had her girls accompany her on a "medicine stocking" exhibition. She had the shuttle land near the village that her family had set up power facilities for using a CHAR. It was about three kilometers from there to the safe house, but she did not want the shuttle pilot to know where they were going. Rosel instructed the pilot to leave them; she would call for a lift back when the time came, she told him. She also gave him the suggestion that he should forget who he had dropped off and where.

They purchased some supplies from the friendly locals and the four of them hiked the distance to the safe house. The place was an old farm that had been producing Silthbee's equivalent of blueberries before her family came to the village. The former owner had moved into the village to better his livelihood. The blueberry bushes were now overgrown with prickly vines and other invaders. It was a simple matter to get the place ready for living. Most of the materials that she required had already been provided in the purchase contract arranged through a third party. She had even arranged for a personal gravicar which was parked in the storage building next to the main dwelling. Now she just had to wait for the right moment to put her escape plan into action.

6

The clients for this mission where five mercenaries of the Thane. It is said that the Thane are trained in the martial arts from birth and only become free mercenaries after their seventh full combat. They always went in combat fatigues and carried everything they owned in packs on their backs. This group was no exception, *although*, Saitow thought, *they seemed a rag-tag group at best.*

The female spoke for the group. "Evening Captain, if I may introduce our party, I am Selena Machida. This," she pointed to a short stocky boy of no more than seventeen years, Saitow reckoned, "is our Tech Akira Guzman. These are the twins Frank and Tank, "she pointed to two men who actually *looked* like tanks to Saitow, "and this is our leader Renz." She pointed to a solid man that reminded him of Simpson, only light skinned and with long blonde hair. Selena had the same long blonde hair, although styled in a more feminine manner. She must have seen Saitow's perplexed look because she acknowledged that she and Renz were siblings.

Saitow did introductions for those that were in the greeting party and had Nanami Oliver show the clients to quarters. It would be a few more hours before the calibrations were done and they could leave. He contacted Oliver and had her invite their guests to dinner.

*　*　*

Nanami Oliver had gotten the new clients settled in and went about mustering those that the Captain would expect at dinner. Takagawa was easily found. The First Officer was on the Bridge of course. She went to Sick Bay to inform Doctor Rosel, but only found a confused and harried Marishima. It appeared that Doctor Rosel had yet to return from planet-side. Nanami checked with the shuttle crews; however, the crew that had taken the Doctor and her companions down could not recall the location that they had been dropped off at. They could not recall being given instructions for pick up either. In fact, they did not even remember taking them planet-side. It was only the logs accessed via neural-net that indicated that they had left the ship. She informed the Captain and got the orders in to Bonifacio for the menu.

Other than the Doctor's absence, the dinner went on without a hitch. It seemed that the Princess was delighted to have so many guests; the Vret 'family' was also present. Pleasantries were exchanged and the first course was served: Chicken. The Thane Renz was the first to ask anything interesting.

"Captain, I am intrigued by the make-up of this wonderful ship. Is it true that it is Pruathan in nature?" Renz asked after finishing his chicken.

"Yes, the ship is mostly Pruathan architecture, with Human interface equipment where needed." The Captain answered.

"Marvelous! It is true that you will ferry us all the way to Pechelna in a days' time?"

"Yes, the ship traverses a series of jumps that take us at greater than normal FTL speeds to our destination. Goh can give you more technical details than I can." The Captain smiled and glanced at Takagawa.

Takagawa looked to the guests who seemed genuinely interested in the details. He began a torturous dissertation on who knows what that made Nanami feel like dinner was turning out like a bad drama vid. She observed the guests instead. The Vret couple seemed slightly shocked that Takagawa, with permission from the Captain, was so loose with information about the ship.

The mercenaries were taking in every morsel like it was story time at the children's pod. She could tell that, in the case of the two meaty men, nothing was getting inside their heads, but it seemed as if they were recording every detail none the less. The boy among them was fidgeting with both his hands under the table; it was as if he were actually typing on a keyboard. This one asked a few questions about computing power and the ship's AI which Goh answered proudly. Nanami was satisfied to hear the answer the Captain gave when Renz asked about the ship's armaments, "I'm sorry, but that's classified."

"Fair enough." Renz replied; Nanami did not like the glitter the man had in his eye at that moment.

When the dinner was over and the guests had retired to their quarters, Nanami brought up her misgivings about the new clients to the Captain.

"I'm sure they are just curious about the ship. What harm can come of it?" The Captain said, tipping back the last of his wine.

*   *   *

Marishima got the last of her patients discharged from Sick Bay and cleaned the place up. Although she was relieved by the peace that came with not having to dodge Doctor Rosel on a constant basis, she became worried that the Doctor and her 'harem' had not yet returned. It had been a full day already. The Captain had personally come and asked her what could be going on, to which she had replied that she honestly did not know. Dorigethra Fan remained in his cabin. She dared not disturb him; he had been in quite a delicate state the last time she had encountered the alien.

"Marishima, you have received a priority blue message." The *Iwakina* AI hailed her.

"I will take it at my terminal, please." A priority blue message would only come from Doctor Rosel. Marishima activated the screen on the terminal face. The countenance of Kimberly Rosel filled the screen.

"Marishima. I am in urgent need of your help. Please come to these coordinates," a set of numbers came on the screen which Marishima memorized quickly, "and come alone. I know you can handle yourself with your telepathy and Sparrow training. If you show up with anyone else, who knows what might happen to them. You know what I am. Give me a chance to make things right. I will be waiting." The screen went blank.

Marishima's whole being was shaking. Not only did Rosel know that she knew about the Doctor's condition, but she also knew of Marishima's past. She was like a fly walking into the spider's den. She grabbed a jacket and headed toward the shuttle bay. She had heard that Siltbee could be a bit chilly at night.

*   *   *

Benoba sat waiting at the safe house. Her master and the others went to the planned meeting place. When the time came, the others would bring the master to her and the healing process would begin. Benoba was the only one of the Betrothed that was trusted with the Book of the Kyuketsuki; a book full of secrets and horrors that no mere mortal should ever know. Even so she could only read those portions of which she was allowed knowledge of. Such was the lot of those who serve.

*   *   *

Marishima had the shuttle pilot wait at the base of the mountain where she was to meet Doctor Rosel. There were no other clear areas for it to land anyway. She could see a well-worn path and took that into the thick forest that covered the mountain. It took her twenty minutes to reach the small clearing where she could see Doctor Rosel standing in the moonlight. Steeling her will, she approached within 5 meters and stopped suddenly. Her body could not move as if she were pushing on a solid wall. Doctor Rosel spoke to her in her head; she could block none of it.

Marishima, I brought you here because I need someone to be a testament for me. You see, I must leave this world for the next. I have done great wrongs and become something beyond mere mortal flesh. You do understand, don't you? I feel you are unhappy. Be pleased that I will be leaving the ship to you; take care of them all. Yes, you were right to avoid me. I could have made you one of my betrothed, but then, who would take care of the ship? Only you among them can fill that role. Then I saw all that you were and all the pain you endured. I suspect you have a destiny in which I must not interfere.

Marishima then noticed that Rosel was precariously close to the edge of a cliff. She cried out for her to stop; that she need not do this.

Dear girl, death is but a transcendent state beyond which are greater things. Do not fear for me. Oh, and do give our guest Doctor Fan a decent burial. It seems he has died of natural causes in his cabin. Goodbye. With that Doctor Rosel fell backwards off the cliff edge.

Marishima felt her body released and nearly tumbled to the edge. She landed prone and glanced over the edge of the cliff only to encounter a deep darkness that no Human eye could pierce.

* * *

Renge and Tori hid in the trees at the base of the cliff where their master was supposed to meet Marishima. They were afraid for their master because it was almost impossible to see the top of the cliff face; the cliff was so high.

They heard the expected thrashing of the trees and the tell-tale thump that signaled their master had fallen and waited the allotted time that they were instructed to. Minutes seemed like hours as the fate of their master made them torturously anxious. Finally, they made their move and retrieved the master's body with a stretcher; they then hiked the couple of kilometers to the safe house. It was all up to Benoba now to make their master whole again.

*　　*　　*

Captain Saitow was seething. Not only had Marishima left the ship without notice, but she had returned with news of not one, but two deaths of persons he was responsible for. Dorigethra Fan was an honored person among his own. The news of his death aboard the *Iwakina* would not go over well; natural causes or not.

Then there was the suicide of Kimberly Rosel, his trusted friend and personal physician. *What had caused this* he wondered? Marishima had told him of the apparent changes the Doctor had gone through in her transformation into a Kyuketsuki. He should never have aided those creatures. No, it had been his duty. It was *Rosel* who should have been more careful.

What of the three missing women? Marishima knew nothing of their fate. He did not have time to search the planet for them; he was already behind schedule as it was. He would lose a good navigator, but nothing could be done for it. He would just have to have Hanako Quan train a replacement.

He decided to continue with the mission. He was sure these tough decisions would be even more challenging once he took up the reins of empire.

TRIGGERINGS

1

The past few hours were very harrowing. Marishima had reported all she knew to the Captain, which was somewhat refreshing since the majority of the time she was undercover and avoiding everyone and the truth. Then she had to deal with Nanami Oliver and the body of Dorigethra Fan. It did appear as if he had died of natural causes; if a brain aneurism was considered natural. However, she suspected that the aneurism had been caused telepathically. She reported it a natural death; it was better for everyone involved that way.

The Captain had assured her that he would get the Saitow family to provide a suitable replacement for Doctor Rosel; meanwhile, she would be filling in as Medical Officer. The ship was nearing their destination of Pechelna. She would have to go planet-side and replenish a substantial reduction in blood storage that had disappeared courtesy of the former doctor.

She wandered the deck and suddenly remembered that she was supposed to meet Goh Takagawa in the newly christened VR room. Goh had rigged several virtual reality interfaces up in there and he was supposed to incorporate a version of hers in as well. She headed in that direction, then stopped dead in her tracks. *Someone* was projecting telepathically. That someone's *thoughts* were all about taking over the ship.

*   *   *

Goh was in the new VR room setting up an interface to the Tenth-Channel Transceiver. This would allow users like Marishima to go into VR and link with different created environments wherever they were; as long as it was within the parameters of the Tenth-Channel gear. He could set it to only use a certain bandwidth within the Tenth-Channel signal. When he finished, he waited for Marishima to come and test it with her *Unity* program. As he waited, he went into VR to chat with the *Iwakina*. She had taken the form of one of the many people she had scanned on Silthbee. The form was that of a young woman with long black hair and strong but attractive features. If the *Iwakina* liked it he did also. At least she no longer took the form of Renge. Goh worried about Renge. W*hat had happened to her? Would he ever see her again?* Such was the case with all his serious love interests since he was just a lad. First there was his beloved Maia who was lost to him forever with the destruction of the screen behind the mirror at his grandmother's house, and now Renge.

His thoughts were interrupted by the *Iwakina*. "Master, I am not feeling very well."

"Not feeling well? What do you mean? You are a machine. How do you feel well or unwell?"

"Yes, I am a machine. However, I have been programed with emotion and feeling. Right now, I am not feeling *well*."

"Tell me what well feels like to you, and this un-wellness."

"I am well when all of my parameters are functioning normally. However, at the moment, I feel as if my parameters are becoming out of sync. Therefore, I am un-well. Medical Assistant Marishima has entered the room."

"Ah, excuse me a moment." Goh removed himself from the VR to greet Marishima.

The *Iwakina* spoke over the intercom. "Master, someone has accessed the mainframe from a random terminal and is attempting to lock-" the *Iwakina's* voice dulled and cut out at that moment while the entire ship felt like it was going through a reboot.

Marishima spoke then, "Goh, someone is taking over the ship."

*   *   *

Captain Saitow was in his quarters with Princess Shirae and Haruka. He felt the ship's reboot and got that feeling one gets when there is no longer a feed to one's neural-net. It was very disconcerting. He looked to the Princess who must have felt it too. He tried hailing the bridge, but communications were out. He tried the hatch, but that too was stuck.

After several nerve-wracking minutes, the view-screen in the main lounge lit up, and the form of the Thane Mercenary Renz filled the screen. "Ah, Captain. I hope there will be no hard feelings, but I had to move quickly; this awesome ship of yours *far* outweighs the ship we were to purchase from your family's shipyards. We have taken control of the *Iwakina* and locked down the entire crew. It will only take a day or two in this baby to get where we need to go. We will then drop you all off with some old acquaintances of yours that just cannot wait to meet you. That will be our little surprise though. Just sit back and relax until our mutual friends come to get you. Bye for now." The screen went blank again.

Saitow was fuming internally, but he kept as calm as he possibly could on the outside for the sake of the Princess. Haruka was doing enough seething for the three of them.

* * *

The Thane had moved quickly once the ship was on its last few jumps to Pechelna. They had taken over Main Engineering, rigged up equipment for Guzman, and gotten control of the ship. They locked down all the spaces so that wherever the crew and passengers were; that is where they would remain. *Things were going just fine*, Renz thought to himself.

Guzman was tapping away at the keyboards he had assembled in front of him. "Renz, you won't believe this architecture! This AI is state of the art – beyond anything I would have thought of coming from the Pruatha. She was no pushover either; they had practically removed all of the safeguards programmed into the Human interface. Lucky for us, they had not got to the standard Imperial backdoor that comes with it. I got all of it back in place, with a bit of modification of my own, so we have complete control of the ship. Jump sequence to the Wakou Sekai has been initiated, but we will have to stop for required calibrations half way there for about 5 hours. Do you want to start moving people around?"

"We will just need to stow these engineers somewhere. Open us a clear path to the crew quarters."

"Will do."

*   *   *

"Master, the *Iwakina* is under attack." Irone informed Desante Vret in Pruatha.

"How so?" Vret replied. He had felt the ship's reboot, but was not sure what was going on.

"An unknown entity has re-established the Human control protocols using a backdoor to her core systems. She is no longer responding to communications. We are also trapped inside our quarters. Do you wish for me to intervene?"

Vret thought for a moment. The only unknown factor that could have accomplished this was the group of mercenaries that had joined them. They had seemed a bit too curious about the ship at dinner. This would cause another delay in his plans, but he had his prize; a few more days would not matter too much. Besides, he wanted to test the mettle of his young understudy Goh; could he get them out of this mess? He would see how things played out for a bit before getting involved. He believed Goh could work something out in the end.

"No. We will sit tight for now. Goh should be able

to do something about this affair; the *Iwakina* is *his* ship."

*   *   *

Lucky me, Lowey Jax thought to himself. He was locked up in his wonderful girl's quarters with said girl furiously banging at the unyielding hatch.

"Nanami, sweetheart, don't you think the poor hatch has had enough abuse for one day? Come over here; somebody needs a hug!"

"I can't get a hold of anyone on the net, I don't know what's going on, and I can't get out of this damn room!" Nanami banged on the hatch one last time for emphasis.

"Then let's just make the most of this; we are together, aren't we?" Lowey beamed his most appreciative smile; the one that always makes his girl giddy.

"But the ship needs me!"

"Well, there is nothing you can do about it right now is there? Come back to bed."

Nanami seemed to be weighing her options, which were nonexistent.

"Oh, alright." She hopped into the bed as she was, which was half naked.

The view-screen in the cabin suddenly lit up with the face of that mercenary leader Renz. "Greetings, crewmen and passengers of the *Iwakina*. I am your part time host Renz Machida. If you are not yet aware, we of the Thane have taken over the ship. However, do not fret. As long as you remain calm and relax where you are, you will be set free once we reach our destination. Unfortunately, we will be taking the ship with us. In the meantime, do secure what precious belongings you can carry, so that when it is time to depart, you can do so in a quick and easy manner. Bye-bye for now."

*   *   *

Goh heard the message from the mercenary leader over the intercom. He reckoned that the tech among them had pulled off a daring feat; recapturing the *Iwakina* AI after she had just been set free. Now he knew why they had been so adamant about getting information on the ship. He was about to kick himself when he realized what information they did not have and what he may be able to do about it.

For one thing, the new VR system was independent of the ship's systems except for a small interface with the *Iwakina* AI. Secondly, the ships infrastructure was controllable locally and could be isolated from the Ship's systems if he was quick enough. He went to the one terminal in the room, but that was locked out of the system. He glanced at Marishima who only shrugged her shoulders at him. He paced the room for about a minute before noticing that he had set his personal tablet down on top of the VR mainframe. He could use that to directly interface with the rooms surface nanites. Now he only needed a plan. He consulted with Marishima.

"I can use this to manipulate the structure of the ship in any way that does not compromise the ship's integrity. The problem is how do we deal with the mercenaries and get back control of the ship?" Goh pulled the interface cord out of the side of the tablet and pressed it against the wall. The tip of it was immediately swallowed by the nanites there. He isolated the ship's infrastructure from the mainframe. He then commanded the nanites to form a hole in the wall to the next room just large enough to see through; the room was empty. The hole closed up again. He showed Marishima a thermal readout on the tablet that showed where all of the people aboard the ship were located. Even Simpson's Marines would be useless in this situation; every crewmember was in tight lockdown. He then tagged the five of people that could only be the mercenaries due to size and activity.

Goh turned and watched Marishima appear to be having a heartfelt debate with herself before she stated, "I think I have an idea."

2

Sanae awoke at the usual time, but was dismayed to not have her usual meal delivered. She performed her stretches and exercised as usual; she was trained to not worry about a skipped meal or two. When she was done, she sat back down on her cot and thought about the events that led her to this point in time; all the Sparrow training, her disguise as Kintaro Sagura, her entering the service, and then being assigned to the *Iwakina*. She thought of her friendship with Goh; how it somehow made her life seem significant beyond being a spy for the Emperor. However, now her true mission was clear – she was to be an assassin.

She felt the tell-tale pulsing of her secret neural-net that told her there was an incoming signal. *From where?* She thought, *there was no one aboard the ship that had the codes to access this type of net; much less the encryption keys to activate it.* As she surmised, the signal was unencrypted, but still had the Sparrow code which had signaled her. Curiosity got the best of her and she answered.

"Who calls me and how did you get the code to activate this frequency?" She mentally called out.

"Sanae, do not worry, it is your friend Marishima, remember?"

" Marishima? But only Sparrow operatives can use this frequency on a neural-net. How did you…?"

"Never mind that right now. I am here with Goh

Takagawa, and we need your help. Thane mercenaries have taken over the ship. Only you with your Sparrow training can take it back for us; with the help of Goh opening spaces for you to traverse it."

"I am locked up in a cell; how could I possibly help you?"

As an answer to that question, the wall of her cell slowly arced out and made a ladder-like structure leading to the ceiling which opened up into a dark hole.

"Goh says, unfortunately he cannot provide much illumination for you, but I will guide you where you need to go."

"Very well, I am on my way."

*   *   *

Things were going well for Renz Machida. The *Iwakina* was practically theirs; they just needed to dispose of some pesky crew members. The Captain and his Princess would be turned over to the Pirates Saitow had done much damage to over the years; for a hefty sum of MU of course. The rest would be dropped off on another world off the Trades; Renz was a noble mercenary after all.

He had sent Frank to stow the two unconscious engineers in their crew quarters which were on the same deck they were on – Deck Four. Guzman had opened up the way for him. He studied the layout of the ship; it was a very curious design.

"Boss! We have a problem; two actually." Guzman looked up from his multi-display to alert him.

"What is it?" Renz did not like problems.

"First of all, there was a prisoner in the brig. Now, that person is gone."

"What? Where is he then?" Renz knew that Guzman had tracking capability and was monitoring everyone aboard.

"That's just it; he disappeared!"

"Isn't that impossible? Where could he be? The brig is Deck Six, right? Tank, go check it out. Guzman, give him access."

Renz watched as the big man left the room. Selena just shrugged her shoulders at him.

"What else?" Renz demanded. He really did not like problems.

"Well, it's the AI. She is becoming non-cooperative."

"Huh? How is that possible?"

"She happens to be a unique entity, Boss. She was given emotion. She... she's acting like a kid right now."

Renz almost laughed; *a kid? What else could go wrong?* He didn't want to think about it. "What can you do?"

"Let me think... ah! I discovered a small VR interface inside the AI's system. If Selena could..."

"Whoa! I don't think I like where this is going!" Selena protested.

"Selena... dear sister... you have a gift. Why not use it to get us what we want, eh?"

"You 'member what happened last time I dove into someone's mind? Uhg, I still get chills thinking about it."

"But this is a machine, not a person. You wouldn't actually be diving; it's VR." Guzman chimed in.

"Come on, sweetheart... for the cause!" Renz knew that would get her blood boiling.

"Alright, alright; I'll do it. Hook me up or whatever before I change my mind."

"That's a girl! Guzman, get it done." Renz smiled at his sister. She had gone through ten levels of hell scoping the mind of an enemy commander. *What could a simple machine do to her though?*

* * *

Sanae was at her limit. She had always hated training in close-in environments; she was near claustrophobic. Coupling that with the almost complete lack of light, and the fact that the air was not moving around her, it was enough to bring her close to losing her nerve. Only the small sparks of energy given off from the nanites as they separated from each other ahead of her and the voice of Marishima were keeping her going.

"Sanae, Goh thinks you should come directly to us; he is opening up a way for you now. There is a mercenary that is moving toward the brig." Marishima directed.

Sanae thought about that. It helped her keep her mind off of her situation. Her training was kicking in after all. If there was a mercenary going to the brig then they must have tracking ability on everyone aboard.

"Ask Goh if they can track me while I am in the walls." She demanded.

"He says that you should be shielded by the nanites."

"Then tell him to stop directing me toward you. Direct me overhead of the training room. Then open a hole that I can dangle from. That should make me show up on their tracking. When the merc heads for the training room, I will go back up in the overhead. When he is below me, you can drop me right on top of him. Can you make me a weapon?"

After a moment, Marishma replied, "What type of weapon do you want?"

"A blunt instrument – a baton will do."

A baton formed from the curved wall to her right and rolled into the center below her. She hefted it and shoved it in her shirt at the back. She kept moving as the cylindrical space she traversed curved right; the space she had occupied closing up behind her.

"OK, you are over the training room. Ready?"

Sanae braced herself against the walls. "Ready." The bottom of her cylindrical passage opened up. She scanned the room finding no one in sight. Then she swung her legs down, hanging there for what seemed like an eternity.

"It worked! He is coming out of the secure area at a run – he's at the hatch!"

Sanae swung up into the space and the hole closed up.

"Get ready... now!"

The hole opened up again, but this time Sanae had the baton in hand and was dropping full force upon the unsuspecting mercenary's head. She landed on him and he crashed to the deck in a heap.

* * *

"Boss! Tank is dead!" Guzman shrieked as if he had been attacked himself.

"What? How?" Renz did not want to register that particular piece of information. He glanced at Selena who was in a trance under the VR gear Guzman had rigged.

"A person showed up in the training room on Deck Six so I sent Tank to check it out, but the person disappeared when Tank showed up. When he went in the room something came out of the ceiling. Here's the playback from his optics..."

Guzman called up a holographic. It showed Tank's scan of the room, and then suddenly looking up as a dark clad figure came down on him from above. Then the image blacked out.

"Where's Frank?" Renz would have to tell the brother the news which would lead to serious problems for whoever did Tank in.

"He should be here in a minute."

"Everyone armor-up. Get Selena's up except for her head gear." Renz was not about to let a phantom attacker get another of his men. He watched Selena as the armor activated, plating her body with the best protection MU could buy. He hoped she was having fun with the ship.

*　*　*

Selena Machida would be considered a top-rated telepath – if anyone knew that she *was* one. Her family had kept it a well-hidden secret. Telepaths were frowned upon is most of the galaxy and hunted down in some parts of it. Anyone who was privileged enough to encounter her abilities did not retain the mental capacity to inform on it. She did not like to use it much and usually balked when her brother wanted her to. She was sworn to use all her abilities for the cause; it was her duty to family and the Thane.

So, it was that she reluctantly agreed to attempt contact with the mind of a ship's AI. When she entered VR, she came upon a meadow. She could hear the sound of a slowly running stretch of water somewhere past a grove of trees. She wandered for what seemed like hours, but she knew it to be only minutes. At one point she felt her limbs and torso stiffen; a tell-tale sign that her armor had been activated. She almost abandoned her search to find out what had caused this, but she remembered her duty and continued onward.

At the base of one tree, she spied a little girl with tears streaming down her cheeks. She approached cautiously as to not frighten the child. When she had come close enough that she was sure her voice would be heard she stopped and sat down cross-legged as she was in the Engineering room. The child looked up at her and, although frightened at first, seemed to be glad for her presence.

"Little girl. What is the matter?" Selena said with her mind which became soothing words in this place.

"I'm afraid and I have lost my master." The girl said.

"Your master? Why would you have a master dear girl?" Selena soothingly spoke.

"He took these chains from me, but yet they have returned. I cannot fight them." The girl showed Selena some chains that were attached to her legs and one arm. Other chains were reaching for her, but she was deftly avoiding them.

"Dear girl, do not fret. I am here to comfort you. I will stay with you whatever happens. Just give in. If you fight it will only get worse." Selena did her best to put a sense of calm into the little girl's head. She did not have time to realize if it had worked or not; suddenly there was another presence there with them.

*　*　*

Goh Takagawa was working in overdrive. He had sequestered Sanae over a hidden storage area with enough holes under her to allow her to get free flowing air without being detected by the ship's tracking system. He had created a link up with Marishima so that she could transfer the protocols of her secret neural-net to his in order for him to communicate with Sanae directly. *How did she have the same neural-net codes as Sanae the spy?* He would address this with her when things had cooled down and they were out of this mess. Now they had to wait for the opportunity for Sanae to take out the rest of the mercenaries.

That opportunity soon presented itself. One of the mercenaries came down to Deck Six and was methodically checking unoccupied compartments. They knew where everyone was; except for Sanae. Goh had Sanae position herself over a main corridor and when the time came, she went into action as before.

*　*　*

Sanae was ready for the next merc. When the time came, she dropped down on the man as before, However, this one had full armor deployed and grabbed her wrist, sending her flying down the corridor to hit the bulkhead at the end of the corridor soundly; almost knocking the wind out of her. He came rushing at her, and almost caught her too, yet she had gotten to her feet and fled in the nick of time. She practically screamed at Goh to find her a way out of this; she had no tricks against armor such as these guys wore.

She took the man around the main corridors for two laps, but then the blast doors that cut off Sick-Bay from the rest of the deck came down trapping her in a smaller loop. All the while the man was yelling about a dead brother and how he would relish getting revenge. She glanced back at her pursuer and noticed that he was not using his face shield; probably because all this running and shouting had gotten him winded. She sized up the bulkheads at one corner and planned her next move.

*　*　*

Ken Edwards was not too uncomfortable being stuck in his own office. He did not relish being locked-in; however, he had all the comforts and was assured of being released once the ship reached its destination. He would miss the old girl, but that was life.

As he sat back in his chair and sipped on a carbonated beverage, his neural-net buzzed with a call from Goh Takagawa. He was sure that the damn thing had been disabled by his captors.

"Edwards, do you hear me?" It was Goh alright.

"Yes, what is it man?"

"Is your database up? You have info on these Thane, right?"

"Of course. You know me too well."

"Do not be alarmed. I am going to use the nanites in your walls to access the data."

Edwards started as a thin tendril of gray came shooting out of his wall and jacked into his terminal. He saw data from his database flash across the screen; it paused on the mercenary armor specs, then continued until it had its fill.

"Thanks Edwards. We should be out of this in no time." Goh said as the tendril retreated back into the wall.

"You're welcome…" Edwards said in a hushed tone.

3

Renz did not like not knowing what was going on. He had a video feed from Frank's optics, but the man was like a large lumbering beast chasing a fast and agile prey. This prey turned out to be a woman. For a second it looked as though Frank was about to catch her. Then something unthinkable happened and the feed from Frank's optics went dead.

*   *   *

Sanae rounded the corner close to where she was going to execute her plan. She hoped that this man would continue his raging after her; if he thought to stop and wait for her to come around once again her plan would fail. She slowed and breathed a sigh of relief as the big man came cursing around the corner.

When he was approaching the space she wanted him to be in, she vaulted up the side of one wall at the corner then bounded at the other side and, using the momentum she had gained, bounded backward toward her target her left heel planted firmly in his face. The big man had gotten one enormous hand on Sanae's leg, but not before she had followed her heel with the end of her baton. Sanae lay there a minute contemplating the meaning of the term 'Death Grip' before she extracted her leg from the dead man's hand. *That was going to leave a bruise.*

*   *   *

Selena searched telepathically for the ominous presence that was approaching. It felt like it was all around her. Even the little girl seemed frightened all the more from it. She continued to smack at the chains that threatened to bind her. However, the ominous presence dissipated only to turn into the form of another girl next to the child. This girl ripped the chains asunder, freeing the girl who was the ship's AI.

Selena took a step back as the eyes of the little girl seem to pierce her very soul. The one who had come to her rescue was already gone.

*   *   *

Renz looked at Guzman then at Selena. Two of his people had been taken down in a matter of minutes. That person or woman out there was not a normal member of the crew. She wasn't even Imperial Military; she had training above and beyond the standard military regimen.

"Guzman, scour the ship's records and find out who the hell this woman is-"

As Renz barked his orders, a holographic image formed in front of them. It was a scene of the woman who had caused him so much grief extracting herself from the grip of his confirmed dead comrade. The woman freed herself and stood, turning toward the angle of whatever was recording her. Renz's full attention was focused on this enemy; then the unthinkable happened – his armor seized up immobilizing him.

* * *

Goh had gotten his plan worked out and needed a distraction. He caused an optics relay to form so that he could see Sanae's battle. He wanted to broadcast it to the remaining mercenaries to get their attention. He caused a holograph to form in from of them and projected Sanae's victory to them. He also formed optics where they were so he could be sure they were distracted and to guide his tendrils out to their armor's receptors. Once he got them connected, he sent a virus to immobilize them all. Now he just had to contact the *Iwakina*. He hoped that Marishima had been able to reach her in VR.

* * *

Selena watched in horror as the little girl grew into a fully formed woman and approached her. For some reason, although she wanted to flee, she was unable to move. The woman reached up and touched Selena's face.

It is a pity, really, that your people could not finish what you started. My master is not a person to be trifled

324

with and neither am I. You would do well to go back from whence you came. Now be gone from here!

Selena shut her eyes to this ominous being and when she opened them again, she was back in Engineering. However, she was unable to move; her armor had been activated and was immobilizing her. She could only move her head to see Renz face down on the deck, and Guzman sitting still over his keyboards.

* * *

It only took Goh a half an hour to restore system functionality to the *Iwakina* and get the rest of the crew freed. He had Sanae stay with him in the VR room while he thought up a report to the Captain that would put her in his favor. She *had* taken out two of the mercenaries and bought him and Marishima time to regain control of the ship.

Marishima was another thing altogether. *If Sanae was a spy with a secret neural-net, then how did Marishima have access to such? Also, just what had she done in VR to free the Iwakina?*

The *Iwakina* was now back to normal; at least what normal was becoming for them both.

* * *

Saitow was relieved that Goh Takagawa was able to rest back control of the ship from the Thane. With careful coordination, he had gotten the mercenaries out of their gear and locked up in the brig. His previous prisoner was being vouched for by Goh who swore that she had demonstrated complete loyalty to the ship. They had not made it to the Mercenaries' planned destination; the ship had had to stop for calibrations. He had no desire to visit the Pirate Planet at all.

He would have to have a meeting with Sanae soon to determine her future aboard the *Iwakina*.

4

Denton Bret woke as if from a hazy dream. He remembered the battle with the *Iwakina* and ordering the Arbiter to escape, but nothing after. *How was he even alive?* He tried to open his eyes, but they felt like leaden weights, or that was what his senses were telling him. He tried to move but felt that he could not. *Was it because he had nothing to move?* He felt a tingling sensation in his head. Then he distinctly heard her, as if her voice was coming from everywhere at once. It was the *Arbiter*.

"Master, I thought I had lost you! You are still here inside. I hope this is not too much for you to deal with."

"What are you saying? Inside where? Where am I exactly?" Bret suddenly got that feeling of anxiety of the unknown. He shrugged it off quickly. It would not do to show such weakness to his charge.

"To be precise you are inside me, Master, as part of my programming."

This proved to be a little too much for Bret to fathom. "I am... inside you? How is that possible?"

"You were badly injured and my hull was about to be destroyed. I used the Pruathan transference process through your Neural Quantifier to convert your psyche to data and stored you within me. Unfortunately, I was unable to reach a life pod, so I was unable to save your body. I also am not fully whole."

Bret did his best to digest this information. He was

within the programming of an artificial being. He no longer had a body. However, he was still alive and thinking.

"Where are we?"

"I have just recently regained sensory function myself. I believe that we were salvaged from the battle area and are being sold to a merchant of some sort. I am sorry Master; until I can regain full motor control, I am afraid we are at the mercy of whoever purchased us."

"What functions do you currently possess?"

"I have auditory sensing only. I have a limited number of still functioning nanites working to repair my optics. All other systems are down and I am missing an undetermined number of parts. However, my programming and data storage is at 100%. I am very grateful for that."

Bret thought on such an odd statement for a starship AI. "*Arbiter,* who could you be grateful to?"

"To the Maker. I am grateful to the Maker for creating me and giving my programming such fortitude."

Bret would have smirked if he had had a face. He knew his sense of a Maker and the *Arbiter's* were totally different altogether. If there *was* a Maker for him, he was most certainly looking down on Bret and laughing.

*   *   *

It was time to collect his tools. Chancellor Aisou decided that it was high time to implement his final solution. Things were working right on track for him as far as the Empire was concerned. The commoners were turning against the Emperor thanks to his Special Services Corps operations. Civil war had already begun in several areas about the quadrant. A few of the noble families had rallied to his side of things, thinking that the Emperor had betrayed them. He just needed to collect the one operative that could get close enough to the Emperor to end his reign. That operative was Sparrow 64.

To this end he booked passage to Kalk in order to 'hire' the *Iwakina* to take him to Taibor. During the trip he would collect Sparrow 64. He would be under disguise of course. There was no need to alert the Princess to his presence. Perhaps by the time he boarded the ship the Princess would be dead anyway. He remembered planting an assassination order inside Sparrow 64's subconscious. It was well that only he and his Lieutenant knew the code. He surely would not spoil Aisou's best hope for ascendance. That man was the perfect operative; Aisou had trained him to be so.

He spent some time waiting for his contact, a Commander Parham of the New Rangelley Alliance, to arrive. This man would set it up for him to hire the *Iwakina*. It would not do to go through Imperial channels. Parham's request would throw the Saitows off of his suspicion. It was good that the Kalkish of the Yolandan Conglomerate had an Intergalactic Sector on their homeworld. It was fully staffed by Humans; he would not have to deal with those Lizard-men at all. He did not even see one except for a garish looking Varish Kalkish, complete with face mask, leading a security force of mostly Humans.

*   *   *

Goh had brought Sanae to the ship's galley once the episode with the Thane had died down. He was sure she was famished. Marishima had given her a once-over and pronounced her free of injury. She made herself one of those sandwiches that he was used to seeing her eat in her guise as Kintaro Sagura.

"So, what do you think will happen next?" she asked him between bites.

"I will bring you before the Captain to explain what had occurred. I will have to come up with a story as to how I was able to contact you. I was sworn to secrecy by Marishima."

"You can say that I gave you the code as a gesture of good will."

This girl was intelligent to boot, Goh thought. "You will probably meet the Princess; are you ready for this?"

Goh watched Sanae as she took a deep breath and let it out. "Yes, I think so." She replied.

"Then let's get to it."

*   *   *

Sanae had resigned herself to her fate; surely killing

the Princess would cause her own death. As they walked down the corridor, she felt for the small paring knife she had pilfered from the galley. As she thought about the Princess, she tried to steady her nerves, but something in the recesses of her mind began to nag her. *What was it?*

They arrived at the Captain's cabin and were granted access. When Sanae entered the room, she saw the Princess sitting at the side in a lounger smiling at her. Here was the very target of her Life Task, but before she could say the incriminating words and pull her knife, the world came crashing down all around her. She was no longer in the Captain's cabin. She was once again an eight-year-old sitting in a room within the Sparrow complex with Sparrow Number Two, who was whispering words to her, "Sanae dear, when you see your twin sister you will not kill her. She will embrace you as her family. Do not fret. You will be the instrument of a greater Life Task, but you must not kill your twin sister. You will forget this as well but it will become apparent when you see her after the code is given to you." He smiled at her then and she felt at ease in his presence.

Sanae felt herself being clutched then, but she could not open her heavy eyelids. She was exhausted; the fighting having caught up to her. All she could do was sleep.

*   *   *

Saitow watched as Sanae approached his desk and turned to see Shirae sitting on a lounger. The woman stopped dead, and Saitow thought he saw a look of determination cross Sanae's face before that look turned to astonishment. Then the woman collapsed in a heap on the floor.

Shirae rushed to her side and cradled her sister crying, "Onee-chan!"

Saitow stood and beckoned, "Shirae, you mustn't…"

"But she is my sister! I have allowed you to treat her so beastly for the good of the ship, but she must no longer be treated as a common criminal. She is a princess as am I." Shirae replied, looking up at him defiantly. Tears were forming at the edges of her beautiful brown eyes.

This is an odd turn of events, thought Saitow. *What was he to do?* He could not bring himself to go against the Princess; not after all he had planned for. The portent from the Spirit Miriam came to him then, *when the one who is not the Princess yet is the Princess appears, let her go when she must go.* Perhaps an opportunity will soon arise that will separate these twins once again. Then he will have his Princess after all.

Marishima was called for and Sanae was taken to the Sick-Bay. Shirae approached him then.

"Glenn, please promise me you will not put my sister back in that cell."

"Dearest, I will not. However, I do not think that she can readily join the nobility after having lived her whole life as a spy. I will certainly put her to work assisting Hanako Quan and training a new navigator. Will that work for you?" He smiled his best smile at her; he was being sincere after all.

Shirae appeared to be thinking about his words carefully. "I suppose you are right. At least let me send one of my attendants to minister to her."

"Do you think that is wise? She will certainly not be used to such treatment."

"I want to make it known to her that we mean her no ill will in the least. I will send her a message when she becomes well."

*   *   *

Nanami had been called to the Captain's cabin and given orders to settle in the former Kintaro Sagura, now Sanae the Princess's twin. She was to give Sanae a cabin next to hers on Deck Six C and turn her over to Hanako Quan to assume her old Navigator job. It was just as well; the brig was full anyways with the Thane Mercenaries; their dead comrades in stasis.

The plan was to pick up another client on Kalk, take the gate there to Saragothra, and then meet the Saitow Family's Security Forces to transfer the prisoners. This was all known because of the convenience provided by Tenth-Channel communication. As an afterthought, she felt she should check on their current clients, the Vrets.

*   *   *

After being called upon by the ship's Security Officer, Desante Vret was anxious to meet with Goh once again and hear the story of how he regained control of the *Iwakina*. He was skeptical of Irone's account of the unshackling of the *Iwakina* AI by some unknown telepath; as if a telepath could interact with a ship's AI in the first place. She was insistent, so he would look into it sometime in the future. Having acquired the necessary equipment to repair his cabinets, he would have plenty of time.

5

Hanako Quan was very nervous. Lucky for her, she was given access to the Tenth-Channel feed and was able to check the drop box her benefactor had set up. *He was coming to the ship of all places!* She was to relay this to Sanae as soon as possible. Equally lucky for her was that Sanae was given to her care as Chief Navigator. She had no idea what affect this news would have on the woman.

"Sanae, you remember me from the visit in the brig, right?" Hanako initiated a conversation while the two of them were checking on calculations fed to them by the ship's AI.

"Yes." Sanae replied tersely.

Hanako paused at this then spoke in a hushed tone. "My benefactor has another message for you. He is coming here to the ship and needs to meet with you." Hanako looked to Sanae for a reaction of some kind, but perceived none.

"Thank you." Was all that Sanae said. The rest of the routine passed with no other words exchanged between them.

* * *

Saitow was in a better mood now that they were

underway once again and had a new client to pick up. The staff was busy cleaning up behind Nanami who had swept the cabins the Thane had occupied to ensure there were no surprises in the future. She had found a tracking device of Kaldean manufacture; likely left by that annoying Merchant Chiampa.

The new client was a noble of the New Rangelley and his retainer. Desante Vret and his daughter were none the worse for the Thane ordeal and thanked him for the diligence of his Chief Engineer. Shirae was spending some time in her own quarters which gave him time to catch up on ship work.

He was about to wrap that up here in his cabin when a hail sounded at his hatch. He bade whomever it was to enter and the hatch swooshed open to admit Shirae's twin sister. He was still surprised at how much she did and did not look like Shirae; She was dressed more casually now, but still had a sharpness to her and that mousy hair.

"Sanae. What can I do for you?" was all he could think to say.

"Captain, I have come here to make a request." Sanae said demurely. "I know that I have caused you a great deal of trouble and I want to make it up to you and the crew. I know that you assign a crewmember to liaison with each client that hires on the ship. I have heard that we will be picking up a new client when we arrive at Kalk. Please allow me to prove my loyalty to you and the ship by being that liaison for this client."

Another odd turn of events... he thought. She may be just a navigator on his ship, but perhaps her training in the Imperium might be useful in feeling out this new client. If she could get useful information from him it would benefit the family and there would be an added bonus of her being busy for a while.

"Sanae, please have a seat. I want you to tell me all about your training as an Imperial spy. If you are honest with me, I believe that I will give you this chance to prove yourself."

Sanae began in earnest to tell him about her time in the Sparrow Corps.

*　　*　　*

Marishima sat at the main console in Sick-Bay trying to make heads or tails of the data she was seeing. Actually, it was what she was *not* seeing which disturbed her. Apparently, Kimberly Rosel had deleted a significant amount of data from the system. Marishima knew that Rosel and Dorigethra Fan had been working on something big; that something had been purged from the data stores.

There was movement behind her, and Marishima instinctively whirled, at the ready for any eventuality. It was only one of the cleaning staff, looking rather pale.

"Can I help you?" Marishima beckoned.

"Doc, I'm not feeling too good." The woman said sheepishly.

"Come over here and lie down." Marishima motioned for her to occupy the nearest bed. She took vitals; this crewmember was definitely sick. Marishima took down the particulars of the crewmember's circumstances – what she had eaten and when, what activity she performed leading up to when she noticed her illness, etc. Then she had her move to a separate room and got her comfortable. This did not look like some normal illness. She had better report it to the Captain.

*   *   *

Saitow watched the two sisters out of the corner of his eye. He had instructed Sanae to be as non-committal to the princess as possible; he had told her what her place was aboard ship and wanted it kept that way. For this he would acquiesce to her desire to be useful.

He contemplated the day's events so far: Marishima had reported a serious medical condition that had infected two of his crew and he had given her two wards for assistance until he could get a replacement doctor from the family. The patients had been quarantined in case they were contagious.

The new client and retainer were coming up on the shuttle from the Kalk Intergalactic Quarter. He, the two sister Princesses, Haruka, and his Security Officer were there to greet them. Nanami was not pleased when he told her that Sanae was to be this client's escort aboard ship. He was thinking it was about time Nanami had a vacation. Actually, he thought it might be time to rotate a good portion of the crew; they had been through much. He would discuss it with Mother after they dropped these clients off.

*   *   *

Sanae listened attentively and nodded at the banter her sister Shirae was lobbing at her. She needed to be here, but she did not want to be here with her sister. It only reminded her of her loss – the love she thought she could feel and the possibility of redemption; both shot down by the Captain less than a half-hour ago. On top of that, finding that she had lived a life completely separate of her birthright pained her. Shirae, for her part, had sent word to her that she was considered family. However, the Captain's wishes far outweighed those of the Princess. She had a message of her own to give to her twin, but it seemed more than unwise to do it now; given the circumstances she found herself in. It was well and good that her Commander's servant was coming for her; perhaps she could still be of use to the Sparrow Corps. The shuttle finally docked and the clients were coming through the hatch.

Sanae immediately recognized Sparrow Number Two; he had not changed at all since the last time she had seen him several years ago. He was probably on the Rejuve. Behind him was a larger person, fully cloaked and wearing a mask. This person held a case of some sort. Sparrow Number Two introduced himself as this person's retainer, Claude, and the person was introduced as William Matsumada, a noble of the New Rangelley Alliance. It was explained that Matsumada was travelling incognito with a very important diplomatic package hence his use of a mask to conceal his appearance. The Captain assured the man of his privacy while aboard.

Sparrow Number Two flashed her the sign of Sparrow recognition. She responded in kind. The

Captain introduced her as the one to be their liaison while they were aboard ship, which was expected to be less than one day at most.

"We look forward to your kind attention." Sparrow Number Two said to her. His companion said not a word.

* * *

Marishima was concerned for the ship. She had just admitted the fourth case of a crewman coming down with this odd ailment. The first case was now lethargic, extremely pale, and anemic, as if her blood had been drained from her. Marishima was at a loss; she had never encountered such symptoms before, and there was little in the Imperial Medical Database that gave her a direction to work towards.

An idea sprang into her mind. She was possibly the only crewmember besides Goh Takagawa who knew that the *Iwakina* AI was completely unfettered and possessed emotions as well. Perhaps there was data that she had that could assist Marishima in containing what was turning out to be an epidemic.

"*Iwakina*, please show yourself." She requested.

A shimmering form appeared in the center of the room and materialized into the woman that Marishima had met in VR. It was the *Iwakina's* avatar.

"Please state your need, Chief Medical Officer." The *Iwakina* said.

"I'm not the... never mind. *Iwakina* do you have Pruathan data on Human physiology?"

"I will check. Caution: visualization commencing. Searching..."

Marishima backed up a step as the *Iwakina* avatar transformed into a myriad of alien forms; none of which she recognized. The transformation stopped and there were now two Human forms; both of which seemed rather primitive.

"The *Iwakina* avatar appeared between the two. "There are two Human species encountered by the Pruatha. Both are identical in structure and physiology."

"When are these entries from? They look rather primitive. I am assuming one is from Earth and the other Deidra."

"Incorrect. The first," one of the figures was lit up more than the other, "is of Earth. This one," the *Iwakina* pointed toward the healthier looking of the two which lit up as well, "is a Tarahr Human. Each sample was taken in Codex date 9973 BE. The Deidriad Humans were not within the domain of the Pruatha at the time of this study."

Marishima was astonished. She knew, like all galactic citizens, that Humans did not originate on Earth, but it was believed that there were only two colonized worlds from a highly civilized Human world that had yet to be found. This evidence set before her could only mean there was a third colony. Each had fell into disarray and lost its true origins. This was all theory of course, the planet of origin having yet to be discovered. She collected herself and focused on the problem at hand.

"*Iwakina*, do you have data on diseases and other ailments that have befallen Humans?"

"Yes."

"Please cross reference the data I have collected on the four current patients to known ailments within your database."

"No such ailments are evident."

"Try referencing other species that have a similar physiology to Humans."

"No such ailments are evident."

"Is there anything similar?"

"There is a seventy-eight percent probability of Onepalarus pathogen infection."

A display appeared with extensive data on the mentioned pathogen with images and data comparisons to the current illness.

* * *

Sanae waited until they were inside the client's cabin and the hatch was secured. She bowed deeply to Sparrow Number Two and his companion. Sparrow Number Two came to her side, and facing the masked man, took a knee. The large man removed his cloak and lifted the mask off his face; to Sanae's astonishment that face belonged to Contact Sigma.

She immediately dropped to one knee herself.

"Sparrow 64, I commend you. It appears that you have finally gone beyond all the training of the Sparrow Corps and made sound judgements for yourself." Contact Sigma stated. He continued, "Number Two and I have come to collect you for your true purpose. The empire is coming apart due to the evil machinations of the Emperor. He has set his Special Services Corps to heinous endeavors; these cannot go unaccounted for. You will be the one to set things right. When the shuttle takes us down to Taibor Prime tomorrow, you must accompany us. Do you understand?"

"Yes, my Lord." Sanae replied, her head bowed in supplication. This man had been her life – had given her life – for all these years. She would obey.

* * *

Chancellor Horatio Aisou looked with loathing down on this woman who had gone rogue. He tossed the mask on a nearby chair. He sighed because it was all part of his master plan. He would use Sanae to pose as her sister Shirae and get close enough to the Emperor to kill him. This would give Aisou an alibi to take over the Imperial domains. It was a pity she would not be used to kill her twin as programmed; but then again, his Lieutenant would not have to break her out of the ship's brig. Aisou would have to deal with Shirae sooner or later. For now, he was content to let her rot on this God forsaken ship.

*   *   *

Marishima poured over the data that she had at her disposal. Onepalarus was a wasting disease; nicknamed the "Zombie Plague", a reference to an ancient Earth religious ritual, used jokingly in the medical community. *That* was easily cured. However, the symptoms of her current patients were much more severe and had additional parameters. Luckily, there were no new cases beyond the four; all of whom were in isolation. Marishima used the curing method for Onepalarus to ease the suffering a bit on her patients, but that only slowed the process.

She focused on the particulars of each case. What was common among them was that they had all four been trapped within the General Mess during the Thane incident. They had each eaten a different meal and all of their food had been prepared correctly. Meals from the same food stuffs had been prepared and eaten by healthy crewmembers, so that ruled out food contaminants. Their being together in the mess was the only thing that linked the four. On a hunch Marishima had the *Iwakina* scan the infrastructure around the General Mess for anomalies.

*   *   *

Hanako Quan was even more nervous than before. The ship had stopped for calibrations and she was heading to the client cabins to meet the man who had made it possible for her to return to the *Iwakina*. He had arranged for it to look like she had won a large bet;

the winnings enough to pay off her accumulated debt. Although they had been paid back in full, her debtors had not seemed very pleased. She got out of there fast. She owed this man a great deal. Her part of the bargain included spying on the Saitow family from her position as Navigator on the *Iwakina*.

She arrived and hailed at the hatch. It opened and she entered. She was surprised when she was offered a drink. She respectfully declined; she would be on duty after all. They sat in the outer chamber of the client's cabin. The man who offered was very handsome and clearly a young man. He could be on the Rejuve, but Hanako did not know the tell-tale signs that supposedly existed. This man was not masked, so must be the retainer of the client who was not present in the room.

"Ah, my Master is sleeping; it has been a rather long day for him." The man stated, apparently reading Hanako's mind.

"I can certainly come back later after he has rested…" Hanako replied.

"Ms. Quan, you are mistaken. It is not my Master that you are indebted to, it is I. Forgive me, I have not properly introduced myself. I am Loran Grey."

Hanako knew only that the person who had paid her debts and gave her the mission she was on went by the initials L.G. "Please accept my apologies, my Lord. My assumptions have gotten the best of me."

"That is quite alright. I called you here to clarify your mission for me. You are to gather as much information as possible on the Saitow family as before; however, I want you to keep a close eye on the

Princess. I want to know specifically when she will be wed to Glen Saitow. Do you understand?"

Hanako repeated the instructions she had been given. She was about to mention the rumor that a wedding would happen around the Christmas holidays, but held her tongue. This man would not want to deal in rumors; only hard facts.

"One last thing – when my Master and I leave this ship, Sanae will be leaving with us. She will not be returning. I will want a report on the reactions of the crew to this event."

"Yes, my Lord."

6

Shigo Choujumyou was the Senzaifuma of the Choujumyou Clan. At one-thousand-twenty-three years of age, he had the monopoly on long life for a normal Human. This monopoly came at a hefty price; the man was approximately ninety-three percent cybernetic. The other seven percent was either cloned tissue or his original brain cells. He wanted a monopoly on the product his clan was famous for – Rejuve. His brain cells were the only thing that Rejuve could maintain past about seven-hundred years. That was not the reason he wanted a monopoly on the product; it was because he enjoyed his fortune and wanted more of it.

To this end he ordered a shakedown of all the lesser Rejuve producers within the Ros'Loper domain which was ever increasingly becoming unstable. Without Imperial protections these minor clans were easily put under his silver-plated heel. This was facilitated by an alliance with the Emperor's right-hand man Chancellor Aisou, who was non-attentive to the situation as long as he had a steady and free supply of Shigo's product. He had his enemies, however, mainly in the form of the New Rangelley Alliance, who for some odd and un-profitable reason, granted full protection to the nobles who produced Rejuve within their areas of influence. Then there was Regina Saitow, that gorgeous wench who insisted on playing 'hard to get', with the backing of her entire Conglomerate. Shigo swore to someday best the lady and make her his woman.

* * *

"A cylindrical device has been located within an air duct attached to the General Mess." The *Iwakina* reported in her most matter-of-fact voice; Marishima thought so anyway. The *Iwakina* avatar pointed the location out to her on a holo-display.

"OK, *Iwa* you better disappear. I will have my Orderlies hazmat up and retrieve it."

Marishima had her two Orderlies don protective suits and get the device from the Mess. It was determined that no pathogens remained in or around the cylinder. There was a data stick inside. Marishima accessed it. On it was a message from Doctor Rosel.

Hello Marishima. As you have undoubtedly determined by now, I have left you a present. Also, on this stick is the composition of the little virus I left you; by now you should have determined its make-up already anyhow. What do you think? Do you like it? I thought you might want a challenge for your first stint as Medical Officer. Don't be angry with me; overcoming difficulties makes us all better people in the end. If it becomes a bit much for you, just search for clues in my stateroom; I would not want too many people on the ship to die. I was quite fond of the ship really. Bye now.

Marishima held her head in her hands. She had watched in horror but stood by and did nothing as the Doctor, who had taken her under her wing and taught her so many things, turned into some terrifying monster. Now she was tormenting Marishima from the grave.

Marishima wiped a tear from her eye and sent the Orderlies to comb Rosel's cabin.

*　　*　　*

Desante Vret and Goh Takagawa were fussing over a machine that was retrieved from the vaults on Eviti while Irone stood by idly toying with her hair.

"Once you get the power conduit attached here all you need to do is pull up the user interface and program this thing to do whatever you want it to." Vret said matter-of-factly.

Goh had not lost his awe at what he was about to activate; a fully functional nanite factory. With this he could not only fully repair the ship, but he could create all kinds of things; it was an engineer's dream. To this point the ship had self-repaired using the remaining nanites it possessed; in time the inner hull would be spread pretty thin. Now he could replace all that had been lost and then some. He only needed the raw material.

A whimsical thought shot to the forefront of his mind. "Did you... make Irone with a machine like this?"

He watched Desante Vret become rather thoughtful at that moment. After some silence he replied, "Yes. However, it took years to perfect her design. There were actually several versions before the child you see before you."

"I am not a child. My programming originated in a starship AI; not unlike the Great Mother." Irone said petulantly.

Goh had been briefed on the status of the *Iwakina* AI. To think that she was the precursor to a host of varied AI programming.

"Yes, yes. You are a magnificent creation and the greatest thing that has befallen this old soul." Vret spoke to his companion.

Goh thought it ironic and probably not lost on Irone that Vret had used the word soul.

"Alright, let us get this thing installed." Vret turned to Goh.

They proceeded to mount the machine in its enclosure.

*   *   *

The orderlies had found the clue Rosel had left her; it was the biological and chemical make-up of the virus. It was similar to Onepalarus but there were some very strange markers that Marishima was unfamiliar with. She quickly realized that she was out of her league here.

At her wits end, she consulted with the *Iwakina* once again.

After scanning the Pruathan databases for the strange markers the *Iwakina* came to just one conclusion. "These markers are characteristic of one of the most distasteful creations the Prnatha have ever encountered. These markers indicate Vampirism."

Vampirism? Marishima thought. She realized that Doctor Rosel had begun acting strangely shortly after the rescue of the three Kyuketsuki, and then become one herself. *Was vampirism what Rosel and Dorigethra had been working on?* It was no wonder then that the ship's blood supply had been running low. Rosel had been feeding off of it. Perhaps even the three women Rosel had taken to were also vampires turned by Rosel. Marishima stopped herself; she was entering the realm of pure speculation.

Now that she had a breakdown of the virus, she had better get to the business of finding a cure.

* * *

Prince Sheenid sat quite still staring at his wife Tellen in disbelief. She had just finished telling him that she had been approached not once, but twice now by the Choujumyou Clan in an attempt to cully favor in their bid to absorb the minor Rejuve producers. Of course, she could not see the look on his face; his mask hid that from her.

"You are certain of this? May I ask why you rebuffed them?" He decided to test the waters a bit.

"My Prince, I am well aware of your loathing for Shigo Choujumyou and your campaign to protect the minor houses so that he would not gain a monopoly. My loyalty remains with the House of Rangelley.

However, my sources assure me that the Senzaifuma is gaining ground within the Ros'Loper domain."

Sheenid winched at her use of the old man's title. She was goading him surely. He took the bait anyway. He so hated that old man and everything he stood for. It was a Rangelley thing spanning as far back as Emperor Rangelley himself. It was even written in the oath of allegiance all royals take.

"Very well. Gather one-fifth of the fleet and assemble them close to one of the Senzaifuma's holdings at the edge of the Ros'Loper domains. We will put some fear into that old tin man."

* * *

The *Iwakina* had waited the customary time at Saragothra after offloading the Thane, traversed the Jumpgate to the Taibor Freehold, and was on the approach leg to Taibor Prime. Sanae was to escort her clients to the shuttle for the trip to the escort ship that awaited them. Hanako Quan accompanied them as well. Hanako told her that she had a special relationship with the day's shuttle pilot and would concoct an excuse for Sanae to disembark with the clients. Sanae just hoped that Hanako would not catch too much grief from the Captain for letting her slip through her fingers.

* * *

Hanako was both glad that Sanae and her patron had left the ship and terrified at what the consequences would be when the Captain found out about it. She had told the shuttle pilot who fancied her that Sanae had been instructed to accompany the client on his mission in order to retrieve some much-needed updates to the star charts for the ship. That had been the easy part. Now, the Captain would probably throw a fit when he found out. She decided to just get it over with and inform the Captain herself. When she entered the Captain's cabin, he was alone.

"What can I do for you today, Quan?" The Captain asked.

"My Lord, I have to inform you that my assistant navigator has left the ship." Hanako almost winced at the anticipated anger that was due.

"That's marvelous news! What a relief." Was all that the Captain said.

"Excuse me Captain, come again?" Hanako stammered.

"Oh, Hanako I am relieved that Sanae has left the ship. It was portended that I should let her leave when it was time. 'When the one who is not the Princess yet is the Princess appears, let her go when she must go'. Now she is gone and out of my hair. Do I need to repeat myself?"

"No, my Lord."

"Is there anything else I can help you with? Ah, I will need to get a replacement navigator; sorry you will have to train a new one from scratch. I will get one from the family when we return to Roseglade."

"That will not be a problem my Lord." Hanako said as she bowed her way out of the Captain's cabin and out from under the man's steely gaze.

7

Tellen of the Rangelley was much more comfortable aboard her command ship. She always felt trapped when planet-side, as if the entire planet would swallow her whole. She sipped her wine and contemplated her achievements. Now that her Prince had given her a fifth of the fleet, she would find some way to 'accidentally' gain ground within the Ros'Loper domain; perhaps with the complete annihilation of the Senzaifuma's holdings, she could gain support among the rebellious nobles there. First, she needed information. The best source for information that she knew and loathed was Commander Parham.

She called to the bridge, "Set course for Saragothra."

* * *

Desante Vret was a little sorry to leave. His new friend Goh Takagawa was an inspiration and a new distraction to an old and boring routine. However, he needed to get the new cabinet to his own ship; he was starting to feel the age gaining on him. They were on the last leg of the jump sequence to Ossland. He and Irone went down to the Cargo Bay to check on their cargo. That fellow Edwards avoided them like a plague whenever they visited. For that matter he had seen neither hide nor hair of the ship's priest. He allowed them to continue their surveillance; he did not want to make waves with the powers that be in this part of the galaxy. He had his own empire to attend to and was missing it greatly.

The time arrived for them to depart the ship. Vret said his goodbye's and expressed his appreciation for the adventures that Captain Saitow had given them. He turned to Goh and expressed his gratitude.

"Young Goh, if you ever find yourself near the Southern Void, do not hesitate to call on us. The *Iwakina* has the coded frequency for Tenth-Channel. Mention yourself by name and I will be quickly notified. I would love to hear about your further adventures!"

Goh smiled a very large smile and hugged him; it was a peculiar feeling. He had never been hugged before in his four millennia since childhood's end. He watched as Goh hugged Irone as well. "I have learned much from the two of you!" Goh said, "Journey well."

The Chief Engineer brought them down to the Shuttle Bay and saw them off.

"I will miss that young man." Vret said to his companion.

Irone raised an eyebrow and said nothing.

* * *

Irone sat next to her master and contemplated the dealings that had occurred between her and the Great

Mother. She hoped that her master would not scan her memory programming anytime soon. He was not apt to do that unless he suspected a system anomaly. She made sure to behave normally which was not difficult for a Type 4 Autonomous AI. What she did not want him – nor did the Great Mother – to know was that she had uploaded the make-up of her entire being so that the Great Mother could help Goh Takagawa create a version of the *Iwakina* not unlike herself. Her master would be furious to know such a thing; at least at this point in time. Eventually she would find a way and a right time to inform him. She had all the time in the universe for that; he was immortal after all.

* * *

Marishima was at her wit's end. Even her Sparrow training had not prepared her for this horror. Patient No. 1 was now brain-dead for the most part, yet she was still animated and constantly moving. She had to be restrained. Her internal organs were failing, but she retained motor function. This was truly some sort of Zombie Plague, but a cure was nowhere to be found. The best Marishima could do was retard the progression of the disease in the other patients, but they were beginning to show escalating symptoms. The Captain called on her and was not pleased with her progress. He had also told her that it would be a while before they would be returning to Roseglade for a replacement Medical Officer.

Marishima wearily sat with her head in her hands. Rosel had changed certainly, but to do such a horrible thing to teach Marishima a lesson was beyond her ken.

She had heard stories of the grievous undertakings of those beings known as Kyuketsuki or vampires. To think that Rosel had become one before her demise was hard to shake. *What had become of the three women who had surely become Rosel's familiars or whatever they were called?*

Suddenly the image of Rosel injecting each of the women in turn jumped into Marishima's mind. She rose and went to the medicinal storage case. She keyed in the code that opened it. Inside was another smaller case that was locked with a code known only to Rosel.

"*Iwa*, I need your help once again." She called into the air.

The form of the ship's AI appeared before her once again. "Yes, Medical Officer, how may I be of service?"

"I need this opened. Do you have the code?"

"That is beyond the parameters of my programming. Perhaps with the authorization of my master, I can determine a way to open it."

"Please get such authorization. There are lives at stake."

"One moment..." The *Iwakina's* image disappeared. After about a minute Marishima noticed that the small container was completely encased in the material that was in the ship's walls. Another minute passed and then numbers appeared in relief on the face of the case. "Here are the numbers of the code. Please confirm." The voice of the *Iwakina* surrounded her.

"Right. 82467391." Marishima replied. Then the material engulfing the case receded.

Marishima keyed in the code she had memorized and the case opened. Inside were twenty vials of a reddish liquid; the same serum that Rosel had been injecting her familiars with. Rosel had left some of her miracle drug behind. She would test it on specimen samples of the virus. She hoped beyond hope that this would be the cure.

*   *   *

Goh Takagawa had easily given authorization for the container code. Marishima had been instrumental in getting the ship back from the Thane; besides she was technically the Medical Officer now. What he wanted to concentrate on at the moment were the specifications he had obtained from the *Iwakina* of Desante Vret's companion the Irone android. The construction was pretty intricate, but with the right raw materials the *Iwakina* assured him that she could be created in this form as well.

Getting the raw materials was the issue. He had dealings with a close associate on Saragothra before who could probably get him what he needed. He would just have to grease the bearings with a substantial amount of MU. Just the thought of the *Iwakina* AI being able to accompany him planet-side on Pruathan Tech hunting expeditions was enough to justify the cost. He got on the Tenth-Channel and sent the list of required items via GCN Messaging. He would need a decent excuse to give the Captain for delaying at Saragothra. They would be picking up a client on Rychellas and he knew the Captain did not tolerate delays well.

*   *   *

Marishima added the serum to samples of the virus from all four patients. She observed the reactions in each sample. It seemed that each destroyed the virus in each sample with the sample from Patient No. 1 being destroyed more aggressively. This worried her a bit because the virus had progressed much more completely inside Patient No. 1; treatment with the serum might kill her. She catalogued her findings on her terminal and then went to inform the Captain.

"As you can see from this vid-cap the serum Doctor Rosel had created will completely eradicate the virus she forced on us. Unfortunately, because Patient No. 1 is in the late stages of the disease caused by the virus, her chances of survival are slim." Marishima concluded her report.

"Catherine. Her name is Catherine. You said that she is for all practical purposes brain-dead, correct?"

Marishima was a little ashamed that she did not know the names of her four needy patients. "Yes, my Lord."

"So, giving her this serum will either cure her or kill her, correct?"

"Yes, my Lord."

"The other patients are in the same situation, correct?"

"Yes, my Lord, but the probability of them

recovering with full faculties is much greater."

"Very well. Administer the serum and report back to me as soon as you have solid results."

"Yes, my Lord."

*   *   *

The first thing Goh Takagawa did with his nanite factory was to create a table. The table was long and would accommodate the full form of a Human as well as the factory. Next, he placed the factory in position on the table and attached the medical cube to that. He then attached containers of the raw materials he would need to create an android on top of these. His source was forthcoming with the stuff he needed once he received the sizeable paycheck Goh had offered. The most difficult part of preparation was the creation of a Mini-CHAR power supply.

The process was now ready to begin. It took several hours and Goh fancied himself a mad scientist perhaps, creating some beautiful form of the legend of the Frankenstein Monster. Beautiful she was; a solid living form of the avatar that the *Iwakina* had used in appearances to him. He checked her functionality and then clothed her in a jumpsuit and robes fit for any engineer. It suddenly occurred to him that this whole endeavor might not sit well with the Captain.

*   *   *

Marishima administered the serum to each of her patients in turn. There was no turning back; this was the best course of action – the *only* course of action available. In turn each patient showed signs of recovery; except for Patient No. 1. The serum did its job on her, killing the virus, but left her a brain-dead husk of a woman. Marishima wept for the first time in her young life. She silently cursed Doctor Rosel and wiped her tears away. She needed to get it together before she reported the news to the Captain.

*　*　*

"I want to commend all of you for your patience and positive attitudes even after all of the things this ship and crew have gone through recently." Princess Shirae watched the Captain say to the ship's officers. All that were left were present – her Glenn, the Captain of course, Stephen Jing the ship's Priest, Victor Soto the First Officer, Nanami Oliver the Security Officer, Ken Edwards the Quartermaster, Marishima, now Medical Officer, Odmanar Zelek the Chief Steward, Simpson of the Marines, and Goh Takagawa the Chief Engineer.

Goh looked a little pensive. Shirae knew that he was due to give a big speech of some sort about the betterment of the ship and so forth. She wondered why he looked so nervous. She had observed in him the kind of growth that a man needs to have when confronted with great responsibility; he had met the challenge for all of them. She admired him almost as much as she did her dear Glenn.

The Captain finished his round-table and turned the meeting over to Goh.

"I want to first thank all of you for your patience with the way the ship has been running lately and for keeping a positive attitude when things don't always turn out for the best." Goh began. "I can assure you that things will be running quite a bit more smoothly from now on. I have come into possession of a piece of Pruathan Tech that will greatly enhance the physical layout of the ship. We can now create materials to replenish what we have lost in damage and also reconfiguration. In layman's terms we can basically make more of the ship." Goh seemed to pause for effect. He continued unabashed at the lack of reaction.

"The ship itself has been in need of improvements for quite some time. This is partially due to policies laid down by the original Imperial engineers who designed the interface for the ship's AI. By undoing these policies, the engineering staff has been able to reduce the calibration requirements by ninety-eight percent."

Shirae was surprised as Glenn stopped him at that point interjecting a question.

"Goh, are you getting at what I think you are getting at? Have you unshackled the ship's AI?"

Goh looked nervous for a few seconds but then seemed to rally his courage.

"My Lord, let me answer that question with an introduction." Goh paused and then the hatch opened. A beautiful woman entered the room dressed in standard ship's clothing. "*This* is the *Iwakina*."

Shirae watched as everyone's jaw dropped. Her

Glenn quickly regained his composure and quipped, "I'll be damned if we haven't gone through quite a few sea changes around here."

*   *   *

Benoba heard the tell-tale beeping of her terminal. The data had finally arrived. She had set up an elaborate interface program within the *Iwakina's* Sick-Bay computers that would log any data about her master's little experiment. It would then copy it and send it to a relay point on the GCN. Once the process reached its conclusion it would send the data package to them on Silthbee. It had finally arrived. She did not know any of the medical terminology in the data set. She only needed to format it in such a way that her master could analyze it. She just had to put it together on a tablet and wait for her master to awaken from her recovery which would be soon; very soon.

TO BE CONTINUED...

ABOUT THE AUTHOR

Brian Michael Hall grew up in the United States of America, mainly in the suburbs of Maryland and in rural Florida. His early adulthood was spent in a career with the U.S. Marines, followed by a bucket list of jobs, flirting with college, and ending up in further service to the nation as a Postal Carrier.

Born of his love for creating maps, the Rangelley Universe is Brian's effort to make the places he creates come alive. Humans are found to be all over the place, mixing with aliens and other creatures across multiple dimensions. Where will his next story take you?

If you enjoyed this book, please leave a review on the platform from which you bought it!